# The Bachelor

## SABRINA JEFFRIES

**ZEBRA BOOKS**
**KENSINGTON PUBLISHING CORP.**
www.kensingtonbooks.com

ZEBRA BOOKS are published by

Kensington Publishing Corp.
119 West 40th Street
New York, NY 10018

All Kensington titles, imprints, and distributed lines are available at special quantity discounts for bulk purchases for sales promotion, premiums, fund-raising, educational, or institutional use.

Special book excerpts or customized printings can also be created to fit specific needs. For details, write or phone the office of the Kensington Sales Manager: Attn.: Sales Department. Kensington Publishing Corp., 119 West 40th Street, New York, NY 10018. Phone: 1-800-221-2647.

Zebra and the Z logo Reg. U.S. Pat. & TM Off.

First Printing: March 2020
ISBN-13: 978-1-4201-4856-5
ISBN-10: 1-4201-4856-7

ISBN-13: 978-1-4201-4860-2 (eBook)
ISBN-10: 1-4201-4860-5 (eBook)

10 9 8 7 6 5 4 3

Printed in the United States of America

*To Starbucks,*
*without which this story*
*might never have been told*

# Lydia's Husbands

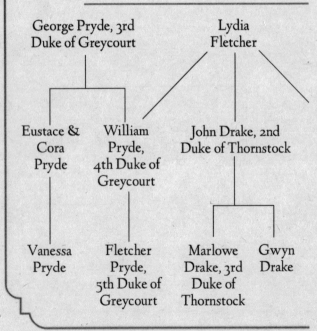

George Pryde, 3rd Duke of Greycourt — Lydia Fletcher

Eustace & Cora Pryde

William Pryde, 4th Duke of Greycourt

John Drake, 2nd Duke of Thornstock

Vanessa Pryde

Fletcher Pryde, 5th Duke of Greycourt

Marlowe Drake, 3rd Duke of Thornstock

Gwyn Drake

# "PLAY ALONG," JOSHUA MURMURED.

And pulling her against him, he covered her mouth with his.

Gwyn froze. Joshua was kissing her. *Kissing* her.

She could see the fellow they'd been watching walk past them, then pause to look at them. With her heart pounding, she closed her eyes and threw her arms around Joshua's neck.

She'd merely done it to throw the stranger off. Or perhaps she'd done it because she wanted a real kiss? Either way, everything changed then. It was as if Joshua forgot his real purpose for kissing her, because a groan escaped him and his mouth began to move roughly on hers.

It sent her pulse beating wildly. He smelled of honey water, soap, and sun-warmed leather. She hadn't expected him to smell so enticing.

Or kiss so well.

Now *this* was what it meant to be kissed. She hadn't expected that from him, of all people.

Next thing she knew, he had her up against the building and had dropped his cane so he could brace himself with a hand on either side of her. Why did the very act of his imprisoning her against a wall make her melt like butter all over the side of the carriage house?

## Praise for *Project Duchess*:

"Jeffries's riveting first Duke Dynasty Regency has a little bit of everything: an independent, forthright woman; a handsome duke with trust issues; and a mystery . . . Complex, intense characters heat up the pages with scintillating love scenes amid the intrigue. Jeffries continues to impress, and romance fans will eagerly await the next book."—***Publishers Weekly***

"Readers will love Grey and Beatrice, and the nicely paced, intriguing plot will keep them engaged . . . An appealing historical romance from a fan favorite."
—***Kirkus Reviews***

"Bestselling Jeffries brilliantly launches her new Duke Dynasty series with another exemplary Regency-set historical brilliantly sourced from her seemingly endless authorial supply of fascinating characters and compelling storylines."—***Booklist***

## Books by Sabrina Jeffries

*Project Duchess*

*The Bachelor*

*Seduction on a Snowy Night*
(anthology)

## Published by Kensington Publishing Corporation

# and Children

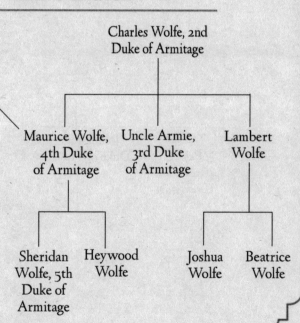

Charles Wolfe, 2nd
Duke of Armitage

Maurice Wolfe,
4th Duke
of Armitage

Uncle Armie,
3rd Duke
of Armitage

Lambert
Wolfe

Sheridan
Wolfe, 5th
Duke of
Armitage

Heywood
Wolfe

Joshua
Wolfe

Beatrice
Wolfe

*London Society Times*

## THE DUCHESS OF ARMITAGE'S TWINS
## TAKE LONDON BY STORM

Once again, dear readers, I have uncovered a delicious bit of gossip for your enjoyment. One would expect the Duchess of Armitage to wait the requisite year before having her daughter, Lady Gwyn Drake's debut, but the widowed duchess is showing, yet again, a shocking lack of regard for the rules of polite society. Her daughter is being presented at court *this very Season.* Tongues will surely wag, and the young lady will no doubt give them plenty to wag about, because one can't help but expect Lady Gwyn to prove a delightful diversion. At least her mama is wise enough to follow *some* of the rules of propriety for a widow of only *six* months, for I am told that she will not attend social occasions with her daughter. Instead, Lady Gwyn is being sponsored at court by the duchess's intimate friend, Lady Hornsby, by most accounts a woman of stellar virtue.

No doubt Lady Gwyn's advanced age of thirty is the cause for her mother's haste in running her through the marriage marts like a prize Thoroughbred at the Derby, although gossip has it that the heiress is infinitely more attractive. Yours truly has also heard she is as spirited as her twin brother, the Duke of Thornstock. So, few gentlemen are likely to balk at her age when such bounty is their reward.

To add to the excitement, Lady Gwyn's half brother, the Duke of Greycourt, will also be presenting his new *wife* at court during the Season. Everyone has wondered about what sort of woman would choose to marry such a haughty man. We also eagerly anticipate the appearance of Lady Gwyn's rakish twin brother. London's ballrooms will simply be teeming with members of the duchess's family, including *two* eligible dukes, if one counts the newest Duke of Armitage, Sheridan Wolfe. Young ladies will be positively frantic to snag one of them. It should be a *very* interesting Season.

# Chapter One

*April 1809*
*Armitage Hall, Lincolnshire*

Lady Gwyn Drake paced the ornamental bridge like a tigress in a crate. What did it mean when one's blackmailer was late? It certainly didn't bode well for the negotiations she hoped to initiate.

Perhaps she was at the wrong spot.

She drew the man's note out of her pocket and read it again:

> *To Lady Gwyn,*
>
> *Tomorrow at 4 p.m., bring fifty guineas to me on the Armitage estate near the bridge that crosses the river if you wish to guarantee my silence. Otherwise, I will feel free to tell such secrets about you and me as will ruin your good name. You know that I can.*
>
> *Captain L. Malet*

Not the wrong spot, then. This was the only bridge over a river on the estate. Did he realize that the house occupied by the estate's handsome gamekeeper, Major Joshua Wolfe, was a short distance away? Or did he just not care?

She scowled. When she'd last seen "L." Malet, ten years before, he'd been only an ensign in the army and she'd been only twenty. But if he was expecting to meet that same wide-eyed, foolish girl, he was in for a surprise.

Balling up the note, she tossed it into the river. Then she slid her hand into her muff to touch the pocket pistol she'd lifted from the closet of her twin brother, Thorn, otherwise known as the Duke of Thornstock. Though the pistol wasn't loaded—she had no clue how to fire a gun, much less load one—the feel of the carved ivory stock beneath her fingers was reassuring. It should look impressive enough to hold off a coward like Lionel Malet.

She heard the crunch of wheels on gravel just in time to see him descend from a phaeton. He probably owed money on it, but you wouldn't know it to look at him sauntering down the hill to the bridge without a care in the world.

Hard to believe she'd risked everything years ago for a pair of blue eyes, a smug smile, and a head of raven curls. Even in a mere ensign's uniform, Lionel had looked incredibly appealing to a woman surrounded by her stepfather's aging friends—or her teasing brother and half brothers.

Today, dressed even more impressively in gentleman's attire, he lacked the power to move her. How could she not have seen the truth back then, that he was debonair and slick, the kind of man who slithered his way into a naïve woman's life, then poisoned her and her future with one bite? If she'd just recognized . . .

It didn't matter. She recognized his true character now. So as he approached, looking utterly sure of himself, she drew out Thorn's pistol and aimed it at him. "That's close enough, sir."

He laughed at her, blast him. "You mean to shoot me, do you?"

"If I have to."

"But you don't." He cocked his head rakishly. "You merely need to pay my price. Fifty guineas is a reasonable amount for my silence, wouldn't you say?"

Her hands shook. She hoped he couldn't see that. "I'm surprised you ask so little, considering what you'd get if you married me."

"Are you still interested in that?" When she merely glared at him, he shrugged. "I didn't think so. What a pity. A marriage would suit both of us."

"I'm sure it would help your finances, but in what possible way could it benefit *me*?" she asked coldly.

He let his insolent gaze trail down her. "You're by no means as youthful as you were at twenty. It won't be long before you're considered an out-and-out spinster, and then no one will marry you."

"Good. That suits me perfectly." Oddly enough, it was the truth. "I'm afraid you have soured me on men, sir." That, too, was the truth. Or part of it anyway. "Nor am I some green girl to fall for your machinations again."

"So why do you need the pistol?"

"My brother has been fearful that you might try to abduct me, as you tried to do with Kitty Nickman at Christmastide on this very estate."

Mention of his failed plan seemed to spark his temper. "I considered it. But I know Thornstock. If I kidnapped you, he would cut you off, and then we'd both be poor. Indeed, he threatened as much years ago."

The memory of that betrayal settled into her chest like a bad cold. That it still had the power to wound infuriated her. "He was trying to protect me, as any good brother would." Still, it rankled that her twin had read Lionel's character so well when she'd been oblivious to it. "And judging from your attempt to blackmail me, he was wise to do so."

"This is not an attempt." He took a step forward. "I mean to get my money."

She steadied the pistol on him. "I don't have it."

He crossed his arms over his chest. "Then I suppose I'll be telling the world about us, starting with your brother."

A sick fear gripped her at the thought of Thorn—or anyone at all—hearing the truth. "I promise I'll get you your funds once the family goes to London for the Season. That's only a few days away. Surely you can wait *that* long."

"Ah, but why should I?"

"Because if I ask Thorn for fifty guineas in the City, he'll think nothing of it, given the ease with which I could spend that on jewelry or clothes. But here in the country, where that would take some doing, he'll find the request suspicious and demand to know why I really want it. There's no plausible lie I can give him. And if I answer him truthfully, he might just murder you."

Lionel chuckled. "You mean you haven't told your arse of a brother what we did?"

"Of course not. And I know you didn't tell him either. Because you wouldn't be here trying to blackmail me if you had. Thorn would have killed you years ago."

"True." The amusement faded from his cruelly handsome face, leaving only the cold glitter in his eyes. Now *that* was the Lionel Malet she knew and hated. "Fortunately," he went on, "I am better prepared to fight your brother these days. Not for nothing have I trained as a soldier. And Thornstock has undoubtedly grown soft with age."

"If you believe that, you haven't had many dealings with him recently."

"In any case," he said, brushing off her comment, "I have no intention of waiting for my money. If you can't pay me today, I'll just have to take something else by way of payment."

He stalked across the bridge toward her, and though she backed up swiftly, he was on her before she could get very far. Only when he snatched the gun from her did she realize it wasn't her he was after.

"You can't have that!" she cried, her heart sinking. "That's Thorn's! It's not mine to give!" It was part of a pair, Thorn's most recent purchase, and he was inordinately fond of it. Her brother would never forgive her if she let it be taken.

"I don't care." Lionel examined the pistol, then snorted as he realized it wasn't loaded. "This will fetch a pretty penny in London while I wait for the rest of my money." He shoved the gun in his greatcoat pocket. "Oh, and the price for my silence has just gone up. It's a hundred guineas now."

When he turned to walk away, she grabbed his arm, trying to prevent him from escaping with Thorn's gun. "I'll get you your dratted money, but you can't have the pistol!"

She'd managed to wrestle it halfway out of his pocket before he gripped her upper arms and shook her. "I will have whatever I want of you, make no mistake. So if you wish me to keep your secrets—"

A shot sounded over their heads. Startled, she and Lionel both looked toward where it had come from, up on the rise behind her where the dower house sat.

Its tenant, Major Wolfe, did something to the barrel of his own gun, then aimed it at Lionel's heart. Honestly, she'd never been happier to see the gruff former soldier in all her life.

"Step away from her ladyship," Major Wolfe called out as he made his way down to the bridge, somehow keeping his weapon trained on Lionel while maneuvering the uneven surfaces of the riverbank path with his cane.

Lionel sneered at him. "Or what? A mere gamekeeper wouldn't dare to shoot a viscount's son."

Gwyn frowned. "How did you know he's a game— Oh. Right." She'd forgotten that Major Wolfe had helped thwart Lionel during that abduction at Christmas. Not that it mattered. "The major is a duke's grandson and a crack shot besides. Not only would he dare to shoot you, he wouldn't miss."

Major Wolfe's gaze flicked to her. He seemed surprised by the remark, though she couldn't imagine why. She'd flirted often enough to make it clear what she thought of him. Then again, she'd ended that after getting more than one surly response. No man was going to make a fool of her. She had let Lionel do that, and it had ended disastrously.

The major steadied his aim on Lionel. "You're standing on *my* land, trying to assault a member of the family *I* work for. So you'd best release the lady, or I swear I'll make you regret it. Not a magistrate in the county would blame me for shooting an armed man on my own property."

Lionel started. "I'm not armed." When Major Wolfe nodded to Lionel's coat pocket, where the ivory handle of Thorn's pistol still hung out, Lionel paled. "The gun isn't loaded," he said, though he had the good sense to release her.

"Not to mention that it doesn't belong to you." She met Major Wolfe's gaze. "It's Thorn's. Captain Malet took it from me."

Major Wolfe arched one dark brow at her. "And what were *you* proposing to do with an unloaded pistol?"

"Never mind that. I'm merely saying I want it back."

"Ah." Major Wolfe gestured to Lionel with his firearm. "You heard the lady. Give it to her."

Lionel's eyes narrowed, and Gwyn's heart nearly failed her. What if he chose to reveal her secret to Major Wolfe? It would be just the sort of thing he'd do to revenge himself on her. And she would die of mortification, which was saying something, because there was little that mortified her these days.

She edged closer to Lionel. "Hand it over." She lowered her voice to a whisper. "I promise you'll have your money once I reach London. But not if you say one word to *him* about our past together."

Lionel glanced from Major Wolfe's weapon to her ashen face. "I'll hold you to your promise," he murmured, then gave her Thorn's pistol and backed to the end of the bridge and onto the path that led to where his phaeton was waiting.

Major Wolfe, who'd been watching their exchange intently, fortunately didn't ask what they'd talked about. She was fairly certain he couldn't have heard them over the roar of the river below, but she still shook from the knowledge of how narrow an escape she'd made.

And would continue to make as long as Lionel was about.

"I wish you'd killed him," she muttered as Major Wolfe approached her, keeping his eye on the retreating Lionel.

Once Lionel climbed into his phaeton and drove away, Major Wolfe relaxed his stance. Then he shoved the large, odd-looking pistol into the capacious pocket of the ragged greatcoat she'd always seen him wear when working on the estate.

"I'll accompany you back to the hall." When she opened her mouth to protest, he added, "Just in case Malet is lurking nearby, waiting to get a chance at you again."

Oh. That was certainly a good point. "Thank you for coming to my rescue."

He nodded, taciturn as always, and gestured for her to go ahead of him. They crossed the bridge and climbed the hill for some time in silence, with her casting him furtive glances every few steps. Lord, but the man was handsome—unfashionably so, with his long black hair tied in a queue by a simple leather cord—but handsome nonetheless.

Some would say his jaw was too jutting and his lips too thin to be called attractive, and that might be true. Personally, she found the combination arresting. But it was his hazel eyes that distinguished him from every other man she'd ever met, even Heywood, whose eyes were also hazel. The major's were the color of dark honey, a golden color so unusual that she could stare at them all day.

Not that she'd had many chances. When his sister Bea had been on the estate, Gwyn had seen him more often, but once Bea had married, he'd seemed determined not to associate with anyone who lived in Armitage Hall.

That didn't keep the maids from whispering about him—how he looked, what he said, what he did. One had even stated that she would marry Major Wolfe in a heartbeat, lame leg or no. Yet he seemed to have no idea of his appeal to the female sex, or surely he'd have taken a wife by now. According to his sister, he was already thirty-one.

"What did Malet want?" Major Wolfe finally asked.

She was glad she had a plausible explanation ready for him. "To make me go with him. That's why I brandished the pistol."

Major Wolfe searched her face. "Since when do you carry a pistol with you on Armitage land?"

"Since Mr. Malet told Heywood that he meant to kidnap me in revenge for something Heywood and his friend did abroad," she snapped.

"Malet made that threat four months ago," Major Wolfe pointed out. "It's odd that he waited until now to attempt it."

"Perhaps he was waiting until our guard was down," she said dryly. "Or perhaps he had tried courting an heiress who wouldn't know all about his wicked intentions, and she didn't prove viable, so he fell back on his old ways."

"And you just happened to be roaming the estate with your brother's unloaded pistol when Malet came looking to kidnap you."

She knew perfectly well that Major Wolfe wasn't credulous enough to believe *that*. Then an idea struck her. "Thorn heard that Mr. Malet was nosing around in Sanforth, so he warned me to keep an eye out."

"Your brother is presently in residence at the hall?"

"Yes. And he gave me his pocket pistol for protection."

"A valuable, unloaded pistol that he didn't teach you how to load or shoot? That seems reckless of him, and your twin has never struck me as the reckless sort."

"You'd be surprised," she muttered. A pox on Major Wolfe and his military mind. This was not going well.

"What's more, you and Malet seemed to know each other, at least well enough to be exchanging confidences."

"Confidences! Don't be silly. Whatever you think you saw isn't what you're implying."

"Hmm. If you say so." Major Wolfe moved along the path through the woods at a surprisingly good pace given his damaged leg. "Why is your brother here anyway? Doesn't he have an estate of his own to run?"

"Of course, but he decided to accompany me and Mama to London for the Season. I am to be presented at court and have my debut in society, you know."

"I'm well aware," he said tensely.

What was *that* supposed to mean?

Oh, he must be thinking of his sister Bea, and the fact that she was being presented as well, but as Grey's new wife, the Duchess of Greycourt.

"Fortunately," he went on, "today's incident will impress

upon Thornstock the need to keep a closer eye on you and
your suitors in London."

The statement was so typically male and arrogant that
she was about to blister his ears over his presumption when the
greater implications of his words hit her. "Surely you don't
mean to tell Thorn about this."

Major Wolfe lifted a brow. "Of course I do. He needs to
know so he can make arrangements to accompany you
everywhere."

She stepped in front of him to block his path. "But you
can't! I don't want Thorn mucking about in my personal affairs. I had enough of that growing up with him in Berlin."

In the darkness of the forest, the major's eyes looked as
brown as oak and just as hard. "You cannot expect me to
keep silent on this matter."

"Why not? It's none of your concern. I'm a grown
woman. I can handle the likes of Mr. Malet in good society,
where I will never be alone."

"*Never?* Even in the Armitage town house? Or going out
onto a balcony at a ball for a breath of air? Or—"

"I will be careful everywhere, I assure you. And anyway,
there won't be nearly as many situations in which he could
effect a kidnapping without drawing attention to himself."

And there'd be even less if the major told Thorn about
Lionel and her twin decided to dog her heels wherever she
went. Then she'd never get to meet with Lionel privately to
give him his money.

Nor could she tell *Thorn* about the blackmail. He would
either kill Lionel outright and end up in gaol, or challenge
Lionel to a duel and end up in gaol. No, Thorn could never
know what Lionel was up to.

"Please, Major Wolfe, you must not tell my brother—"

"Your brother may heed your pleas, Lady Gwyn, but I
know better than to do so. Either you tell him in my presence,

or I will tell him myself. But one way or the other, he is going to hear what Malet attempted. That's the end of it."

Good Lord, he was like a dog with a bone. And now, thanks to him, her ability to pay Lionel his money and put an end to this madness had just become ten times harder.

# Chapter Two

Joshua couldn't believe he and Lady Gwyn were having this discussion. Even his sister wouldn't be so reckless as to court danger in such a way.

*But she would keep the news of danger from you. And did, too, before Greycourt married her. So perhaps Lady Gwyn and Beatrice have more in common than you think.*

It didn't matter. He wasn't about to keep Lady Gwyn's secrets for her. And he could tell from how she'd reacted to his questions that she definitely had secrets. He recognized fake outrage when he saw it.

The fact that she didn't want to involve her brother said a great deal, too, probably having something to do with Malet showing up on the estate today. So not telling Thornstock of the encounter truly would be imprudent. What if Malet harmed her because Joshua hadn't informed her brother of the danger?

No, he wouldn't take that chance. The sight of Malet manhandling her had nearly stopped his heart. Not because he cared about her. Feeling anything but disinterested concern for the wealthy sister of a duke would be absurd. Even though, according to his sister, Lady Gwyn was thirty, she looked no older than Beatrice. She would have her pick of the men once she reached London. Best to remember that before he let himself slide into anything foolish . . . like desiring her.

He looked over at her and noted that she'd gone a trifle pale, quite a feat for a woman whose skin was already as creamy as alabaster. She probably used some sort of cosmetic, like the ones Beatrice had always been trying, although God only knew what Lady Gwyn used to make her lips that fetching shade of peach and her eyes that provocative shade of green. Emerald green, he would call it, because they glittered like the gemstone itself.

Damn it, he was waxing poetic about her. Best to be careful about that. He might be the grandson of a duke, but his father had been the youngest of three of that duke's sons, and a wastrel besides. From birth, Joshua had been ineligible for the coddled—and yes, beautiful—daughter of another wealthy duke. He was even more so now that his damaged leg kept him on half-pay, incapable of pursuing his ambition in the Royal Marines.

Besides, if he couldn't serve his country, he preferred to live as far out of range of so-called "good" society's frivolous maneuverings as he could manage.

"You're suddenly very quiet," he said, unaccountably annoyed by that.

She sniffed. "I don't see much point in speaking when you refuse to listen."

"I listen. But that doesn't mean I will automatically heed your commands. That's what has you angry—the fact that every other gentleman does your bidding, while I refuse."

She halted to glare at him. "Thorn doesn't do my bidding, and neither do my half brothers."

"The important word being 'brothers.' A woman's brothers always see her more clearly than other gentlemen."

"Oh? You wouldn't have thought your sister could become

a duchess, yet you were wrong." When he bristled at that bit
of honesty, she added, "And in case you hadn't noticed, I
didn't exactly have Mr. Malet in my thrall there on the
bridge."

"I did notice. Which is why you should take more care
with him, before you find yourself dragged into a carriage on
its way to Gretna Green."

She planted her hands on her hips. "So which is it, Major
Wolfe? I'm spoiled because all men fall at my feet or I'm in
danger because they don't?"

Damn the woman for pointing out his lack of logic. She
muddled his thinking—made it impossible for him to argue
rationally with her.

He didn't want to examine too closely why that was.

Then she added, "You've only ever seen me with my
brothers and Mr. Malet. You know nothing of how I behave
with other gentlemen. Yet you presume to know my character." Steadying her shoulders, she walked on. "You should be
ashamed of yourself."

He shook his head. The woman had the ability to use her
tongue in flaying a man's very flesh from his bones when she
didn't get her way. And he wasn't about to rise to the bait.

When he didn't answer that at once, she huffed out a
breath. "I never understood why Bea got so frustrated with
you all the time. I certainly do *now*."

The remark about his sister pricked him as nothing else
could. "Speaking of people presuming to know people, you
don't even know my sister well enough to realize she dislikes
being called Bea."

The profound silence provoked by his words stretched on
so long that he looked over at Lady Gwyn, then wished he
hadn't. She wore an expression of such embarrassment that
he wanted to take back his words.

"Is that true?" she asked in a mortified tone. "Or just . . . something you're saying to vex me?"

He considered lying, if only to wipe that look off her face. "Forgive me, Lady Gwyn. Beatrice would throttle me for having told you that."

"Why did *she* not tell us? We would never purposely . . . That is, we all thought . . . No, there's no excuse for it." A frown creased her forehead. "Except that Mama called her that from the beginning because your Uncle Armie called her that in letters."

Joshua could well imagine why. Their uncle, the previous holder of the title of Duke of Armitage, had belittled Beatrice in every way, even to the extent of giving her a nickname she didn't care for. It was his perverse way of forcing her into doing what he wished. Fortunately, the bastard had died before he could succeed in the worst of his plans.

But Lady Gwyn couldn't have known that. And despite everything, her mortification over not using the right name for Beatrice softened him toward her. Because clearly she did like his sister and regretted doing anything to hurt her.

"Still, we should have asked her what she wanted to be called. It was very wrong of us not to." Lady Gwyn's color receded a bit. "Although that does explain why Grey always calls her Beatrice. I'd assumed he was being his usual formal duke self, but she must have told him what she preferred. I can't imagine why she didn't tell the rest of us."

He sighed. "She wanted to fit in, wanted to be liked by you and yours. So she wasn't about to ruin that by informing you all—especially our aunt—that she didn't like that version of her name."

"Well, then," she said softly, "I will apologize to her as soon as we go to London day after tomorrow. I realize that

Bea . . . *Beatrice* . . . isn't my blood relation, but I consider her as family all the same. And I want to make her feel welcome with the rest of our motley crew."

Now he felt like shite for bringing up the matter in the first place. Especially because he actually liked his aunt and knew perfectly well she never intended to offend.

Joshua and Beatrice's Aunt Lydia was also Lady Gwyn's mother, having married into the Wolfe family after Lady Gwyn's father died. Aunt Lydia had married Uncle Maurice, who had almost immediately taken up a position in the foreign service in Prussia and had eventually become ambassador.

That was why Joshua and Beatrice had only recently met Aunt Lydia and her two sons by Uncle Maurice. They'd returned to the estate after Uncle Armie had died, leaving Uncle Maurice to inherit.

Then Uncle Maurice had died, and their cousin Sheridan had become the new Duke of Armitage. Sheridan's younger brother, Heywood, would be heir to the title if Sheridan didn't spawn an heir himself.

Being the son of the youngest Wolfe brother, Joshua could only inherit the title if Sheridan and Heywood died without siring heirs. Because they were both young and healthy, that wasn't likely to happen.

Not that he cared to be duke. Having seen Sheridan struggle to keep the estate from falling into arrears, Joshua wanted no part of it. What he wanted was to be taken off half-pay so he could return to the Royal Marines. Unfortunately, the state of his leg made that unlikely, especially when the Secretary of State for War and the Colonies wouldn't even answer his letters.

Suddenly he realized that Lady Gwyn was speaking to him. "Hmm?" he asked.

"We're here."

He gazed up at the imposing Armitage Hall and sighed. "Right." Time to have an uncomfortable conversation with her brother, the Duke of Thornstock, whom he barely knew.

They entered the hall and were told that the duke was in the writing room. Joshua wondered what use Thornstock was making of the cramped space fitted with only a writing desk and a bookshelf containing almanacs going back some years. Somehow, Joshua doubted that the man was doing any reading. Thornstock didn't seem the type.

As it turned out, the duke had found the very excellent brandy that was kept there. He was also writing intently, and apparently not being too pleased with the result because balls of crumpled foolscap littered the floor.

"Don't tell me—you're writing a play like your namesake, Marlowe," Lady Gwyn said. "Mother will be so proud."

It was the only time Joshua had ever heard Thornstock's Christian name, which, he must assume, had been chosen in homage to Christopher Marlowe, the playwright. One of Joshua's favorites, in fact.

Thornstock's head shot up, and he scowled at his twin. "Dukes don't write plays, remember? But we do write a bloody great number of letters."

Joshua didn't miss how the duke slid the one he'd been writing into the top drawer of the writing table.

Smirking at her brother, Lady Gwyn gestured to the balls of paper. "It must be quite the important letter to require so many drafts."

Lady Gwyn was clearly poking at Thornstock as usual. Those two had a contentious relationship, rather like the one between Joshua and Beatrice before she'd married so well. Except that his and Beatrice's had been fueled by the desperation of their situation, whereas Lady Gwyn and her brother were both rich. So what was it that fueled *their* acrimony?

No, he didn't care. It wasn't his problem. Lady *Gwyn* wasn't his problem.

Thornstock rose to acknowledge Joshua with a nod. "So, what brings Sheridan's gamekeeper and my favorite sister here to grace me with their presence?"

"Favorite? Do you have another sister I don't know about?" Lady Gwyn asked archly.

"I hope not. One is all I can handle."

Joshua had seen the twins spend hours sniping at each other. He had no patience for it today. "Forgive the intrusion, Your Grace, but we just encountered Lionel Malet on the grounds."

"*What?*" Thornstock hurried to the small window to look out. "Where? How long ago?"

Lady Gwyn leaned close to whisper, "You could have broken it to him more gently."

"Unlike the two of you, I don't have all day." Joshua faced the duke. "Malet accosted your sister on the bridge near the dower house. Fortunately, I saw them and threatened him with my pistol before he could do more than that. I made sure he left the estate, but I can't promise he won't return."

"It wouldn't matter if he did." Lady Gwyn sniffed. "We'll be in London by then."

"All the more reason to keep an eye on him," Joshua said. The woman was more stubborn than greyhounds rooting out a hare.

With his brow furrowing, Thornstock strode back to the writing table. "Was Malet armed?"

"Not that I saw," Joshua said. "He did try to steal the pistol you gave Lady Gwyn to carry for her safety."

Thornstock's gaze shot to Lady Gwyn, and a muscle worked in his jaw. That was proof enough for Joshua that the woman had been lying about how she had acquired her brother's pistol.

"Did you think to *load* the pistol I gave you, Gwyn?" the duke said, with sarcastic emphasis on the word "gave."

There was a certain defiance in the way she looked at her brother. "Of course not. Loading it would require some knowledge of how to use the thing, and you haven't bothered to teach it to me."

Joshua was impressed by how she'd turned her dangerous act into a fault of her brother's. Thank God Beatrice hadn't picked up that skill.

"Right," Thornstock said blandly. "In that case, perhaps you should return it, because it's always unwise to brandish a weapon you aren't prepared to use."

"Exactly what I told her," Joshua said.

Thornstock smiled at him. "I see you are growing used to the fact that my sister rarely listens to what she is told."

"Now see here—" Lady Gwyn began.

"Not to mention," Thornstock went on, ignoring her, "that the pistol is worth a bloody fortune."

"Then I suppose it's a good thing I didn't allow Malet to steal it," Joshua said.

"Indeed." Thornstock cast his sister an enigmatic look. "Hand it over, Gwyn."

Lady Gwyn smiled. "Wouldn't it be better if you simply taught me how to shoot?"

"I shudder to think of you armed to the teeth for your debut." Thornstock held out his hand. "Give it over, Sis."

"Oh, all right," she grumbled, and slapped it into his hand hard enough to make him wince.

Thornstock narrowed his gaze on her. "Wolfe, would you mind giving me a few moments alone with my sister?"

Joshua bowed, glad to finally leave the twins to their own

devices. "Take as much time as you need. I have work to attend to."

But when he turned for the door, the duke said, "Actually, Wolfe, I'd like you to wait in the hall until I've finished my discussion with Gwyn."

Her ladyship paled. "Why?"

Joshua wondered the same thing but had the good sense not to ask.

Thornstock ignored her question anyway. "If you don't mind waiting, sir."

Joshua wasn't fool enough to tell the man the truth—that the prospect of being around Lady Gwyn any longer would unsettle a saint. "I can wait."

"I promise it won't take long." Thornstock headed over to open the door.

With a terse nod, Joshua walked out, tensing as the door shut behind him. Nothing like being summarily dismissed. He wasn't certain which was worse—being treated like a servant by a man his own age or being asked to wait around for her bloody ladyship.

Not that it mattered. Beggars, especially lame ones, couldn't be choosers. All the more reason he had to find a better situation for himself soon. Because his life at the Armitage estate became more intolerable by the day.

Gwyn glared at her brother. "You didn't have to be rude to him."

"Was I rude?" Thorn paused. "Ah, you're simply trying to change the subject. But I know better than to fall for that."

"You caught me," she lied. Because she'd never be able to explain to her twin the anger that had welled up in her when Thorn had shut the door practically in Joshua's face.

Thorn pointed to the only other chair in the small room. "Take a seat," he ordered as he sat down behind the writing table. "I want to hear the truth about what went on between you and Malet."

"I already told you the truth."

His eyes turned a stormy gray. "Not the whole truth, I suspect."

A pox on Thorn for knowing her so well. The blessing—and the curse—of being twins was their inability to hide much from each other.

Wondering what to say to put him off, she ambled over to the chair. Thorn absolutely could *not* learn the "whole truth" of this. But a version of it might suffice, especially one that made her sound like a fool. Brothers always seemed to consider their sisters fools, and Thorn clearly had thought her one since the day he'd paid off Lionel in Berlin.

"I received a note from Mr. Malet this morning," Gwyn said. "He told me he wanted to talk about renewing our former . . . acquaintance."

Thorn shot to his feet. "And you agreed to meet him, just like that? What possessed you to do such a damned foolish thing when you *knew* he'd tried to kidnap an heiress before?"

"I borrowed your pistol. I figured brandishing it would keep me safe enough."

Thorn stalked up to her chair. "Obviously, it did not."

"Which is precisely why you should teach me how to use the thing," she said, meeting his irate gaze with her steady one.

"Over my dead body," he growled.

"Or mine."

A flush rose in his face. "I am never teaching you to load or fire a gun, so put that thought right out of your head!"

"Then do not be surprised if I get into trouble in London."

Looking positively apoplectic, he paced the room before halting in front of her. "Trouble with Malet, you mean."

"Of course not." Or at least not the kind Thorn was thinking of. "I assure you, I lost any fondness for Mr. Malet years ago."

Thorn looked skeptical, which was rather ironic because she meant every word. "Then why did you go alone to meet him?"

"To tell him what I just told you—that I want nothing more to do with him and he must leave me alone. I knew if I didn't give him an emphatic refusal in person, he would assume you were forcing me to refuse him and then he'd continue to plague me. But I made myself very clear. He just didn't like what I was saying."

Thorn crossed his arms over his chest. "Then what did you mean just now when you spoke of getting into trouble in London?"

"I meant that with men being the reckless, unpredictable creatures they are—and with my being an heiress—I might experience some difficulties during my debut. And having a weapon for protection might solve that."

"Having me around all the time would be more likely to solve it," he growled.

Her heart skipped a beat. "Absolutely not." If Thorn was constantly about, she'd never be able to pay Mr. Malet his money. She rose to face down her brother. "I can't have you hovering over me during the entirety of my debut. Not only will it frighten off all my suitors, but you don't even like marriage marts, so you'll be bored, which always makes you annoying. I prefer more pleasant company when I attend balls, thank you very much."

He opened his mouth, then thought better of whatever he meant to say. Instead, he released a heavy sigh. "What am I to do with you, *Liebchen?*"

The familiar endearment didn't dissuade her from her

purpose. "Be my brother, not my father," she said softly. "I already have a nosy mother; that's parent enough for me. I'm thirty, for pity's sake. Don't you think it's about time you stopped hanging about me like a matron acting as my chaperone?"

Though he stiffened at the insulting comparison, he said, "I only wish I *could* stop, believe me."

"Perhaps if you trusted me for a change—"

"I do trust you. It's all the fortune-hunting arses in society I don't trust. Like Malet. And speaking of him, did Wolfe overhear enough of your conversation to realize that you were once nearly engaged to the bastard?"

"I don't think so. The major wasn't close enough to us for that."

Thorn released a breath. "Thank God. It wouldn't do for people in society to learn that you were once involved with Malet. The gossip about his being cashiered—and why— has already filtered out to those in the highest ranks of society, and he is persona non grata there. So people might make unfounded speculations about you if it becomes known that you almost married the scoundrel ten years ago."

She blinked at Thorn. "Being cashiered? I know nothing of that. What happened?"

A shadow crossed her twin's face. "Ask Heywood and Cass if you want the whole story. Suffice it to say, Malet isn't in any way an acceptable suitor for young women."

"As I recall, you made sure I figured that out on my own," she said tersely.

At least her brother had the good grace to look guilty. "Still angry with me over that, are you?"

"Don't be absurd. You saved me from a dire fate—being married to Captain . . . Mr. Malet." *Never mind that you nearly destroyed my future in the process.* "It's all water under the bridge."

"Liar," her twin said softly. When she didn't repeat her claim, he sighed. "In any case, we should keep your past association with Malet a secret from Wolfe. We'll just let him continue to assume that Malet was trying to abduct you today because of his conflict with Heywood. Don't you agree?"

"Of course." The very idea of Major Wolfe knowing what a fool she'd been in her youth put a knot in her stomach, though she wasn't sure why. It wasn't as if she would see much of the former officer from now on. Her family was leaving for London in a few days, and he would be stuck here.

"I'm glad you concur," Thorn went on. "I honestly don't think Wolfe is the gossiping sort, but the less said about the matter to anyone, the better."

"Most assuredly."

When her twin walked over to the door and opened it, she belatedly remembered that Major Wolfe was awaiting them outside. But why? Did Thorn mean to offer him a reward for rescuing her today?

She hoped not. The major was as proud as a lion—and twice as snarly. He wouldn't take that well.

"Come in, sir," Thorn said. "I have a proposition to put to you."

Oh no. That didn't sound good.

Judging from Major Wolfe's wary expression as he entered, he agreed with her. "What sort of proposition?" he asked, shooting her a questioning glance.

She gave a helpless shrug. She had no idea what her brother was cooking up.

"As you may know," Thorn said, "the entire family will be decamping to London in a few days. We leave the day after Easter."

"I'm aware," the major said, crossing his arms over his chest.

"When we do, I would like you to join us."

"I daresay there's not much call for a gamekeeper in your London town house," Major Wolfe said suspiciously.

"True, but I don't need you for that. I need you to be Gwyn's bodyguard."

# Chapter Three

Bloody hell. Now *that* was unexpected.

Did Lady Gwyn know what her twin had planned? One look at her incredulous expression told Joshua that she didn't.

"While I agree that under the circumstances your sister could use a bodyguard," Joshua said, "surely you, sir, would be enough to frighten off Malet."

The duke drummed his fingers on the writing table. "My sister says she doesn't want me 'hovering about' because it will also 'frighten off' the men courting her," he said acidly. "But most people don't know of your connection to our family. So you can keep an eye on her suitors without people realizing you're doing so."

Lady Gwyn stiffened. "I don't need a nursemaid for my debut."

Thornstock arched a brow. "I would hardly call a marine officer a nursemaid. Protecting you will be rather dull for him, I expect. Fortunately, I don't mind paying him handsomely for such work."

Joshua could use the money, but given his lack of endurance for loud noises, the very thought of London made him shudder. "There are other considerations, Duke. Like my inability to pursue Malet very quickly on foot should he attempt to abscond with her in that fashion. You may prefer to hire a more able-bodied fellow."

"You can shoot, can't you?" Thornstock asked. "And use a blade? Grey said you knocked around one of Malet's minions so well at Christmas that the fellow could barely walk afterward. So it seems you can use fisticuffs, too. Apparently, running is about the only thing you *can't* do."

"I can shoot, stab, and slug a man, yes, but that's not—"

"It's good enough to satisfy me." The duke cast a furtive glance at his twin. "As long as you protect my sister by any means at your disposal, I am content."

It began to occur to Joshua that despite the difficulties he might encounter, this chance to go to London could also work in his favor. His letters clearly weren't reaching the War Secretary, but if he could visit the office in person, he might convince the man to put him back in the Royal Marines at full pay.

Before Joshua could ask any questions or even agree to the proposition, however, Lady Gwyn cleared her throat. "I suppose I have no say in this."

"Of course you have a say in it," Thornstock told her. "You can either have me hovering about you in society, or you can have Wolfe doing so more discreetly. But one of us *will* be accompanying you during your debut. So you'll have to decide which it's to be."

"That's not much of a choice," she said, casting Joshua a look he found impossible to read. Alarm? Anger? Attraction?

He scoffed at that last one. The woman might flirt with him occasionally, but that didn't mean she desired him. She'd been preparing for her debut for months. Practicing her flirtation skills was undoubtedly part of that preparation.

Still, he held his breath as she seemed to consider the two possibilities. He wanted her to choose him . . . but only because he needed to go to London to see the War Secretary.

It had nothing to do with how lovely she looked wearing something other than a black gown for the first time in months. Nor did it stem from how the light from the window turned her hair redder than flame, or the way her plump lower lip quivered a bit as she considered her brother's proposal.

God, this was a mistake he'd be a fool to make. Going to London was already a potentially disastrous running of the gauntlet from which he might never recover. But to risk having it happen around her? He could well imagine his reacting to some sudden sound in the street and having her witness the full extent of his vile temper.

So he opened his mouth to withdraw his willingness to serve as her bodyguard, but she spoke first. "Very well. I choose the major."

Her words so took Joshua aback that he nearly missed the satisfaction flashing across her brother's face. What was Thornstock planning, and why would he want Joshua to be part of it? Granted, the duke was known to be a rakehell, the sort of chap more preoccupied with debauchery than debuts. But even if escorting his sister about society would curtail his fun, surely he'd rather do it himself than rely on a virtual stranger.

As for Lady Gwyn . . .

No point in trying to figure out *her* reasoning. She rarely made sense to him. She liked to shop—he sometimes saw her in Sanforth picking out reticules and such. She liked to tease and cheer people up—she'd attempted it with Joshua time and again. But when it came to her brother, she seemed to feel naught but anger. The duke must have thoroughly provoked her ire at some point, and she was still punishing him for it.

Joshua should take that as a warning. The lady held

grudges, even against her own twin. So he mustn't lower his guard around her. It was never wise to expose one's jugular to the enemy.

The duke turned to him. "And you, too, agree to the scheme?"

If he didn't, he might end up sentenced to a life in the countryside forever. And even though it was peaceful, which was probably better for his temper, he would rather be at war where no one cared about that. "I agree."

"Excellent," Thornstock said. "With that decided, we should settle a few details." He ran a critical gaze over Joshua. "I do hope you have clothes suitable for going into society."

"Thorn!" Lady Gwyn exclaimed. "Don't be rude."

"How is that rude?" Thornstock asked. "You don't want him to stick out in society any more than necessary, do you?"

She thrust out that lush lower lip. "It's just . . . I merely think . . ."

"I don't mind the question," Joshua put in, amused by the fact that she was trying to defend him. Her brother's inquiry was reasonable, given the ragged state of Joshua's greatcoat. "I still own a dress uniform, as well as an undress uniform that would probably be appropriate for daytime social affairs."

Thornstock looked surprised. "I thought you had left the marines."

"I'm on half-pay. It's not the same as being discharged. Technically, I am still an officer, and still capable of being called up to serve. But in reality, a man with my . . . difficulties would be overlooked when it came to calling up soldiers on half-pay."

"Ah, I see," Thornstock said. "As long as you can legitimately wear the uniform, that's fine with me. And ladies do find officers in uniform appealing, don't they, Sis?"

Something flared in her gaze. "So I've heard."

The duke smirked at her before continuing his interrogation of Joshua. "What about regular attire? You'd hardly want to wear your uniform to accompany Gwyn on her shopping jaunts, for example."

"Oh, Lord," Gwyn said. "He'll be going with me on those, too?"

"As long as Malet is a threat," Joshua said, "I will be going with you everywhere." He returned his attention to the duke. "I have regular clothes that should be perfectly appropriate." Granted, some of them might be moth-eaten and out of fashion, but he wasn't about to admit that to Thornstock, duke or no.

"If you need a tailor," the duke said, "let me know, and I can recommend one who can fit you out."

Joshua fought the urge to laugh in his face. A tailor. Thornstock clearly hadn't ever had to deal with a dearth of funds or he would realize how absurd his offer was. Lack of a reliable tailor was the least of Joshua's problems. "Thank you."

As if Lady Gwyn guessed the reason for Joshua's terse reply, she said, "Or if you'd rather, one of my half brothers could loan you a few things."

"I appreciate the thought," he said. This conversation had begun to grate, and the one thing he must not do in front of these two was lose his temper. That would very quickly ruin any chance he had of going to London with them. "I do have one question for the duke. Where will I be residing while in town?"

Thornstock frowned. "I assumed you'd be willing to stay at the Armitage town house with Mother and Gwyn. Knowing that you're there to look after them will relieve me, and because

Mother is also your aunt, that should make it perfectly respectable. And Sheridan will be there eventually."

"Why wouldn't Major Wolfe stay with *you*?" Lady Gwyn asked.

Was she blushing? Impossible. Unlike his own sister, Lady Gwyn never blushed. Still, her cheeks seemed scarlet just now, and the mere thought of her blushing sparked an unwise fire in his blood.

The duke narrowed his gaze on her. "Because I don't want him to, for one thing."

"Of course not." She flashed her brother a calculating look. "How silly of me to think you might give up some of your bachelor habits for a month or two."

"How typical of you to assume that's why," he said lightly, though his eyes were ice. "The truth is, Wolfe can't very well protect you if he's living in another household."

"It *would* be best for me to reside with you and your mother, Lady Gwyn," Joshua said. "Though I don't know about the propriety of it."

"It's not the propriety I care about," Lady Gwyn bit out. "It's the idea of having my every action scrutinized!"

"I'll do my best to give you your privacy at the town house," Joshua said, "but when we're in public, I should accompany you most plainly, so that Malet doesn't even attempt an attack."

The woman seemed unsure how to answer that.

"I agree with Wolfe," Thornstock said. "Now, on to another matter, sir. Have you a weapon smaller than that flintlock pistol I see peeking from your greatcoat pocket?"

"Actually, it's a seven-barreled Nock pepperbox."

"Good God, I've never seen one, though I knew they existed." Thornstock held out his hand. "May I look at it?"

Joshua handed over his weapon. He was proud of it,

having purchased it from a fellow marine officer when the man had retired.

Thornstock looked it over with a clearly admiring gaze. "This is quite a pistol. No wonder you frightened Malet off. I take it you have to turn the barrels manually?"

Joshua nodded.

Thornstock handed the pistol back to Joshua. "Unfortunately, you can't go hauling *that* about in society. The ladies will swoon to see a mammoth weapon like that."

Lady Gwyn snorted. "Men! We don't swoon at everything."

"*You* don't," Thornstock said, "but even you must admit that you're not the average lady."

Truer words had never been spoken. Shoving his pistol back into his greatcoat pocket, Joshua smiled thinly. "In any case, my Nock pepperbox should do for circumstances outside of society. Though it appears rather the worse for wear, it still fires effectively."

"What about a firearm for when you are within society?" the duke asked. "Don't suggest a sword. You may not realize this, but these days officers at balls are not allowed to carry their swords beyond the cloakroom."

"I carry my own sword everywhere without being discovered." Joshua pushed a button on his cane, and the handle slid out to reveal the blade inside it. "Since I always need my cane, I prefer that it serve a dual purpose."

Thornstock whistled low. "How clever is that? I'm impressed, Wolfe. You are prepared for every contingency."

"I've heard they make canes with small pistols in the handle as well. I hope to buy one in London." Another good reason to accept Thornstock's offer.

"You could use *my* pistol for the time being. It's one of a pair, so you and I could each carry one." The duke picked up the pocket pistol he'd set down on the writing table moments before. "What it lacks in the quick firing of your pepperbox, it makes up for in ease of use. Although I don't know if it could be hidden inside a dress uniform."

Joshua stared covetously at the firearm's gold-chased barrel and intricately carved ivory stock. "Trust me, I could find a way to hide it." Damned right he could, if only to get his hands on it. "Though it appears to be rather too valuable to use as a weapon, Your Grace."

"I did pay two-hundred pounds for it only last month."

Bloody hell, that was the equivalent of Joshua's salary on the estate for five years.

Thornstock held it out to him. "I assume I can trust you to keep it safe."

Joshua should refuse to accept the costly piece. God only knew what would happen if the damned thing proved more ornamental than useful. But he couldn't resist its sheer beauty. "I will do my best to return it intact," he said as he took it.

Thornstock lifted a brow. "You can keep it as payment for guarding my sister . . . as long as you return *her* intact."

Joshua was still reeling at the incredibly generous offer when Lady Gwyn said loftily, "I am not a gun, Thorn. Nor do I belong to you, to be loaned out to the major on consignment."

"More's the pity," the duke grumbled. "He might actually be able to keep you in line."

Joshua wasn't touching that statement for all the gold and ivory pistols in England.

Lady Gwyn's eyes flashed at her twin. "And you wonder why you have so much trouble with respectable women."

"I deal perfectly well with respectable *married* women,"

Thornstock drawled. "It's the unmarried ones trying to leg-shackle me who drive me mad."

"So, are we finished with this highly inappropriate discussion about how to manage me in London?" Lady Gwyn quipped.

The duke smiled thinly. "I doubt many men could 'manage' you, *Liebchen*. I wouldn't even attempt it."

"Good. Because if you did, I'd hand you your bollocks in a box."

Bloody hell, even Beatrice wasn't that outspoken. Lady Gwyn had quite a mouth on her, one he wouldn't mind explor—

*Don't even think it, man. That's asking for a world of trouble.*

"Only one more matter needs mentioning, Wolfe," Thornstock said. "You mustn't tell Mother why you're traveling with us."

"Much as I hate to agree with my brother about anything, he's right." Lady Gwyn's face looked shuttered. "It would alarm Mama to hear that my very . . . er . . . future could be in danger. And with her so fragile since our stepfather's death . . ."

Eyes narrowing, Joshua looked from one twin to the other, sure that they were hiding their reasons for keeping it from his aunt. But if they were, he couldn't imagine why. "So what am I supposed to tell her?" he asked testily. "She'll find it odd that I'm leaving my post on the estate for no reason."

"Tell her you wish to see Bea." Lady Gwyn colored again. "I mean, Beatrice. Tell Mama that you wish to attend the ball where your sister is presented as Grey's duchess." She clapped her hands. "Yes, that's perfect! Mama will be delighted by *that*."

"But Beatrice will find it suspicious," Joshua grumbled. "She knows I am not one for crowds." And she knew why, too.

"Just let me handle your sister." Lady Gwyn's smile turned impudent. "I will describe how you've pined for her ever since she left, how you get terribly lonely over there at the dower house, and how you just *had* to see her in her shining moment."

Joshua eyed her askance. "Beatrice will laugh in your face if you spout any such fustian. She knows me better."

Although he *had* been lonely and he *had* missed her, he wasn't about to admit that to her lofty ladyship. Or to Beatrice, for that matter.

"Oh, very well," Lady Gwyn teased. "I'll have to work on making it sound more manly. God forbid a man should miss his sister." Her smile vanished. "Right, Thorn?"

Thornstock stared hard at her. "Watch it, you termagant. I don't want to run Wolfe off before he even begins."

"And on that note," Lady Gwyn said frostily, "I believe I shall leave. I have packing to do, and the major undoubtedly has matters to settle with the servants under him and with Sheridan." She turned to Joshua. "Oh, and Major Wolfe, if you don't mind, I'd like a private word with you before you head back to the dower house."

With a tight nod, he followed her out into the hall.

"This way," she said. After peeking into the blue parlor, she led him inside and closed the door.

That gave him pause. "I believe this is a bit more private than propriety would allow, your ladyship."

"Pishposh. This will only take a moment. But I don't want my brother to interfere any more than he already has." She lifted her pretty brow. "And by the way, when you say 'your ladyship' like that, it sounds awfully sarcastic."

"I'll attempt to make it sound more respectful in future," he said, though this time he'd been unable to keep the sarcasm out of his tone.

"That is not what I meant!" she protested. "You know perfectly well you are not a servant."

"I beg to differ. Your brother referred to me as a game-keeper not once but twice." When she winced, he softened his tone. "*You* may not think of me in that light, but Thorn-stock certainly does. With good reason. I do the work of a gamekeeper. And thanks to the agreement I just made, I will do the work of your bodyguard in London. So obviously I don't mind being employed by your family."

What a bare-faced lie. He did mind. He wanted to do something of more worth than managing the kennel and wooded property of a ducal estate.

"If you say so." She sighed. "But that's not what I wish to discuss. Once we reach London, I want you to teach me to shoot."

He muttered an oath under his breath. "Because your brother wisely refused to do so?"

She waved her hand dismissively. "He's merely being his usual overprotective self. But you taught Beatrice, so I don't see why you can't teach me."

He crossed his arms over his chest. "I taught Beatrice out of necessity, because she was occasionally alone in the dower house at night and I wanted her to be safe. Somehow I doubt that putting a loaded gun into *your* hand would keep anyone safe, even you."

"Then I have a surprise for you, Major," she said with a toss of her head. "Unless you agree to teach me to shoot, I will walk back into the writing room and tell my brother that I prefer to have him accompany me about London after all. Because you are only of use to me if you do as I ask, at least in this instance."

Damn. She seemed determined to force the issue. He could wash his hands of her right now and refuse to do her bidding, in which case he would also lose the chance to go to London with Sheridan's blessing.

*Or* he could try another time-honored tactic: deflection. Hmm. That *could* work. A plan formed in his mind.

He nodded as if to concede defeat. "Fine. Shooting lessons, it is."

# Chapter Four

The day after Easter, their party set out for London in Thorn's comfortable traveling coach, with Gwyn and her mother on one side and Thorn and Major Wolfe on the other. Thorn was exerting himself for once, trying to entertain Mama by giving her riddles to solve.

Gwyn was more interested in watching Major Wolfe.

The truth was, Gwyn had been dreading her debut until Thorn had hired the major to accompany them. That day in the writing room, she'd poked the bear, and it had been so much fun that she could hardly wait to do it more. Whenever she teased the major, the cloud of gloom lifted from his brow and he turned sarcastic. It meant she was able to affect him more than he let on, which had quite surprised her.

Today he'd managed to surprise her again. After all the talk about his lack of acceptable clothing, she'd expected him to wear his uniform at the very least. But although his travel attire was somewhat unfashionable—few gentlemen wore dove-gray greatcoats or smoky gray trousers these days—he looked so glorious in it that it hardly mattered.

Even without a uniform, every inch of him shouted "officer," from the ebony locks he kept tied in a queue to his gray kid gloves and black leather jackboots.

And oh, how those boots made her salivate. It didn't help

that the toes of the boot on his right leg were, of necessity, nearly touching her skirts, because he seemed unable to bend that knee very well due to his injury. She wished she were daring enough to run the toe of her half-boot over the toe of his. Perhaps that would tempt him to stretch his feet *beneath* her skirts, at least enough so that they could touch boots more . . . er . . . intimately.

Perhaps it would *finally* make him look at her. He'd kept his gaze trained out the window for an hour now, although she couldn't figure out what he found so fascinating out there. With Easter having been early this year, the Season was early as well, so spring had not yet sprung. Some trees were budding, but the weather was so damp and cold, even in the carriage, that her wool cloak still didn't keep her warm.

She shivered, and her mother reached over to take her gloved hand. "Oh, dear," Mama said, "your hands are like ice. We simply *must* buy you a thicker cloak in London. This one is fetching, I'll grant you, but—"

"My cloak is perfectly adequate for spring, Mama," Gwyn said, not wanting to reinforce the major's opinion that she was spoiled. "Besides, I'd never even had a chance to wear it when we went into mourning. I'm not going to pass up the chance now just because it's a bit chilly today."

"Well, when we stop to change horses," Mama said, "I'll ask that they give us some heated bricks. I always find that warming one's feet helps keep one warm all over."

"We don't have time for heated bricks, Mother," Thorn put in irritably. "We're expected at the Golden Oak Inn in Cambridge at dusk, and I want to make good time. Besides, I'm not cold. Are you, Wolfe?"

"I'm fine," he said, not even turning his head from the window.

"Well, of course *Joshua* is fine." Her mother sniffed. "He's probably been in all sorts of weather as a soldier."

"I dare say he has," her brother remarked. "Weren't you at the glorious Battle of the Nile, Wolfe?"

At last he turned his gaze from the window. "Yes," he said tersely. "And it was hardly glorious, trust me."

Thorn shifted on the seat to gaze more fully at the major. "The British won spectacularly, didn't we? I'd say that's glorious."

Major Wolfe grimaced. "We lost nearly two hundred men on our ship, many of them my fellow marines. So forgive me if my image of the battle is colored by the blood I saw running on the decks of the *Majestic*. At one point, the *Majestic* was between two of the French ships, which is how we lost our captain and two of our masts, not to mention how our hull became severely damaged. It did not feel very glorious at the time."

"All the same," Thorn persisted, "Sheridan told me last night that you are quite the war hero. That you were promoted to captain on the strength of your performance in that battle alone. I had no idea."

Neither had Gwyn. How it must chafe the man to be brought so low as to be a gamekeeper. No wonder he was always grumbling.

"Is that where you were wounded?" Gwyn asked, eager to hear anything he might say about his time in the Royal Marines.

A faint smile lifted the corners of his mouth. "Given that the Battle of the Nile took place ten years ago, no. I haven't been languishing in Sanforth as long as all that, your ladyship."

"Forgive me," Gwyn muttered. "I don't know that much about the war against France."

"Clearly," Thorn drawled.

"To be fair, I *was* living in Berlin at the time," Gwyn shot back.

"And we all know newspapers don't exist in Berlin," Thorn said caustically.

Mama glared at them, then turned her attention to Major Wolfe. "You know, Joshua, you needn't speak so formally with us. As my nephew, you're family."

"Ah, yes, my good chap," Thorn added, "I meant to mention that yesterday. You'll stand out like a green lad in society if you keep using 'your ladyship' and 'Your Grace' and such. I know Gwyn and I aren't actually related to you, but as Mother says, you're part of the family, especially now that your sister has married our half brother. Besides, you're the grandson of a duke yourself. So stop with the honorifics, for God's sake."

"I tried to tell him that two days ago," Gwyn said, "but he wouldn't listen."

The major lifted a brow. "Forgive me, Lady Gwyn, but it was hard to keep up with the many instructions—and requests—you were giving me."

He was veering dangerously close to mentioning her wish to be taught to shoot. Judging from the glint in his eyes, he knew it, too.

"That's Gwyn for you," Thorn said. "Always instructing people."

"Me!" Gwyn said, crossing her arms over her chest. "You were the one going on and on about his clothing."

"Hush, both of you," Mama said. "I don't want to listen to this bickering all the way to the Golden Oak Inn."

Thorn rolled his eyes. "We're not children anymore, Mother, and haven't been in some years."

"You could have fooled me," she said. "My nephew is the only one behaving with some decorum."

"I don't think anyone's ever accused me of behaving with decorum, Aunt," the major said. "Not even my sister."

The mere mention of Mother's favorite niece softened her. "I meant to tell you—it is such a sweet thing you are doing, attending Beatrice's debut ball. Does she know you're coming?"

Major Wolfe slanted a querying look at Gwyn. When she gave a small shake of her head, he said, "It's a surprise."

"That's even better!" Mama exclaimed. "Oh, I can't wait to see her face when you stroll into the town house."

"Then I shall attempt to stroll, if only to please you, Aunt," he said without rancor, although he wouldn't meet Gwyn's gaze.

The remark went right past Mama, as excited as she was at the prospect of surprising Beatrice, but Gwyn noted it at once. It made her heart hurt for him. How many times in a day did people speak such things heedlessly? How often did he have to pretend not to notice their slips?

"It's just a pity that you can't attend the presentation at court, too," Mama went on cheerily, "although perhaps Grey could get an invitation for you if he spoke to the right people."

"Please do not put him to that trouble," the major said in what sounded more like a command than a request. "Attending Beatrice's debut ball will be quite enough for me."

Gwyn winced. This must be sheer torture for him, being forced to go into society when he didn't want to. But that might work in her favor. Perhaps he'd let her talk him into staying at the town house once or twice while she went with friends into society. Friends she could get away from easily. Once was all she would need to get Lionel's money to him.

"What made you decide to join us in London in the first place?" Mother asked. "Bea was sure you would not come even if she asked."

His gaze flicked to Gwyn for the briefest of moments before he jerked it away and said dryly, "I missed her."

Gwyn barely suppressed a snort, and she could see her brother trying hard not to laugh.

"Well, that is lovely." Mama leveled a dark gaze on Thorn. "I wish the twins were so close to each other. But Thorn has never forgiven Gwyn for not coming back to England with him when he returned to claim his title."

"*Mother*," Thorn said in a pained voice.

"What? It's true."

"Perhaps so, but it's of no interest to the major, I'm sure," Gwyn said. "He doesn't want to hear about our family squabbles."

"On the contrary," Major Wolfe said, "I am all ears."

And all eyes, too, apparently, for he was now watching Gwyn with an intensity that did odd things to her insides.

"It began when Gwyn had this particularly troublesome suitor," Mama said.

Gwyn shot Thorn an imploring look, but for once he seemed at a loss for words.

"I forget the fellow's name," Mama went on. "Was it Hazle-something?"

Hazlehurst had been another of Gwyn's suitors. Thank heaven for Mama's spotty memory. And for Gwyn's rather lengthy history of being courted by men whom she ended up not marrying.

"Yes, Mama, it was Hazlehurst," Gwyn said, lying for all she was worth.

"Anyway," Mama went on, "I gather that Thorn was nasty to him, so the man went off to join the navy. And Gwyn never forgave him."

"Hazlehurst?" Major Wolfe searched Gwyn's face. "Or Thornstock?"

"Both," Mama said. "Washed her hands of them both."

"Can you blame me?" Gwyn said with a sniff. "Thorn had no business running Hazlehurst off, and Hazlehurst had no business allowing himself to be run off by Thorn."

"Especially for something as trivial as your brother being

nasty to him," the major said. "If this fellow Hazlehurst couldn't hold his own in such a circumstance, the navy must have given him quite the rude awakening."

"I'm sure it did," Thorn said, apparently *finally* getting his wits about him. "I've heard that floggings are common on a man-of-war. Is that true, Major?"

The man shrugged. "It depends on the captain. I've seen it happen a great deal on some ships, and not at all on others."

Thorn had apparently found a subject that interested the major, for they launched into a discussion about how marines were treated on naval ships, the battles Major Wolfe had been in, and all sorts of other manly military subjects.

Under other circumstances, she would have found the conversation fascinating, too. Today, however, she listened with only half an ear, unable to concentrate on anything except her relief that the disaster had been averted.

But for how long? What if her mother revealed something else about the past that forced her to lie? Or was Mama now satisfied that she'd said her piece on the subject?

Clearly, Gwyn's debut was going to be fraught with more peril than she'd expected. Because the last thing in the world she wanted was for Major Wolfe—or anyone in her family—to learn the truth about her past with Lionel Malet.

# Chapter Five

They had stopped to change horses every hour, and occasionally one or the other of the ladies had disembarked to use the necessary. But that had not been often enough for Joshua to get out and exercise his bad leg. Normally, he wouldn't have needed the exercise until they stopped for the night, for he would have stretched out his leg enough to keep it from cramping.

Unfortunately, that was impossible while he sat across from Lady Gwyn. He wasn't about to thrust his booted foot beneath her elegant green carriage dress. For one thing, he didn't wish to soil it, or the expensive-looking cloak she wore over it. For another, even if she didn't misinterpret his actions, he feared the very idea of having his boot beneath her skirts would start *his* imagination roaming to other forbidden places.

Yet no matter how he tried to arrange matters so he sat across from his aunt, who probably wouldn't care if he encroached on her space, he always ended up across from Lady Gwyn. Either his aunt or Thornstock or both were behind that. He couldn't imagine that Lady Gwyn had anything to do with it. She'd been quiet ever since he and Thornstock had begun discussing the military.

After a while, she fell asleep. Only then did he dare to

slide his boot beneath her skirts, but it was too little, too late.
So when they stopped in front of the Golden Oak Inn, he
practically leaped from the carriage in his eagerness to
escape the confined quarters. All he wanted now was a short
walk to get the feeling back in his leg, a fine meal, a glass of
brandy, and a chance to sit before the fire soaking his bad
foot and calf in a bucket of warm water.

He was glad he would get to do all of it alone if he wished,
because the duke had informed Joshua that he would have
his own room. Being a "war hero" apparently had its advantages.

"Where are you going, Gwyn?" he heard his aunt ask.

"For a walk, Mama. I need some fresh air. I won't be long."

Bloody hell, the woman was even now heading across the
innyard in her fancy cloak and hat, bound for the archway
they had just come through. Thornstock, who was already escorting Aunt Lydia into the inn, halted long enough to nod to
Joshua. Obviously, Joshua's post as bodyguard started *now*.

Barely suppressing a curse, he altered his course to head
for the young woman. "Lady Gwyn!" he called out.

She paused to look back, clearly surprised. "No need to
come with me, Major. I'm sure you want a mug of ale as
badly as Thorn."

"You cannot walk in a strange town unaccompanied,
madam."

"Why not?" She turned to continue on. "I walk alone in
the country all the time. And it's not even dark yet."

"It will be dark shortly." He caught up to her. "And
anyway, dark or not, Malet could have been following us the
whole way, watching for just such a chance to kidnap you."

"I doubt that. He—" She halted, as if realizing she'd been
about to say something unwise. Then she drew her cloak
more closely about her. "Fine. But I fully intend to see Great

St. Mary's Church before I return. So are you sure you wish to go that far? That walking with me won't . . . um . . . pain your leg?"

He debated whether to speak the truth, and finally decided he had nothing to gain by lying. "*Not* walking would pain it after such a lengthy ride in a coach. My leg cramps if I sit for too long in one spot."

"Oh, dear," she said, sounding genuinely upset. "I had no idea. Is there anything we could do to help?"

*Let me thrust my foot as far under your skirts as I dare to-morrow? Take my leg in your pretty hands tonight and knead it until I fall asleep?*

Damn. "No," he said curtly. "It's something I'm used to dealing with."

"Well, I do hope you'll tell us if we can make it better."

"I will." Time to change the subject before the image of her making it "better" in any number of lascivious ways sent his mind down unwise passages. "So, I'm curious about something. What exactly did your brother do or say to this Hazlehurst fellow that made the man run off to war instead of staying around to marry you?"

"First of all, it wasn't certain that Hazlehurst would have married me even if he *had* stayed around."

"Were you an heiress back then?"

"Yes."

"Then he would have married you." The minute the words left his mouth, he realized how insulting he sounded. "My God, that was not—"

"For your information," she clipped out, "I didn't mean that he might have chosen not to marry *me*. I meant that *I* might have chosen not to marry *him*."

"Of course. Pardon me, Lady Gwyn. When it comes to

matters of marriage and the heart, I tend to be cynical. It colors every word out of my mouth."

Silence was all he got for that answer.

He tried again. "It goes without saying that *you* would have your pick of the men, but I figured any man would be a fool not to marry a woman as beautiful and accomplished as you, especially when a fortune was also involved. You and your brother had already made it clear that this Hazlehurst didn't have the sense God gave him, so—"

"Oh, do stop, Major. My feelings aren't so bruised that I would fall for that balderdash. I can tell when someone is flattering me."

That took him aback. Though her tone was peevish, it certainly didn't sound insulted anymore. Bad enough that he'd gushed like that to a woman who probably received compliments as a matter of course—he wasn't about to admit that he'd meant every word of that "balderdash."

They walked a little way in silence, past the carriage house and the stables next to it until they emerged onto the main road in Cambridge. Their inn was in a less-populated part of town, so they were mostly alone for their walk.

He understood why she was so concerned about his leg holding up, but honestly, he walked great distances on the estate every day. He merely had to walk them slower than most.

As they were entering the area that contained the university buildings, they approached two men unloading trunks from a cart in front of a tavern, laughing and joking as they carried a trunk inside. It was the kind of idyllic scene that could take place in any town in England.

Joshua and Lady Gwyn had just passed by the cart when a loud crash sounded behind them.

It instantly catapulted Joshua back to the deck of the *Amphion*, to the explosion cutting through their rigging . . . and both side's men. Instinct sent him whirling into a crouch and, scarcely aware he did it, he drew his flintlock and cocked it. It took him a few more precious seconds to notice the open trunk with its pewter mugs clattering over the cobblestones.

The two fellows who'd dropped the trunk froze at the sight of his pistol. He froze, too, disoriented.

Suddenly, he felt Lady Gwyn's hand covering his. "I think there's no need for the gun just now," she murmured.

An agony of shame swamped him. Damnation, what was he doing? "Remove your hand, Lady Gwyn," he said tightly. "I have to uncock the pistol."

She did. He rose and went through the complicated process of uncocking his weapon safely.

Then he rounded on her. "For God's sake, never, *ever* touch a man's hand when he's got a cocked pistol in it!"

She swallowed hard. "I—I'm sorry. I was just—"

"I could have shot them." He couldn't seem to calm himself. "I could have shot *you*. If I had turned—"

"But you didn't," she said, though her flaming cheeks showed she'd taken his warning to heart. She grabbed his arm to draw him away from the two men, who were now watching with avid curiosity. "Everything's fine."

"Everything is *not* fine." He was still quaking at what he could have done. "We should return to the inn."

"Not until you're calmer." Still clinging to his arm, she continued on toward Cambridge proper.

He went along, even as his heart hammered in his chest. "This is why I shouldn't be going to London, shouldn't be acting as bodyguard to *anyone*, damn it. I need quiet places, preferably with no one around." Or he needed to be in the Royal Marines again, where his behavior would seem normal.

"Balderdash. You realized what you were doing pretty quickly, I'd say. No harm done."

He lifted a brow at her. "You're still gripping my arm as if to keep me from hurting anyone. Don't tell me it's no harm done." When she released his arm self-consciously, he said, "Now you know why the residents of Sanforth steer clear of me."

Especially the women, who had begun to regard him with alarm whenever he went into town.

Yet Lady Gwyn wasn't doing so. "Have you reacted that way before? At home in Sanforth or on the estate, I mean?"

"Unfortunately, yes."

"How often?"

He gritted his teeth, though she had a right to know. "A few times."

"Have you ever shot anyone? Hurt anyone?"

"Not yet. But—"

"Then you are dealing with it as best you can. And for what it's worth, I, too, jumped when they dropped that trunk behind us."

"You didn't shoot anyone."

"Neither did you." She smiled doggedly. "Now, we're going to change the subject and finish our walk."

He stared hard at her. "You're rather high-handed for a woman."

"You've *met* my family, haven't you? When we're all together, it's the battle of the dukes, everyone struggling to get their own way. I have learned that if I want my own wishes considered at all, I have to throw myself into the fray with the rest of them."

In spite of everything, that made him smile. Her assertion reinforced the impression he'd gained of her family himself.

They walked a short distance more.

"Magnificent sunset, isn't it?" she said, apparently determined to cheer him up.

He hadn't noticed. But now he made himself pay attention to where the sun sank low on their right, washing the sky with swirls of pink and orange and purple. "It is." He nodded toward an impressive building. "Is that the church you wished to see?"

"Yes. I try to visit it every time we come through here. I've always admired the Late Perpendicular Gothic style of Great St. Mary's. I like the clean lines, the symmetry, and the lack of stained glass. And because of the latter, what I like best right now is how the dying sun looks like red flames in the reflection of the plain windows."

He mustered up an answer. "I sometimes forget that sunsets are more than mere indicators of coming weather at sea. 'Red sky at night, sailors' delight. Red sky at morning, sailors take warning' and all that."

"Given your years aboard ship, do you find the red-sky thing to be true?"

"Generally."

She sighed. "I often wish I could paint a sunset, but I can't do it justice."

"No one can. Nature has the monopoly on sunsets. I've yet to see one in a painting that didn't look forced."

"That's rather harsh, don't you think?"

"Perhaps. I haven't seen many paintings." He glanced at her. "I didn't know you were an artist."

She gave a rueful laugh. "To call me an 'artist' is to call my cloak a sail. I can sketch plans for a ha-ha or a folly in no time, but to paint a reasonable approximation of such a building and do it justice? I'm hopeless at that."

"Ah, yes, I forgot about your interest in architecture."

"That's because you hardly ever see us," she said lightly. "Mama has invited you to dinner countless times and you never come. Just think of the riveting conversation you're missing. Only last week, Sheridan and Mama got into an extended argument about how a cravat should be tied."

Grimly, he shook his head. His life seemed miles away from theirs.

She tucked a curl under her fancy hat. "So now that you've been reminded of my love of architecture, you must tell me what *you* have an interest in. Because somehow I doubt that it's catching poachers and breeding retrievers and whatever else a gamekeeper does."

"You guessed that, did you?"

"It was hard not to. You're so grumpy whenever I see you that I can only assume it's because you don't like your post."

"My post is fine. It's just . . ."

"Not what you thought you'd spend your life doing," she said.

"Exactly."

"But you keep doing it because you're afraid of hurting anyone if you do anything else," she persisted.

"Yes." Surprised by her insight, he shot her a dark look. "I thought we were going to change the subject."

"Right," she said, smiling faintly. "So what *did* you think you would spend your life doing?"

"Leading men into battle. Discussing strategy with other officers. Traveling to new places that were . . . were . . ."

"As far away from England as possible," she finished. "I know the feeling. I truly did not want to return to England myself, although I am learning to be content. With the war going on and all my family living here now, it's unlikely I'll ever be able to return to Berlin, no matter how much I miss it."

"Is that the real reason you didn't come back with Thornstock when he asked? Because you didn't want to leave Berlin and your parents?"

"Partly." She dragged in a heavy breath. "And partly because Thorn was returning to an estate and title and great wealth. Whereas I would have been returning to—"

"Nothing. Except a position as the sister of a duke with an estate and title and great wealth."

"When you say it like that I sound spoiled," she muttered.

"I didn't mean it that way." Bloody hell, every time he opened his mouth, he insulted her. He thought for a moment, trying to choose his words carefully. "Everyone wants something that is theirs alone. If you had returned with your brother, you would have lived in his shadow the way I live in your family's shadow. If anyone understands why you didn't want that, it's me."

Looking gratified by his words, she slid her hand in the crook of his elbow. His blood warmed at the touch. God help him, how he wished he didn't respond to her like this.

Then again, he felt amazingly calmer now. No doubt her chatter, her very presence, had something to do with that.

So he allowed himself to enjoy it for the moment as they moved down the cobblestone street, his cane tapping the stones rhythmically.

"Why, sir," she teased him, "is that a smile I see tugging at your lips? Oh, now I really do wish I could paint. I would love to capture the image of Major Wolfe's smile in the wild. Otherwise, no one will believe it exists."

"*Joshua's* smile in the wild." He allowed his smile to broaden as he stared down at her. "You heard what your mother said. 'You needn't speak so formally.'"

Her eyes shone as green as the commons they were skirting. "Then you must call me Gwyn."

He hadn't really been serious, but now that he'd spoken the words, he rather liked the idea of calling her by her given name. And they *were* sort of family.

No, not family in the least. Even his family had not seen him do what he'd done earlier in the street. "But no given names in public," he said.

"Right," she agreed, with an unaccountable softness in her voice. "Only in private."

The word "private" sent his heart pumping. The idea of her being with him in private made a wild exultation course through his veins.

An *unwise* exultation.

Then, as if to remind him that desiring her was madness, his stomach growled.

She laughed. "*Now* I think we should return to the inn. You seem calm enough. And perhaps that's why you reacted so . . . violently earlier. A fellow as tall and muscular as you can't go too long without a meal."

"True," he said, though despite his hunger he found himself oddly loath to return.

They turned and headed back for the Golden Oak.

"You know," he said, "you never did tell me what your twin said to run off that Hazlehurst fellow."

She frowned. "You're correct. I didn't."

"Gwyn, tell me. I want to know."

For several moments, she was silent. Then she dragged in a heavy breath. "Oh, very well." She walked a few more steps. "Thorn paid him to leave Berlin. For all I know, he paid him to join the . . . er . . . navy, too."

Joshua gave a low whistle. "If I had tried that with Beatrice, she would have, to use your phrasing, 'handed me my bollocks in a box.'"

"I *should* have," Gwyn said blithely. Although she sounded nonchalant, he couldn't help noting the heightened color in her cheeks.

"Surely your brother's reason for paying the man off was sound," he said, imagining himself in such a position. "Once the fellow took the money, he proved himself a fortune-hunter, and you would not want such a man as a husband, would you?"

"Of course not. But it was still presumptuous of Thorn."

"Clearly. Although your brother must have offered the man a great deal of money indeed to have made Hazlehurst willing to turn down a chance at your dowry."

"It wasn't just the money, to be honest, because Thorn offered him only a few thousand pounds. But Thorn also told him that if . . . er . . . Hazlehurst *did* attempt to elope with me, he would cut us both off."

"Ah. Do you think he would have done it?"

Her shoulders slumped. "It hardly mattered. Hazlehurst wasn't willing to gamble on losing my fortune, so he grabbed his bird in the hand and ran for all he was worth." She looked up at Joshua. "You say that *you* are cynical about love and marriage? Well, I'm beyond cynical. Knowing that most men see me as a walking bank has a way of keeping me from liking them."

"So that's why you're thirty and still unmarried. I did wonder. You seem to be exactly the kind of woman gentlemen in society want."

She laughed bitterly. "You clearly haven't been in society for a while or you would realize I am nowhere *near* the kind of woman gentlemen want. They prefer wives who will hand over their dowries and never attempt to have a say in how the money is used. They want women who keep silent about anything that matters and who only speak to say, 'Yes, dear,' 'Whatever you want, dear,' and 'You are my lord and master, dear.'"

"It can't be as bad as all that," Joshua said. "I don't like high society any better than you apparently do, but Grey seems to listen to Beatrice, and that's impressive, considering that Beatrice is the most impudent woman I've ever met."

"More impudent than I?" Gwyn asked, looking expectantly at him.

Bloody hell. "I . . . er . . . believe it would be wise of me to refrain from comparing the two of you. I can imagine no situation in which my answer would please you. And though you may not know how to shoot, that pin sticking out of your hat looks downright lethal."

Just as he'd hoped, that made her laugh. "Why, Joshua, you can be almost charming when you please."

"Don't get used to it. According to my sister, I only manage that feat once a month or so."

"Surely it's at least twice a month," she said with a grin.

But he'd stopped listening. "Does that fellow ahead of us look suspicious to you?"

"What fellow?"

"Don't glance around." He covered her hand with his. "We're going to stroll past the carriage house now. Look up at me and talk."

"About what?"

"It doesn't matter. I don't think he can hear us. I just need an excuse to stare in your general direction while we walk past so I can see what this chap is doing inside."

She gazed up at him. "Don't you think you're being a bit overly suspicious? Perhaps you're still reacting to what happened earlier."

"No. The fellow entering the carriage house isn't wearing the inn's livery, and if he *were* on the staff of the inn, he would be scurrying to help change the horses on that coach that just pulled through the archway. What's more, before he went into the carriage house, he surveyed the area to see if the ostler or the grooms were watching."

"I . . . I hadn't noticed any of that."

"It's a hazard of being a Royal Marine. I notice everything."

"Did *he* notice *us*?"

"No. He was looking down toward the archway and not up the road to where we were. He was too busy checking to make sure no one hired by the inn was around to see." He smiled at her even as his eyes were scanning the inside of the carriage house. "Now laugh, if you can make it sound natural."

"Tell me a joke, and I will."

"Your hat is on backward," he said.

She laughed. "It is not. And that isn't a joke."

"It got you to laugh, didn't it?" He glanced behind her, but with no lanterns yet lit inside the carriage house, it was too dim to see much. "You should go into the inn proper and join your family while I get a better look at what that fellow is doing inside."

"Not on your life," she said. "Besides, two sets of eyes are better than one."

"True. Except that I will have to follow him once he comes out."

"Why?"

"I'll need to determine who his master is."

"All right." But she looked confused by why he was so intent on figuring out who the chap was.

He understood that. It was merely a gut instinct that told him this fellow wasn't to be trusted. But he'd learned in battle never to question such instincts.

After they had fully passed the carriage house, he tugged her over to the side of the entrance and looked around the edge. Fortunately, Thornstock's carriage had been the last one in, so it was close by. Unfortunately, while Joshua could tell that the suspicious fellow was altering something on the equipage, Joshua couldn't see exactly what he was doing. He'd have to return later and examine the coach thoroughly, after he'd followed the fellow.

Suddenly, the chap hurried toward the entrance. Damn, he was coming out right *now*. There was nowhere to hide and not enough time to run, even if Joshua could. In seconds, the fellow would see them and wonder why they were lingering so close to the carriage house when they'd sauntered past several minutes before.

Joshua looked down at her, his mind racing. Then he did the only thing that would both hide their faces and make it believable that they were still close by. "Play along," he murmured.

And pulling her against him, he covered her mouth with his.

# Chapter Six

Gwyn froze. Joshua was kissing her. *Kissing* her. Although, come to think of it, he wasn't kissing her so much as putting his lips on hers. His mouth wasn't moving, and his free hand sat lightly on her waist. What's more, they both had their eyes open, which was unlike any kiss she'd shared from any other man.

That was why she was able to see the fellow they'd been watching walk past them, then pause to look at them. With her heart pounding, she closed her eyes and threw her arms around Joshua's neck.

She'd merely done it to throw the stranger off. Or perhaps she'd done it because she wanted a real kiss? Either way, everything changed then. It was as if Joshua forgot his real purpose for kissing her, because a groan escaped him and his mouth began to move roughly on hers.

It sent her pulse beating wildly. He smelled of honey water, soap, and sun-warmed leather. She hadn't expected him to smell so enticing.

Or kiss so well. This kiss wasn't tender so much as it was thorough, with great, hungry forays meant to conquer her. And when she parted her lips for him, he took the invitation with wild ferocity, driving his tongue into her mouth over and over and leaving thrills in his wake.

Now *this* was what it meant to be kissed. She hadn't expected that from him, of all people.

Next thing she knew, he had her up against the building and had dropped his cane so he could brace himself with a hand on either side of her. Why did the very act of his imprisoning her against a wall make her melt like butter all over the side of the carriage house?

She didn't know, didn't care. She just wanted more. Joshua's kiss was a glorious feast that she gobbled up greedily. The surprising softness of his mouth contrasted with the brush of his whiskered jaw against her skin.

The first fierce thrusts of his tongue now slowed to seductive strokes that made her weak in the knees. She clung to his neck like a cloud to a mountain. He moved one of his hands beneath her cloak to her ribs, then slid it up and down in a slow, sensual glide that sent a cascade of sensations along her nerves. She wanted him to touch her in other places, more private places.

Lord, but the man knew how to kiss a woman, *hold* a woman. How delightfully unexpected.

So when at last he pushed away from her, a keen disappointment burned in her throat. His eyes seemed to search her face in the dusk that thankfully hid them from anyone near the inn.

"He's gone, isn't he?" Joshua rasped.

Her brain was so fogged by enjoyment that she nearly said, "Who?" But she caught herself in time.

She surveyed the road beyond them. "I'm afraid so." She hoped Joshua couldn't tell how her voice shook.

"Damnation." Frowning, he glanced down the now empty thoroughfare. "I got caught up . . . I forgot . . ." He bent to pick up his cane. "Never mind. I lost my chance."

"To do what?"

"Follow him."

"Oh. Right." She struggled to hide the hurt his angry words inflicted.

Like a fool, she'd thought their kiss actually meant something to him. She should have known better. This was Major Wolfe, for whom everything was a marine mission, even the clattering of pewter mugs in the street. Their kiss had merely been a means to an end.

No, she couldn't be *that* wrong about the effect she had on him, could she? She'd been kissed often enough to be able to tell the real from the false. Theirs had been a real kiss. And the fact that Joshua had deepened the kiss and caressed her . . .

That said a great deal.

As did the way he avoided her gaze now. "Wait here," he said, "while I go inside the carriage house to figure out what he did to your brother's coach."

She scowled. Obviously, he didn't intend to talk about their kiss or what it meant. Obviously, he hadn't really intended to kiss her at all, even if he *had* responded enjoyably once he was in the midst of it. She'd learned early on that men were like that. They could enjoy a kiss without necessarily having it mean anything. Certainly that had been true of Lionel.

Very well. If he wanted to ignore their passionate kisses, she'd do so, too. But she wasn't going to let him run roughshod over her in the process.

"You are just as high-handed as I, Joshua, but I am not one of your soldiers to be ordered about. I'm going in there with you." When he looked as if he might protest, she added, "No one is around to see. And after all the trouble we took to hide that we were watching him in the first place, I think I deserve to know what he was doing."

Take *that,* Major I-Am-In-Charge-of-Everything Wolfe. She, too, could act as if the kiss had meant nothing whatsoever.

His eyes glittered at her in the light of the rising moon. "Fine."

"Good."

Turning on his heel, he entered the carriage house.

"Our coachman keeps a flint and some tinder to light the carriage lamps in the boot under his perch," she offered as she followed him.

"How the hell did you know that?" Joshua asked.

She shrugged. "You notice danger; I notice where servants put things I might need some day."

He shook his head as if that made no sense to him, then tried to open the boot. It didn't open easily, so he pulled hard on it, and the perch shook a bit.

"Wait a minute," he said, eyeing it suspiciously. "This may be what the fellow did." He examined the bolts that fixed the perch to the carriage. "Damn him to hell, he loosened the bolts just enough so the seat would fall off once the carriage got moving at a sufficient speed."

"How awful!" Gwyn said, rather shocked.

"Not just awful but dangerous." He rummaged in the boot until he found the toolbox kept there. "Once the perch fell off, taking the coachman with it, the horses would be spooked and driverless. We could quite easily have ended up in a runaway carriage." He found a screwdriver and tightened the bolts on the seat.

"But now that you've discovered it, everything will be fine, right?"

"It depends." He restored the screwdriver to the toolbox and the toolbox to the boot. "I'm assuming our villain was hoping for a chance to abscond with you in the confusion."

A chill ran through her. "So you think Mr. Malet is behind this."

He dusted off his hands. "Unless it was a highwayman bent on robbing Thornstock. It's difficult for a duke to travel without that being noted by criminals."

"Which do you think is more likely the case?"

Facing her, he shrugged. "Probably Malet, if he's still bent on kidnapping you."

Lionel wasn't bent on kidnapping her. He himself had said he knew better. But he might be hoping to rob Thorn, to revenge himself on her family for their perceived slights. Or perhaps he'd decided this would be a quicker way to get his funds.

"Anyway, we've done all we can tonight," Joshua said. "But I think I should ride on the perch with the coachman tomorrow, in case the culprit *is* a highwayman and he brings friends."

"I thought highwaymen were rare these days."

"They are. Which is why I'm inclined to believe that Malet engineered this so he could spirit you off."

"But how would he know when we'd break down?"

"He'd have to follow us. For that matter, so would any highwaymen. In either case, my pepperbox flintlock will be at the ready. And your brother can keep you safe inside the carriage."

Gwyn hid her disappointment. She'd been looking forward to traveling in close quarters with him again tomorrow. It would have given her a chance to question him about his past—how he'd become wounded, whether he'd ever had a sweetheart, and what made him so grumpy and prone to sudden bursts of anger.

What had made him draw a weapon on two bewildered townspeople.

"We'd best go into the inn," he said. "Your family is sure

to be wondering where we got off to. And I'll need to apprise Thornstock of the situation."

She nodded. So that was that. Nothing at all said about their kiss. Clearly, she'd been imagining he'd felt something.

The realization that he had not—or hadn't felt deeply enough to act further upon it—gave her the most disappointment of all. But it was for the best. She could never be happy married to a man with such a mercurial temperament. And once a rigid fellow like he knew the truth about her, which she couldn't hide forever, he wouldn't wish to be married to her anyway.

So no matter how much she'd enjoyed it, she would simply have to consider their kiss nothing more than a shared mistake.


The next morning, with Thornstock's blessing, Joshua took a position up on the perch with the coachman. At first, the fellow, whose name was Peabody, seemed annoyed to have him there. He would only grunt in answer to Joshua's remarks.

So much for taking Joshua's mind off the kisses he and Gwyn had shared yesterday. He'd already spent half the night replaying them, so he'd been hoping not to spend the day replaying them, too, and wondering what had possessed him to be so reckless.

At the very least, he should have apologized for pawing her like a half-starved hound. It had seemed wisest at the time just to pretend it hadn't happened. Pretend it to *her,* at any rate. He couldn't pretend it to himself. He still smelled her lemony perfume, still relished the sweet sounds of contentment she'd made . . . still tasted her mouth, which had been even softer than he imagined.

After holding her perfect, shapely body in his arms, he

*wanted* her more now than he had before. And she probably knew it, too. She would almost certainly use it to twist him this way and that. Damn it all.

To Joshua's vast relief, Peabody chose that moment to speak. "His Grace says you wanted to ride up here on account of there might be highwaymen on the road." The man's words were clipped. "But it's like I told His Grace, that's what my Brown Bess is for." He reached behind him to pat what looked to be a musket. "I can take care of any highwaymen or other scoundrels right well all by meself. So there ain't no need for you to trouble yerself, Major."

It hadn't occurred to Joshua that Peabody might resent his interference, but now that he thought about it, it made sense. "It's no trouble. To be honest, I'd rather be out here in the wind and rain any day. A stifling coach, with a duchess, a duke, and a duke's sister for company, is no place for a soldier like me."

The coachman chewed on that a moment. "I was a soldier meself once upon a time, you know." His resentment seemed to have lessened a fraction.

"I did not know. Army or navy?"

"Army. I was a sergeant in the Nineteenth Regiment of Foot till I got a load of grapeshot in me chest and shoulder and nearly died."

"Looks like you came out of it well enough in the end," Joshua said. "You must have a constitution of iron."

Peabody shrugged. "My chest pains me from time to time, especially in the winter. But at least I didn't lose a limb."

*Or damage one irrevocably*, Joshua thought.

The coachman shifted on the perch. "You were in the Royal Marines, right?"

"Still am."

"Ah. You're on the half-pay list, then. That's lucky."

Only officers had the choice of going on the half-pay list, so Joshua supposed he *was* lucky. He'd never looked at it that way before.

Peabody clicked his tongue at the horses. "I would have had a rough go of it if His Grace hadn't given me this post. He's a good man. For a duke."

Joshua chuckled. "Indeed."

They rode a while in silence.

"Tell me something," Joshua said. "I gather that you come this route often now that His Grace's mother lives at Armitage Hall."

"Often enough." The man expertly tooled the horses around a sharp curve.

"Have you ever encountered any highwaymen?"

"Not in some years, sir. That's why I was so surprised to have His Grace be worried about it when he ain't been worried before."

Joshua debated whether to tell the coachman the truth of things, but he figured he owed it to the fellow. "Actually, last night I caught a man attempting to tamper with this perch. I'm just not sure who he was or why he was doing it. He . . . er . . . got away from me before I could find out." When Peabody looked alarmed, Joshua added hastily, "Never fear—I tightened the bolts he'd loosened. But you might want to keep a close eye on things whenever we change horses."

Peabody nodded. "And ye're thinking it was highwaymen what done it? Don't seem like that's how they work. How would they know where to make us stand to?"

"I'm assuming that the villain would simply follow us at a distance until we were stranded. It's been so dry of late that the dust we kick up would hide anyone behind us."

"True."

"In any case, *someone* wished to halt the coach—or cause

it to have an accident. We're simply not sure of who or why."
He paused a moment. "Have you ever heard His Grace speak
of a man named Malet?"

The coachman frowned in thought. "Can't say as I have.
Is he the one you think is behind it?"

"Perhaps. Whatever the case, we need to be especially
alert." He patted his greatcoat pocket. "I've got a pepperbox
pistol here that would give them hell. Between that and your
Brown Bess, no one is coming near this coach to do anyone
harm."

Peabody puffed out his chest. "Aye, sir. We got our own
army here, don't we?"

For the next several hours, Joshua and Peabody dis-
cussed their lives in the military. Fortunately for Joshua,
Peabody had a flask full of brandy to keep himself warm,
and he was willing to share. But Joshua did notice that the
fellow was careful only to sip the liquid fire, so he could keep
alert and aware of any impending threats to the coach and its
occupants.

To Joshua's relief—and surprise—there proved no need
for caution. If someone *had* been lying in wait for them, he
never showed himself. Perhaps he'd grown tired of eating
their dust, waiting for them to break down.

Or, what would be infinitely worse, perhaps the fellow
hadn't ever intended to follow them. Perhaps he'd hoped for
a fatal accident that killed everyone involved.

A chill ran down Joshua's spine. It seemed unlikely. Who
would wish to kill *him*, for instance? Then again, who would
have thought that the third and fourth Dukes of Armitage
would die within months of each other, both of them murdered, according to Sheridan?

By the time they reached the outskirts of London, it
became clear that whatever the villain had been planning had
not come to fruition. So, for now, Joshua wasn't going to be

able to thwart the fellow. He could only hope he got another chance to do so in the City. Because he did not like the idea of Gwyn and her family being vulnerable to attack.

As they pushed farther into the City proper, Joshua began to relax. What's more, he realized that London had changed a great deal in the decade or more since he had last come here. It had grown filthier, but that was to be expected as it grew. Yet there were more exciting developments, like the gas lighting on Pall Mall, which he'd heard about but hadn't witnessed.

And the area of Mayfair, which Park Lane skirted, had become very built up with elegant mansions. They soon pulled into a semicircular drive in front of one such mansion, which Peabody informed Joshua was called Thorncliff. It, of course, belonged to the dukedom of Thornstock.

"It's grand, ain't it?" the coachman said with obvious pride. "His Grace oversaw the renovation of it himself. Before that, it wasn't near so grand."

Joshua gazed up at the sumptuous marble and Palladian architecture and felt his stomach drop. "Grand" didn't begin to describe it. Magnificent, perhaps. Palatial even. What it was *not* was the home of a man who would let his sister marry the likes of a lame Royal Marine with a tendency to explode into anger for little cause.

Not that Joshua hadn't already realized he was beneath Gwyn, but this . . . He could never belong in such a place. He could never belong with *her.*

Thornstock climbed out of the carriage. "You might as well take my spot inside, Wolfe," the duke said cheerily to Joshua. "Peabody is carrying the three of you to Armitage House farther south."

Joshua declined the offer. He wasn't about to climb down from the perch while Thornstock looked on. He still had *some* pride, damn it. But as Peabody pulled the carriage around, it belatedly dawned on Joshua that now he would have to climb down while *Gwyn* looked on. And that would be even worse.

He turned to Peabody. "How far are we from Armitage House?"

"Once we round Hyde Park on that corner up ahead, it's about a mile straight down that side of the park."

Joshua glanced back, relieved to see that Thornstock had already gone inside. "If you don't mind, sir, would you pull over and let me down? I need to stretch my legs some before I reach the place."

"Of course, Major. I understand."

Since it took Joshua a few minutes to disembark using his cane, his aunt and Gwyn were already poking their heads out of the carriage once he reached the street.

"What's wrong?" his aunt asked.

"Nothing," he said genially. "I just thought I'd walk the rest of the way."

"I'll come with you," Gwyn said, and before he could even dissuade her, she had called for the footman on the back perch to put down the step so she could climb out. "We'll be there shortly after you, Mama," she said, and then waved as the carriage started off again.

"I could use a bit of exercise myself," she said as she joined him. "As soon as we're inside, Mama will want to go right into unpacking, and then we'll head down for dinner, and I will lose my chance to talk to you privately."

Damn. Private conversations with her never went particularly well. "Talk to me about what?"

"You know. Our lessons."

He gave her a blank look.

"Our *shooting* lessons. I wanted to know when they would commence."

"After what happened yesterday in the streets of Cambridge, you still want to learn to shoot?"

"Well. Yes." Then a frown knit her brow. "I mean, not if it will . . . not if you will . . . you know, have trouble with it."

He had half a mind to lie and tell her that teaching her would be too upsetting for him, but the idea of her thinking of him as a half-mad soldier or milksop society fellow who couldn't endure the sound of a pistol didn't sit well.

Besides, he'd already made a plan for dealing with her "lessons." Better to continue on the way he'd started than to chance her looking for someone *else* to teach her, some tall and handsome marquess or duke who didn't have a hair-trigger temper and wasn't on half-pay.

That train of thought alarmed him. It implied jealousy, which he surely wasn't foolish enough to feel. "I won't have trouble with it. If I know to expect the noise, it's not a problem."

She released a long breath. "Then I hope we can start tomorrow."

"*Tomorrow?*" Damn it all, he would have to shift his plans.

"Well, yes. Beatrice and I are to be presented at court in a couple of days, and once that happens, a steady string of social events will follow—fêtes and balls and musicales and such. I won't have time then."

She thought he could train her to shoot in one day? She was the one who was half-mad. Or she believed him to be a magician.

But he did find her urge for speed curious. "You never said *why* you wish to learn to shoot. I'm assuming you have no weapon, and because your brother hired me to protect you, you don't need one. So why insist on this nonsense?"

She stiffened. "Never mind that. It's my business, not yours."

Nothing like putting him in his place. If he'd been starting to feel guilty over how he was planning to thwart her tomorrow, her answer squelched that. She didn't want to confide in him? She wanted to use her exalted rank as an excuse for hiding the truth from him?

Fine.

"Well, then," he said, "we can meet tomorrow morning at ten. Just tell your mother we're going riding. We'll have to, actually, in order to practice shooting. That has to be done in the country."

"I suppose you will provide the firearm?"

"I will provide everything," he said.

But she was not going to be happy when she saw *what* he provided, although at the moment, he honestly didn't care. He didn't. Absolutely not.

"By the way," she said, "did you spot anything odd on the trip today? I mean, concerning that fellow you thought might follow us?"

"Afraid not. I looked for him, but even if he were trying to catch us in a moment of distress, I wouldn't have been able to see him, with the horses kicking up so much dust. And because we didn't break down—"

"He probably gave up before we reached London."

"Precisely."

"Not to change the subject," she said, "but there is one thing I should warn you about Armitage House before we reach there. Sheridan is trying to avoid having to rent it out until after the Season, so at present it is in a state of some disarray. Most of the rooms aren't open, for example."

"The way it was at Armitage Hall."

"Precisely. While that will save the dukedom money, it makes finding one's way around a bit . . . disconcerting. It took me nearly a week to figure out where the servants' quarters are."

Obviously that veiled reference was meant for him. "I assume that is where I will be staying."

She blinked. "Don't be ridiculous. You're Mama's

nephew—you'll be in a room upstairs, probably in the wing where Sheridan's room is, though you and he will be the only two in it."

An entire wing? Bloody hell, another mansion, then. He kept forgetting that the dukedom extended back to the early 1700s. "I did wonder if Sheridan would be coming for the Season."

"We're not actually certain." She glanced away. "He will need a wife at some point, so he might as well start the process now. But he seems to be dragging his feet."

"Can you blame him? Faced with the prospect of assessing all the—as you put it—'walking banks' in society, he is probably not eager to begin looking. Few men enjoy being fortune hunters, despite what women think."

Her gaze shot to him, full of curiosity. "If you say so. You don't . . . see yourself as a fortune hunter, do you?"

"How can I? Unlike your brother, I own no property to support." He wouldn't say more than that. She didn't need to know about his hopes to return to the Royal Marines. He could hide as much as she could, and be better at it besides. She would find that out soon enough.

After another moment staring at him, she sighed. "Fortunately, we won't be doing any entertaining ourselves because Mama is still in mourning, so we won't have to deal with the gossip about why Armitage House has so many closed rooms, even during the Season."

He nodded. He was not in the mood for casual conversation with her. *You're being the grumbler she always accuses you of being.*

Yes, he was. To hell with it. To hell with her.

# Chapter Seven

Gwyn awakened far too early. She generally did during her first day back in London. The excitement of being in the City was so palpable, she could hardly sleep. But she had even more cause for it today. At last, she was going to learn to shoot! It was all she could do not to shout it to the rooftops.

Instead, she leaped from the bed and dressed in her favorite riding habit, careful to tell her maid that she was riding with Major Wolfe and they would be suitably chaperoned by a groom. Then she tripped down the stairs to breakfast well before nine a.m. To her surprise, the footman serving at table informed her that Joshua had not only already eaten but had gone for a walk.

"I was that taken aback, I was, my lady," the footman confided. "I didn't think the major would wish to walk, with his leg like that."

"He's actually quite the walker," she said. "Apparently, it helps loosen up the calf muscles." When the footman eyed her with thinly veiled astonishment, she added, "I believe his sister mentioned it."

His face cleared. "That reminds me, my lady—the duchess paid us a visit yesterday to leave a message for you and the mistress. She intends to call on you this evening with the duke. I am to send a note if that is not convenient for you."

"That is perfectly convenient, thank you." The footman nodded, then went off to fetch her coffee.

Her thoughts wandered back to Joshua. How curious that he would be walking this morning when surely he needed to save his strength for riding. Indeed, she'd been shocked to learn yesterday that he *could* ride, because she'd never seen him do so on the estate. But if a woman could ride side-saddle, then it made sense that Joshua could ride with only one good leg. The principle was the same.

"Oh, Gwyn," her mother said from the doorway, "I'm so glad you're up already. Eliza wanted to say good morning before she goes shopping."

Gwyn rose, as always delighted by a visit from the Dowager Countess of Hornsby, the woman who'd be presenting her and Beatrice for their debuts. Though Gwyn hated that Mama couldn't, Lady Hornsby was the next best thing.

"Gwyn, my dear," Lady Hornsby said as she entered with Gwyn's mother. "How wonderful to see you in something other than black or gray at last. You look positively radiant in that jonquil color!"

"Thank you," Gwyn said as she kissed Lady Hornsby's perfectly rouged cheek. Gwyn only hoped that *Joshua* would find her new riding habit attractive. It stuck in her craw that he could kiss her and afterward seem as unaffected by her as before.

Lady Hornsby patted her gray hair, which was carefully coifed into a mass of ringlets that fringed her very fashionable pink turban. "How I wish I had your natural curls. Mine take my maid forever to create."

"Yes, but you wouldn't wish to have my outrageous color, I imagine."

"Instead of my gray? Absolutely." Her blue eyes twinkled. "Besides, as your mother can tell you, redheads have more fun. Particularly in the bedchamber."

"Eliza!" Mama said.

"What? Gwyn's not some blushing schoolgirl. I'm sure with a brother like Thorn, she's heard a few salacious stories. And met a few salacious gentlemen."

"It does me no good when I do," Gwyn quipped. "Thorn acts as if I'm a nun whom no gentleman should sully. He would certainly never introduce me to anyone salacious." And he'd had no trouble running off the only salacious gentleman she'd ever known. Though much as she hated to admit it, that had probably been wise.

"Such a pity," Lady Hornsby said. "What are brothers for, if not to give their sisters a look at how gentlemen really behave?"

Mama cast her eyes heavenward. "I'm beginning to regret asking you to present my daughter, Eliza. I forgot how . . . brazen you can be."

"What fustian," Lady Hornsby said. "You could sing a bawdy song in your youth as well as the rest of us, Lydia, and you know it."

Gwyn's jaw dropped. "Mama? Singing bawdy songs?"

Lady Hornsby patted Gwyn's hand. "It was a different time, my dear. We all sang the occasional bawdy song, didn't we, Lydia?"

"Oh, Lord," Mama muttered, her cheeks stained a bright red.

"I promise not to tell anyone," Gwyn said. "If you will promise to sing me a few of them."

"If she won't, I will." Lady Hornsby then added, sotto voce, "And by the way, have you heard the latest on-dit?"

She paused for dramatic effect, and Gwyn had to swallow her laugh. Lady Hornsby was a shameless gossip, and despite Mama's protests that she didn't approve, she secretly lapped up every word.

Lady Hornsby lifted one brow. "Lady Winslow is breeding again. What does that make, ten children now?"

"Good heavens," Mama said. "I can scarcely keep up with my five. I can't imagine managing twice that number, poor woman."

"Meanwhile," Lady Hornsby said, "your daughter there can't imagine managing even one, I daresay."

In response to the woman's laugh, Gwyn smiled weakly. Ah, but she *could* imagine . . . and had, many a time. That was the problem.

Lady Hornsby was still laughing when Joshua entered the breakfast room.

"Joshua!" her mother said. "You've arrived just in time to meet my good friend, Eliza Brock, the Countess of Hornsby."

Gwyn tensed when Lady Hornsby turned to study Joshua with a critical eye. Once again, his attire was old-fashioned: a brown coat of the style popular several years before, a nondescript waistcoat, and riding breeches of buckskin. But if the countess sharpened her wit on him based on how he was dressed, Gwyn would never forgive her. He looked handsome no matter what he wore.

And if it were his battle wounds that Lady Hornsby wanted to criticize . . . Well, Joshua didn't deserve to be judged by his lameness, though clearly he expected such, because he wore that stony stare designed to keep people at arm's length.

"Lady Hornsby," Gwyn said hastily, "this is Major Joshua Wolfe. He's Mama's nephew by marriage."

To Gwyn's relief, the countess smiled like a cat in the cream. "So this is Beatrice's brother. I can see he will make a charming addition to our party."

When she looked him over again with more interest, Gwyn gaped at her. Wait, was she *flirting* with Joshua? Why, she had to be twice his age!

And Joshua clearly was aware of the woman's flirtations, for he relaxed his rigid stance. "I can assure you, Lady Hornsby—no one has ever called me charming."

"Except me," Gwyn said.

He met her gaze, his rare smile sending a delicious frisson down her spine. "Forgive me, Lady Gwyn, but you called me '*almost* charming.' There's a vast ocean between that and 'charming.'"

Gwyn felt the weight of her mother's gaze on her. "True. And that's because I see you surly more often than not."

"Surly is my middle name, I confess," he said. "So let me attempt to amend my ways and compliment you on your attire." Before she could do more than smile, he added, "It has more gold braid across the front than I have on my entire uniform."

"Major!" Gwyn cried, torn between laughing and chiding him. "Except for the color, this is a virtual copy of one worn by the Queen of Prussia. It's Hussar braiding, which you, of all people, should recognize."

"I believe you are confused, madam. I'm not a Hussar. I'm a Royal Marine. Hussars serve atop horses. Marines serve aboard ships. They are hardly the same branch of the military."

"I wasn't saying they—" She caught the twinkle in his eyes and huffed out a breath. "You're teasing me. That is so unlike you, sir."

Clearly, he could barely contain his mirth, for his lips twitched. "I did say I wished to amend my ways."

"Mocking me is not a good way to start."

"Very well." He bowed slightly. "You look exceedingly lovely this morning, Lady Gwyn, gold braid or no gold braid. Forgive me for implying otherwise."

Then he turned to Lady Hornsby. "I'm pleased to have met you, madam. Now, if you'll excuse me and Lady Gwyn,

I promised to take her riding this morning, and I'm already late for that engagement."

"I would not wish to keep either of you," the countess said, a new gleam in her eyes. "And Gwyn, I cannot imagine why you don't find the major charming. He seems perfectly delightful to me."

That was because Lady Hornsby had never seen Joshua rude or insulting or overbearing.

Mama was still searching Gwyn's face. "Where's your maid, Gwyn?"

"One of the grooms is accompanying us, Aunt," Joshua said.

"I suppose that's fine, then," her mother said. "Just be sure to be back in time for Bea and Grey's visit. I'm hoping to persuade them to stay for dinner."

"Yes, Mama," Gwyn said.

She headed for the door, not wanting to wait one minute longer for her lessons in shooting. After bowing to the two ladies, Joshua followed her out.

"What has put you in such a good mood this morning?" she asked him as they headed down the steps. "It's not like you at all."

"Are you sure?" he drawled. "Lady Hornsby said I'm 'perfectly delightful.'"

"What she means is she would find it 'perfectly delightful' to have you in her bed," Gwyn said dryly.

Joshua turned a sharp gaze on her. "You're not serious."

"Oh, trust me, she is famous for taking young lovers now that her husband is gone." And up until this moment, Gwyn had rather admired her for it. Why shouldn't an older woman take young lovers? "The countess has a particular fondness for officers—Hussar and otherwise. Or so I've heard anyway."

"Hmm," he said lazily. "Forgive me, but I'd say you sound jealous."

"And I'd say you're daft." She sniffed as she walked down the steps. "I don't care whom you bed, Joshua. It's all the same to me if you bed half the widows in London."

"That would take more energy than I possess," he said. "I'm going to have enough trouble keeping up with *your* antics."

"What antics?" she asked caustically.

"Forcing me to teach you to shoot, for one."

Well, she could hardly deny that. So she hurried down the steps to mount the gelding being held for her next to the horse block. As the groom brought her horse forward from the block, she looked up to see Joshua moving even more slowly than usual, scanning the street as he came down the steps.

Oh, dear, might he have trouble mounting? Perhaps he was dreading having to do it. But to her surprise, once he did reach the street, he climbed the horse block, seized the mare, and was in the saddle in a matter of moments.

She was impressed. How many other physical feats could he accomplish despite his bad right leg? She couldn't wait to find out. After he taught her to shoot, that is.

He rode off at a good clip, and she trailed him, watching his riding with interest. The mare responded well to him, and before long, Gwyn was having to ride hard just to keep up. But as she turned down the road he'd taken, she realized she'd lost him. How could that be?

The groom, who'd been following them at a respectable distance, rode up to stay right by her side.

"Do you know where we're going?" she asked him.

"Yes, milady. Went there this morning with the major."

So *that* was where Joshua had gone so early. "Where is he? Has he ridden on ahead?"

"No, milady. He's checkin' to make sure nobody's fol-lowin'. Don't look, but I saw him and his horse down that alley we just passed."

She caught her breath. Joshua was lying in wait for Lionel. Depending on what Lionel did once Joshua caught him, that could be either bad or good. In any case, there was naught she could do about it now.

The two of them hadn't ridden more than half a mile when she heard hoofbeats behind them and turned to see Joshua riding hard after them. As he came abreast of her, he nodded to the groom, who dropped back.

"Did you see anyone following?" she asked, her heart in her throat.

"No. I thought sure Malet would take this chance to come after you, but I guess he has other plans for the day. I only wish I knew what they were."

She wished the same. Because she had no idea how to reach Lionel to tell him when or where she would meet him with the money. Why, she hadn't even had a chance to ask Thorn for it. She would have to do that soon.

Before long, they reached a field near a stretch of woods in the countryside northwest of Hyde Park. When she spotted the target set up in front of the woods, her pulse leaped. She really was going to learn to shoot!

Joshua reined in his mount. She noticed that there was a horse block out here, too, of all places.

"Where are we?" she asked as she followed suit.

"Believe it or not, we're on land belonging to Greycourt. I asked him where we could do a bit of shooting, and your half brother recommended this property. I already knew of it, anyway, from my youth."

"Is that where you were this morning, at Grey's town house?"

"Last night actually." He dismounted, using the block.

"This morning I was here making sure it would suit all our needs."

Just then, the groom came alongside them, and she realized he'd been carrying a large, wrapped parcel tethered to the side of his horse. With her curiosity thoroughly roused, she dismounted. The parcel looked far too long and thick to contain a pistol. Was it a musket? Was that what she'd be shooting?

She couldn't carry a musket about London, for pity's sake. But just as she was about to ask Joshua what it was, he took the parcel from the groom and opened it to reveal a bow and a quiver full of arrows.

What the devil?

It took her a minute to realize why he had brought it, but when she did, her temper exploded. She pointed to it with a trembling finger. "You *said* you would teach me to shoot, curse you! Not that you would teach me to . . . to . . ."

"Shoot?" he said, annoyingly smug. "I never specified *what* I would teach you to shoot, just that I would do so. You were the one to assume it would be a gun."

She gaped at him as his words sank in. Of all the sneaky things! So *that* was why he'd been in such a fine mood. He'd been anticipating this . . . this *trick* he meant to play on her.

Her anger rose, fueled by the realization that she couldn't even accuse him of lying to her because he hadn't actually done so. "You knew what I meant. And you deliberately ignored it."

"I did. Nor do I make any apology for it." He ordered the groom to secure their horses, then stepped toward her. "A woman like you shouldn't be carrying a pistol to protect herself."

Oh, the audacity of the man! "A woman like *me*? An heiress, you mean? A duke's daughter? A young lady? Seems to me that being those things gives me all the more reason to carry a weapon in a city famous for its crime." She crossed her arms over her chest. "Unless you meant something else by 'a woman like you.' Perhaps you think I'm too stupid to know when it's appropriate to draw a weapon."

He narrowed his gaze on her. "If you choose to think so, that's your affair. But you know damned well I don't consider you stupid."

"Then why shouldn't I carry a pistol, if I learn to use it properly?"

"Even men seldom carry pistols, and certainly not to the sort of activities you and I will be attending."

"Yet *you* intend to carry one."

"To protect you, which is my job." His tone was infuriatingly calm, as if he were arguing with a child. "Thornstock is paying me well enough for it, so let me make sure he gets his money's worth."

"What about when we leave London to return to Armitage Hall? Do you mean to spend the rest of your life protecting me?"

That seemed to produce a ripple in his calm. "Of course not. But after this Season, you'll have a husband to protect you. And Malet will no longer be trying to kidnap you because you won't any longer be an heiress, just a rich wife."

She could hardly reveal that she never meant to marry. Even if she dared to tell him why, he would never understand her reasons. He wasn't a woman. "You sound awfully sure that I'll snag a husband this Season. I wish I could be as certain. At my age, even a tidy dowry doesn't always guarantee a quick marriage."

"You'll snag a husband, trust me."

The bitterness in his voice took her aback. It implied he might actually—

No, not Joshua. By refusing even to acknowledge their

kiss yesterday, he'd made it quite clear how he felt about her. And as he'd said before, he regarded marriage cynically.

Not that it mattered what he did or didn't feel for her. He would not want a "woman like her" once he learned the full truth of what that meant.

Suddenly, the groom returned from tying off the horses, effectively putting an end to their rather personal conversation.

"So," Joshua asked her, "do you want to learn to shoot a bow and arrow? Or should we mount up and return to town?"

His smirk and his lifted brow told her he expected her to say no and march off in high dudgeon. It wasn't as if she could threaten again to choose Thorn over him as a bodyguard. Because that wouldn't gain her anything but her twin watching her every move, keeping her from paying Lionel.

She and Thorn had played hide and seek too many times as children—they knew each other's tricks. She had a better chance of slipping away from Joshua than she'd ever have from Thorn. But that meant she had to trick the major into letting down his guard, which required figuring out his weaknesses. Archery lessons might provide a good chance for that.

Though she began to wonder if he *had* any weaknesses. So far, she'd only found one—his difficulty with loud noises. But using *that* against him would be cruel.

"How about this?" he said. "Shooting arrows and shooting pistols aren't much different when it comes to aiming, so you could use some of what you learn in archery in learning to aim a pistol. Archery also strengthens the arms and shoulders, which is helpful when dealing with a pistol's recoil. So if you can prove yourself capable of excelling at archery, I might—*might,* mind you—consider teaching you how to shoot a pistol one day. In the far distant future."

Was he actually trying to coax her into staying by

dangling the prize in front of her that he'd initially denied her? She simply *had* to see where this went. But she wasn't about to let him know how eager she was to do so.

"Oh, very well, if you insist," she said coolly. "We're here already, and archery is supposedly a popular—and respectable—pastime for ladies these days. So why not?"

Why not, indeed? She would make Major Joshua Arrogant-As-Hell Wolfe show her every possible lesson in archery, until he was sick to death of it and she was proficient. Because that was the only way she could think of to get some of her own back on him for his trickery.

# Chapter Eight

It didn't take Joshua long to recognize the gross miscalculation in his strategy. Gwyn was an agony to teach. And not because of her ability—or lack thereof—to learn archery.

"I know I'm holding the bow wrong," she complained. "My arrows keep missing the target entirely."

"I told you, it has nothing to do with your grip on the bow. It's because you keep trying to draw the bowstring too far back."

"Oh, right. Show me again how far to draw it. I promise I'll pay better attention this time."

Gritting his teeth, he came up behind her and put his arms around her to place one hand on her bow hand and the other on her draw hand.

"You don't need as much force as you think," he said. Again. "You can work on sending your arrows farther and faster once you've strengthened your drawing arm sufficiently to sustain the draw while you aim."

Was she really this interested in learning archery? Or was she deliberately trying to get into his embrace so she could torment him for the trick he'd played on her?

If the latter was her strategy, it was working. This close to her, he could smell her light, lemony scent and feel her satiny curls brush his neck.

God help him, but having her lush body against his made him want to—

*Concentrate, man. Don't let her get the best of you.*

"You draw it back like this," he said. "You see? Not that far. I told you, there's no need to bend the bow in half."

"Blast! Now I've dropped the arrow."

She bent over to pick it up, and he thought he'd died and gone to heaven. It would be so easy to put his hands on that sweetly shaped bottom of hers and then—

Bloody hell. He slid back from her as she straightened. He had to get some distance or find himself doing things he'd later regret. Unfortunately, now that he was to the side of her, he could see how the tip of her tongue slipped out as she focused on nocking the arrow into the bowstring.

He wanted that tongue twirling with his so badly he could taste it.

"This is harder than it looks," she muttered. "Who would ever guess that keeping an arrow positioned properly in a bow would be so difficult?"

"Try parting your lips—" He groaned as her startled gaze shot to him. "Your fingers, I mean, so that your index finger is on top of the arrow shaft and the rest of your fingers on the bottom. It's called split-finger shooting. You can put all of them on the bottom, but you may find it easier to hold the arrow in place the other way."

"All right." She repositioned her fingers and let the arrow fly. This time it actually hit the edge of the target.

She beamed at him. Seeing that sunny smile, he would have thought she'd hit the bull's-eye. Her palpable delight did something dangerous to his peace of mind. Like make him wonder how it would be to see that delight come over her face in bed. *His* bed. Preferably soon.

God, she was driving him mad, which was undoubtedly her purpose.

"Give me another arrow, if you please," she said.

He handed her one from the quiver, but as she reached for it, she paused to regard her gloved hand with a frown. "I wish you'd told me what we were really doing today. I would have worn thicker, better gloves, instead of these old worn ones. Now the glove on my draw hand is getting cut up from the bowstring."

"Here." He tucked the arrow under his arm so he could look at her hand.

When he drew off her glove, she blinked at him. "What are you doing?"

He pulled off both of his gloves. "You can use mine. They're sturdier."

"Very well," she said, and took off her other glove.

But before he let go of his, he looked closely at her draw hand to make sure she hadn't cut her skin. She breathed in sharply, and suddenly he became aware of the intimacy in holding her bare hand. His was calloused and rough. Hers was . . . not. The delicacy of her soft skin fascinated him, and he wished he could feel it on his face, his chest . . . his cock. Damn.

He dropped her hand and thrust the gloves at her. "See if they'll do."

After she put them on, she laughed. "They're huge." She held up her hands, which looked clownishly large with his gloves on them.

He fought a smile. "But will they work?"

"I think so." She nocked another arrow in the bowstring, once more sticking out a bit of her tongue.

This time, however, she ran it along her lips. He groaned as his body responded to that little motion. Bloody hell. One would think he'd never been around an attractive woman.

"Am I doing it wrong?" she asked. Clearly, she'd heard his groan.

"No, but let's try it with your thumb here." He put her thumb into the position so she could get a feel for it. "How is that?"

She let her arrow fly, then crowed her satisfaction when it hit closer to the bull's-eye.

"Well done," he choked out. "See? You're already getting the hang of it."

"Only because of your teaching." She drew out an arrow from the quiver herself this time. "I still don't feel as if I know what I'm doing."

He heard a sigh to the right of them. He glanced over to see the bored groom sitting cross-legged on the ground.

Joshua headed over to hand the young man a sovereign. "Take this," he said. "There's no point in you suffering through our practice when you can be having a pint at that tavern we passed on our way here."

The groom jumped to his feet. "Milady? Do you mind?"

"Not in the least." She didn't even look at him, waving him off with her arrow before nocking it into the bowstring. "We may be here a while longer, given how bad I am at this."

The groom bowed. "Thank you, milady. Thank you, Major." Then he ran off.

Joshua returned to her side.

"How do you know so much about shooting with a bow and arrow anyway?" she asked. "It's not as if anyone uses them in battle or hunting anymore. Or do they?"

"They don't. But my grandfather was a member of the Royal Toxophilite Society in London. Toxophilite means—"

"I know what it means, Joshua. It's a fancy word for a skilled archer." She lifted a brow at him. "As your sister once told you, 'I *can* read, you know.'"

"Forgive me," he said coldly. "I didn't intend to question your reading abilities."

"Don't get all grumpy over it. I was merely pointing out

that you aren't the only one who knows something about books." She nocked her arrow and shot it wide of the target. "And go on with what you were saying about your grandfather, the old duke."

He shook his head at her. She was the only woman he'd ever met who was never put off by his being "grumpy." "Grandfather was quite the archer; he taught me everything I know. That's how I became aware of this place. It's where the Toxophilite Society used to have their matches. I shot in one of those matches before I was shipped off to the Continent."

"How old were you when you left?"

"Sixteen." Before his leg was damaged forever. It seemed like a lifetime ago.

"So young?"

He shrugged. "I was lucky to have a grandfather willing to buy me a commission even though my father had died fighting a scandalous duel over a lady of ill repute. And sixteen is the usual age to start in the Royal Marines. At least I wasn't in the navy. There, you start at twelve."

A pensive expression crossed her face as she held the bow to her bosom. "I can't imagine sending off my twelve-year-old son to battle."

"Yet you would send him to Eton without a thought?"

"That's different. There aren't any cannonballs volleyed at you at Eton." She cleared her throat. "So, is this bow your grandfather's?"

"Actually, it's Beatrice's. I had it made for her when she found his old bows and wanted me to teach her. I believe she had a mind to get me interested in something—anything—after I was finally able to be up and around."

"You mean, after you were wounded in battle."

"Precisely." And he did *not* want to talk about that with her. He couldn't bear to see the pity in her eyes. "Anyway, I went over to Greycourt's mansion last night to borrow it from her. I told her you wanted to learn to shoot."

He knew he'd said too much when she narrowed her gaze on him. "So what you're telling me is you had already planned this charade when we arrived in London? That you actually told Beatrice the truth of it, and she didn't bat an eye?"

The look of betrayal in her eyes unsettled him. "Don't blame her. I . . . um . . . didn't *exactly* tell her the truth of it. She didn't know you wanted to learn to shoot a pistol."

"So you tricked her, too." She faced the target, her expression grim. "Next time I see her, I intend to inform her of the full truth about that."

It began to irritate him that she couldn't understand why he'd done it. "Go right ahead. She will side with you in the matter, I'm sure. Though I daresay her husband will side with me."

"I wouldn't bet on that if I were you," she mumbled.

She might be right, actually. Greycourt wasn't like any duke he'd ever met. The man had married Beatrice, after all, and at the very least that required keeping an open mind about what sort of woman would make a good wife.

Gwyn would make a good wife for any man who didn't give a farthing about what society thought. A man like him, come to think of it.

He scowled at that fanciful, impossible idea. "Let's work on aiming for a while."

The abrupt change in subject had her glancing at him. "I thought we'd been doing that already."

"No. We've been working on your drawing of the bow."

She sniffed. "Then you'll have to show me how to improve my aim because I don't see how I can do it any better."

He really *had* got her dander up, hadn't he? "All you do is draw back the arrow to your cheek so it's directly lined up below your eye, the way I showed you before. Now line up the end of the shaft with the tip of the arrow and the center of the target—"

"How am I supposed to do that when I have the end of the arrow against my cheek?" she complained. "That makes no sense."

Her arm shook a little, making it clear she was coming to the end of her stamina. Drawing a bow was harder work than most people realized, especially the way *she'd* been trying to draw it.

"Perhaps we should continue this another time." Right now, he would happily join the groom in a pint.

She steadied her arm. "Just a few more shots. Honestly, I'm fine. I want to aim correctly at least once before we leave. If you could just show me—"

"Certainly." He stood behind her again, this time trying to put more of his energy into holding the bow for her and less of it into holding *her*.

It didn't work, especially because he wasn't wearing his gloves. Putting his hand on her draw hand meant his bare hand was resting against her cheek. Her soft, silky cheek.

Swearing silently, he positioned the arrow the way he'd described. He released her hands. She shot the arrow. It went wide.

"Why didn't that work?" she asked.

"Because it's nearly impossible for me to aim properly when I can't put the end of the shaft up to *my* cheek."

"Oh! You're right, of course. Here." She thrust the bow into his hands and withdrew another arrow from the quiver. "Why don't *you* aim as if you're going to shoot at the target, and I will observe how you do it."

Thank God she didn't want him touching her again.

He did as she'd asked, shifting his weight onto his good leg so he could stay upright. Once he'd drawn back the bowstring, she peered closely at his bow and arrow from one side. Then she did it from the other. Finally, she took off his gloves and moved behind him.

But when she reached around him to cover *his* hands with *hers*, thus pushing her breasts into his back and her lower half against his arse, he'd had enough.

Dropping the bow and arrow, he rounded on her. "Damn it, Gwyn. What are you about?"

"I'm trying to learn how to aim," she said, sounding bewildered.

He knew better than to believe that. And he refused to fall for her tactics. "That's not all you're doing, admit it."

"I honestly have no idea what you mean."

Snorting, he grabbed his cane and advanced on her. "You're cozying up to me. Bad enough you were forcing me to put my arms around you every other shot, but now you're pressing your body up against mine, which is even worse. It's all meant to tempt me into doing something rash so you can punish me for misleading you about the shooting lessons."

"Why on earth would I choose that method to punish you?" she asked, backing away until she came up hard against a large birch. "You've made it quite clear you don't find me appealing in that way."

That caught him off guard. "How in God's name did I make *that* clear?"

She jutted out her chin. "By refusing to speak of our kiss. By pretending it never happened, as if it were some . . . vile thing you'd endured for the sake of your 'mission' to protect me."

Could she really be that unaware of the many ways she made him lust after her? Did he dare believe her?

He leaned in to plant one forearm against the tree next to

her head. "Has it occurred to you that perhaps my 'mission' to protect you means *not* doing things like kissing you?"

"Why should it? It isn't as if you'd do anything ungentlemanly to me. We both know you aren't attracted to me. You think I'm a silly, spoiled female who—"

He kissed her. He couldn't help it. She was blathering nonsense, and he had to make it stop. It was either that or lose his temper at her for thinking he would fall for her blatant lies.

But the longer he kissed her, the more he wanted to kiss her. Her mouth was so giving, so . . . so tempting. He could stand here all day like this, one hand on her waist, one knee rubbing hers through her gown.

God, when had he dropped his cane to put his hand on her? It didn't matter. He wasn't about to stop unless she made him. She tasted like ambrosia, whatever that tasted like. Food of the gods. Fruit of the forbidden. And she was forbidden as hell. He just didn't care.

"Does this . . . clarify my attraction to you?" he murmured, his lips close enough to her mouth that he could feel her breath quickening. That he could use his tongue to trace her perfect bow of an upper lip.

"I'm not sure," she said, her voice low and husky. "Show me again."

That was all the encouragement he needed to seize her mouth once more, this time driving his tongue harder and deeper. When she moaned low in her throat, his need for her spiked unbearably high.

And hard. He was hard for a woman who, with one word, could ruin his reputation as an officer and a gentleman.

"You've got to stop doing this to me," he rasped against her mouth. Her oh-so-delectable mouth.

She bit his lower lip. Lightly. Maddeningly. "So now it's *my* fault you can't control yourself?"

"You can't control yourself either," he pointed out.

"True. But that's to be expected." She cast him a look that was pure seduction. "I'm a woman—weak and helpless in the arms of a man, at the mercy of my lascivious urges."

Even if he hadn't heard the faint sarcasm in her tone, he would have known better than to believe that rot. "Yes, I noticed how weak you were when you were drawing back that bow to its farthest extent. As for being at the mercy of your urges . . ." He covered her mouth with his again, this time so he could slide his hand up over her breast, just to see how she'd react.

Right. Like *that* was why he did it. Not because he wanted to, needed to, damned well couldn't help himself.

Her breast was plump and soft. God, how he wanted to taste it. But for now he would settle for caressing it, kneading it . . . imagining having it in his mouth. Clearly, he had lost his mind.

If she was trying to manipulate him using feminine wiles, it was too late to stop her. Because he'd already succumbed. He would march right along with whatever she wanted . . . as long as he got this brief chance to fondle her senseless.

She tore her mouth free. "Do you think that's wise?" Her eyes were wide, their green shining darker and deeper here in the woods.

He could read what she wanted in those beautiful eyes of hers. Or perhaps that was just wishful thinking. "No, it's utterly unwise. But I don't care. Do you?"

"Not one bit," she whispered, placing her hand over his.

That sent the last bit of his sanity flying into the ether.

# Chapter Nine

Gwyn had never expected to have this with a man again. She certainly shouldn't be allowing it. But Joshua . . . oh, his hands on her breasts felt heavenly. Not intrusive or ruthless, just . . . exploring. And when his thumbs rubbed her nipples, sending the wildest sensations rocketing through her, she tore her lips from his with a gasp.

"Yes," she whispered. "That feels so . . . *good*."

"It certainly does." His caresses were thorough, not frenzied, as if he were testing how best to please her. Unlike Lionel.

Never mind about Lionel. And who would have guessed that the major was as good at touching a woman intimately as he was bad at suffering fools?

Kissing a path to her ear, he whispered, "This is what happens when you . . . tempt a man beyond his endurance. He does things he shouldn't."

"For the last time, I wasn't trying to tempt you," she felt compelled to remind him. "And you seemed to resist . . . my 'temptations' well enough at the coaching inn."

"They took me by surprise," he admitted before tugging on her earlobe with his teeth. "*You* took me by surprise."

"Because you enjoyed our kiss?"

"Because *you* enjoyed our kiss," he murmured. "I didn't expect that."

His beard stubble, rough against her cheek, reminded her that he was a man, one whose body she would very much enjoy exploring.

She slipped her hands inside his coat and up under his waistcoat so she could feel his muscles flexing through his shirt. "I can't imagine why not, Joshua. You are very adept at kissing."

He drew back to pin her with a smoldering look. "And this? How am I at *this*?" He fondled her breast so expertly that she let out a strangled sigh.

"You're . . . very good at that, too," she choked out.

His breath came in ragged gasps now. "So you like it."

"Too much." Yet she didn't resist when he unbuttoned the jacket of her riding habit. She even shamelessly helped him by undoing the hooks that kept her jacket attached to her skirt and thus not easy to open.

Then he was confronted by her chemisette. He pulled on it, but it didn't give, yet he could clearly tell it wasn't an actual shirt. "What in God's creation is this confounded thing and how does it unfasten?"

Though she shared his frustration, she couldn't help laughing at it, too.

He scowled at her. "You find my being thwarted by a piece of linen amusing, do you?"

"I wouldn't *dare*," she said with mock seriousness, then laughed at his lowering look. She reached behind her. "It unfastens with buttons, but you'll have to do it."

"Show me," he growled, in a perverse echo of what she'd been demanding of *him* for the past few hours.

Taking his hands in hers, she brought them back to the only button she could actually reach. But apparently, that was all he needed, for he deftly undid each one and unfastened the ties so he could draw off the chemisette.

At last he had what he apparently wanted. He gazed at the tops of her breasts with a famished look that delighted her. It seemed he wasn't entirely immune to her attractions after all. And though she shouldn't care—because she knew he would never marry her if he knew the truth about her—she did take satisfaction from it.

But he wasn't done with his foray. "I want to taste you."

*Yes, please.* But she merely said, "If you wish."

That was all it took to have him pulling down her corset cups and untying her shift so he could draw that down enough to bare her breasts. He took a long, admiring look at them, hunger clearly flaring in his eyes. And then he bent to put his mouth on one and his hand on the other.

Something feral seized her, making her moan and thrust her breasts at him in a half-conscious bid for more. He sucked one breast like a starving man set before a feast, while he fondled the other in silky strokes that had her growing warm and wet between her legs. She let out a shuddering breath of pure pleasure. The only thing better than this would be having his hand caressing her in that aching spot down below.

Could he tell that she'd shared such intimacies with a man before? Well, not *these* delicious caresses exactly. Lionel had been too impatient to be thorough. Or tender, for that matter.

But to her shock, Joshua was patience personified. As he moved to the other breast, licking and teasing it even as he thumbed the damp, hard nipple of the one he'd just been sucking, she clutched his shoulders and let the thrill of his actions course through her, sweep her away if only for a short while.

That reminder of how little time they dared take made her want to keep him with her. Burying her hands in his hair, she arched her back and held him to her. His queue frustrated her, so she untied it to allow her to run the silky, raven strands through her fingers.

Having him like this was beating down all her carefully constructed defenses, making her want to touch *him*, fondle *him*. Lord help them both if anyone came upon them while they were behaving in this reckless, mad fashion.

As if he'd read her mind, he said, "I should stop. *We* should stop."

"Yes," she agreed, though she wished they could stay here forever. Forget about her past and his. Just do . . . this.

But he was already straightening to pull up her shift and tie it.

Not quite ready to give up their enjoyment, she clung to his shoulders. "Do many people know about this place?"

"I don't believe so. Just the members of the Society, and they only come here for matches or to practice as a group." He pinned her with his steely blue gaze. "But since Greycourt owns this land—and knows we're out here together— it probably wouldn't do to tempt fate."

She sighed and looked away. "No."

With her heart clamoring in her chest, she helped him restore her clothing to its proper place and then donned her gloves. What would he do now? Pretend again that they hadn't kissed? Ignore those magical caresses she would never forget?

"We should go," he said, avoiding her gaze as he put on his own gloves and retied his queue.

When he started to move away, she grabbed his arm. "Joshua, don't."

He tensed. "Don't what?"

"Act as if nothing happened. We should talk about—"

"Why?" He stared at her with a stoic expression. "Do you wish to marry me?"

The blunt question took her off guard. Afraid she might spill her soul to him, she made a feeble attempt at humor. "Not if you're going to make light of our intimacies every time they happen."

"Answer the question, and not with a jest."

"It's just that—"

"If you're seeking to explain it, I know the answer." He started to turn away.

"Now see here, Major Grumbler. Why don't *you* answer the question? Do you wish to marry *me*?"

"I'm not marrying a woman who would use her feminine wiles as a way to get around me. To get what she wants."

"What are you talking about?"

"I know better than to think you actually desire me." He scowled at her. "You merely want to wrap me around your finger so you can do as you please while we're in London— not let me know where you're going, not allow me to accompany you, head off on walks and rides without any escort but a groom."

She gaped at him. "That's what you think of me? That I'm the worst sort of flirt, the worst sort of *woman,* who would manipulate a man by using my 'feminine wiles' to get my way? No wonder you have no wish to marry me, if that's how you see me. And that's precisely why I have no wish to marry a suspicious fellow like *you,* Joshua Wolfe!"

Stalking away from him, she headed for her horse. The man was impossible, unbelievable! She refused to put up with him and his groundless suspicions. Only think what he would say if he knew *why* she hesitated!

"Damn it, Gwyn!" he growled, scooping up his cane so he could hurry after her. "Hold up, for God's sake!"

Thank heavens she could mount without him. As soon as she was in the saddle, she rode off, leaving him to his own devices.

Cursing a blue streak behind her, he apparently managed to mount his own horse using the horse block, for he galloped after her. By the time he caught up to her, he was clearly livid. "You can't go running off like that. Malet might even now be watching us."

"I don't think Mr. Malet is the problem at present," she said in icy tones. "I rather think it's your warped ideas about women—how they behave, how they *should* behave."

"It has nothing to do with behavior," he ground out. "You're the daughter of a wealthy duke and the sister of another such. I am but a retired soldier on half-pay, and a damaged one at that. Logic dictates that you can't help but be aware of that difference."

"So now you think it's *logical* to assume I'm toying with your affections? Is that it? Or is it that you simply don't like the idea of a woman like me having a say in such things as her own desires?"

Not that his ideas were any different from everyone else's. Even Thorn would despise her if he knew everything that had happened years ago with Lionel.

When Joshua remained silent, proving he was like the rest of them, she stiffened and cantered ahead. This time he let her.

She rode in a fury, fighting to hold back tears. How dare he rouse her . . . desires and then accuse *her* of toying with *him*! He was the one doing the toying. Just like Lionel, he wanted to have his cake and eat it, too. Men!

As they neared the tavern where he'd sent the groom, he rode up beside her once more. "We have to stop here. We dare not return to Armitage House without your groom."

That was true. It would raise questions neither of them wanted to answer. "Fine," she said and reined in.

But when she remained in the saddle as he dismounted and tied off his horse, he came around to the side of hers.

"We both go in or neither of us do. And I don't know about you, but I can't stand here for the remainder of the day."

Letting out a heavy breath, she dismounted as well, then strode into the tavern, leaving him to limp after her. But before she could so much as look for the groom, the youth came running up to them.

"Thank the good Lord you've come, milady," he said. "Almost went after you, but I figured I best not lead the gentleman to you. So I just been sittin' here biding me time, hopin' you came soon."

Joshua instantly went on the alert. She could see it in the stiffening of his spine, the way he gripped his cane, the hard glance he cast her way. "What gentleman?" he asked the groom.

"Didn't give his name, though one of the maids called him 'Cap'n.' He said he was a friend of milady's. Used her name properlike and everything."

It had to be Lionel, blast it. A pox upon the man! She would never get his money to him if he didn't stop putting Joshua on his guard.

"I don't know how he got this far." Joshua rubbed his chin. "He definitely didn't follow us out here."

"Told me he got your direction from the butler, he did, but I knew better'n that," the groom said. "Our butler don't tell nobody nothin' unless he knows 'em."

Joshua frowned. "There's any number of servants he could have questioned to find out what he needed to learn, although he wouldn't have received answers, because I was careful who I told."

"What about the servants at Grey's house?" Gwyn pointed out. "You said you went there last night. One of them might have overheard you."

The groom bobbed his head. "The gentleman did say he

was told that her ladyship wanted to practice at archery at a place near this tavern."

"He wouldn't have been told that at Armitage House," Joshua said. "But Greycourt mentioned the tavern when he told me he knew of a place." He looked over at Gwyn. "Your brother clearly has an overly talkative servant working for him."

"Perhaps. Though that doesn't sound like someone Grey would hire."

"Do you and the lady fancy a drink, sir?" asked a buxom maid as she approached. "We got the best ale this side of London, and there's a table back there if ye want privacy." She pointed to the back of the tavern.

"Yes, we'll take it," Joshua said. When Gwyn eyed him askance, he murmured, "I need to know everything Malet said to your groom before he forgets it."

Clearly, Joshua had returned to his bodyguard stance. Gwyn only hoped that Malet had been discreet enough not to hint to the groom at how much he knew of her past.

As soon as they'd sat down and the maid had taken their order, Joshua resumed his questioning. "Now, tell me word for word exactly how the conversation went with this captain fellow."

"Lemme see, sir." The groom lifted his eyes to the ceiling as if consulting his memory there. "First, he come up to me, acting all high and mighty, and asked where me mistress was. I thought he was tryin' to be high in the instep about me sittin' at a table all grand, like the quality, so I told him 'tweren't none of his affair where she were. Then he turned all smiles and told me he knew me mistress, that he recognized me livery, and that's why he asked after her."

A chill ran through her. If Lionel had recognized the Armitage livery when he was nowhere near the town house, he must have familiarized himself with it. And though it shouldn't surprise her, it made her uneasy.

Judging from Joshua's grim look, he apparently felt the same way. As soon as their mugs of ale had arrived and the maid had gone, he took a big sip, then leaned over the table. "What did you say to the fellow then?"

"I told him she were down the road, learning archery from Major Wolfe. Once he heard *your* name, he didn't look too pleased."

"I would imagine not," Joshua drawled. "He thought he was going to catch her alone. Hard to kidnap a woman when a presumably armed marine officer is about."

"Kidnap!" the groom exclaimed. "He was out to kidnap her ladyship? I'm that glad then that I didn't say anythin' about where you were."

"I am, too," Joshua said. "And feel free to spread the news of Malet's villainy among your fellow servants, in case Malet approaches any of them."

She stiffened. "If he tells the staff, Mama is sure to hear of it. And you promised not to let that happen."

He set down his mug hard enough that some ale splashed out of it. "Damn it, Gwyn, how am I supposed to protect you if I have to keep everything secret?"

"I don't know," she said truthfully. "But I trust that you will figure that out."

The groom had been watching their interchange with avid interest and now ventured to add his own opinion. "Never fear, milady. I can just tell the others that a villain named Cap'n Malet is after Major Wolfe, so they should inform the major if the man comes nosin' around."

"That will work." Joshua gazed at her. "Don't you think?"

"*Now* you want my opinion?" she snapped. Then, realizing she sounded like a scold, she sighed. "Yes, that's fine."

She took a sip of her ale but could barely swallow. This day wasn't going the way she'd hoped.

Joshua turned back to the groom. "Did Malet say anything more after that?"

"No, sir. Just walked out, all in a miff. But now you see why I didn't go back to where you and milady were. Couldn't risk the fellow followin' me."

"Very good tactic, thank you." Joshua took a long swig.

Gwyn smiled at the groom and took out her purse. "I must thank you, too." She handed him a guinea. "How clever of you to be careful of what you said."

He took the guinea, eyes widening. "If'n you ever need help, milady, you just let me know," he said fervently.

"I will keep that in mind." She looked at Joshua. "Can we go now?"

"Of course." He rose and put some shillings on the table. Then he nodded at her mug. "You barely touched your ale."

"I'd had enough."

She stood, and Joshua came up beside her to offer her his arm. She didn't take it. Their recent argument was still too fresh in her mind. Nonetheless, she needed to make sure of one thing. "I would appreciate it if you wouldn't tell Thorn about this."

"I wasn't planning to," he said as they walked toward the door.

That took her by surprise. "Why not?"

"Because first I want to see how Malet learned where to look for you. It might give me a hint to where he's hiding himself in London, and I could then tell your brother so he could handle the fellow himself."

Blast him for being so good at his job as bodyguard. "Oh. That makes sense."

"Why don't you *want* me to tell him?"

"Thorn will insist upon following me around, too, and then I'll have two watchdogs instead of one. It will make it a jot difficult to have suitors."

"I don't know what you're worried about," he said testily. "Everywhere you go you make another conquest. First Malet and now the groom. And you haven't even had your debut yet."

"I notice you don't include yourself in that number of conquests. Apparently, I'm very bad at using my feminine wiles. You saw right through them."

"Gwyn," he said, "I didn't mean to—"

She didn't stay to hear whatever feeble apology he offered, *if* he offered one. She was rapidly learning why Beatrice had a contentious relationship with her brother.

Because despite his laudable bodyguard skills, Joshua could be a real arse sometimes.

# Chapter Ten

The next day at Armitage House, Joshua came down for breakfast late, which never happened in the country. He had expected the constant racket in the street to keep him awake, but somehow it was doing the reverse. That made no sense to him.

He was still musing over it when he entered the morning room to find Thornstock there reading the paper. Normally, that would be odd—the duke had his own town house, after all—but today Thornstock was accompanying Gwyn and Lady Hornsby to Gwyn's presentation at court. In fact, nearly the whole family would be converging on Armitage House soon, because Greycourt was to accompany Beatrice, and Aunt Lydia wanted to see everyone's court regalia before they headed off without her.

Some years ago, Queen Charlotte had laid down the law regarding proper attire for presentations at court. Men had to wear powdered wigs and breeches, and ladies had to wear ridiculous dresses with trains and enormous hoops, not to mention as many tall feathers in their coiffures as they could manage. The unmarried ladies had to wear white. The wives of peers being presented for the first time could wear whatever color they pleased. But both were expected to adorn themselves with a great deal of their most expensive jewelry.

Or so Joshua had read. He hadn't seen Gwyn or Beatrice in their gowns yet, but Thornstock certainly looked uncomfortable in his wig.

"Wolfe!" Thornstock said as Joshua sat down with his plate of toast and sausages. "Didn't you hear me? I'm done with the *Times* if you want it."

"Sorry," Joshua said. "I was distracted by that enormous sheep on your head."

The man chuckled as he handed Joshua the paper, then picked up a gazette. "I shall have to remember that one. Perhaps your witticism will get back to Her Majesty, and she'll realize that wigs went out of fashion a decade ago. I don't even make my footmen and coachman wear them anymore, for God's sake."

Thornstock carefully inserted one finger under the wig. "I forgot that they itch, too. Or perhaps that's the powder. I can't believe we used to wear the bloody things all the time."

Joshua ate some toast. "You do look very important in it."

Thornstock gave a mirthless laugh. "If you say so. Just be glad you don't have to be at court today."

"One more advantage to not being a peer."

He used to see nothing *but* advantages to that. But last night's wildly erotic dreams about Gwyn had made him rethink his opinion. Over and over, he'd taken Gwyn to bed—in every way a lover could.

Or a husband. One who would have a better chance with her if he were a peer.

Bloody hell, what was wrong with him? She was destined for greater things, something she obviously realized in her more rational moments, when she wasn't letting him—

He had to stop thinking of that.

Thornstock poured himself some coffee, then held up the pot with a questioning glance.

Joshua shoved a cup toward him. "Thank you."

"I'm surprised you drink it at all," the duke said as he poured Joshua a cup. "Most Englishmen prefer tea."

"I picked up a craving for coffee in the marines," Joshua said, adding a generous amount of milk to the cup before drinking.

"My friends think it's odd that I prefer it, but I got in the habit of having it for breakfast while growing up in Berlin." The duke sighed. "And I need whatever sustenance I can get because I have to play bodyguard to Gwyn in your stead today."

Joshua sipped some of the bracing brew. "You have my complete sympathies."

Thornstock narrowed his gaze on Joshua. "Is she giving you trouble?"

Absolutely, but not in the way Thornstock probably thought. "No more than usual," Joshua said evasively. He merely needed time away from Gwyn to get his reckless urges under control.

"Well, I doubt any questionable gentlemen will approach Gwyn inside the palace, even if they *could* get near her with that huge gown she'll be wearing. So I'm not carrying a pistol in this coat. If Malet shows up, which is highly un-likely, I'll just thrash him. I've wanted to do that anyway."

Joshua tensed. For all his seeming indolence, Thornstock was a skilled duelist and regularly went to Gentleman Jackson's academy for lessons from the famous pugilist. So the duke could certainly thrash Malet many times over. And if Thornstock ever heard how Joshua had behaved with Gwyn . . .

No. That must not happen. Joshua's father had died in a senseless, scandalous duel that had devastated Beatrice and resulted in Joshua being sent off to war. Not that he regretted becoming a Royal Marine, but his life would have been vastly different if his father hadn't died and left his children without a penny. So Joshua wasn't about to fight Thornstock in a duel, not if he could avoid it.

"In any case," the duke said, "I'm told these affairs go on for hours, so we probably won't return until evening. Fortunately, the ball Grey is throwing for Gwyn and Beatrice is at his town house, which means Sheridan doesn't have to worry about hosting it here." He regarded Joshua steadily. "I intend to make only a brief appearance, so I do expect you to be present when we arrive at Grey's."

"Of course. It's supposedly my reason for coming to London, remember? To see my sister's debut ball?"

"Ah, yes. I forgot about that." Thornstock sipped some coffee. "Malet isn't invited, of course, but he might try to attend anyway, so we'd best be prepared."

"I agree. The man can be unpredictable." As evidenced by the bastard's showing up yesterday at that tavern.

Pure rage coursed through Joshua whenever he thought of how close Malet had come to her. He actually *wished* Malet would trespass this evening, so he could use that as an excuse to shoot the devil.

It still gnawed at him that he didn't know how Malet had learned about their archery lessons. Last night he'd questioned the servants here, and then the servants at Greycourt's mansion. None had spoken to Malet. Or rather, none had *admitted* to speaking to Malet.

That reminded him of his initial suspicion that Malet and Gwyn had known each other in the past. "Speaking of Malet, do you know if he and Gwyn ever met before that day he tried to kidnap her at the estate?"

Looking grim, Thornstock straightened his newspaper with careful movements. "If they have, I was unaware of it."

Thornstock was lying, damn him. Joshua was tempted to mention Malet's appearance yesterday, but the duke already knew Malet was attempting to kidnap Gwyn. That would not be news enough to make the fellow confide in him.

And there was always the possibility that Joshua was wrong, that what he read as conspiracy between the two siblings was really just the closeness twins shared. No point in raising his benefactor's hackles unnecessarily.

"Because you won't need me until evening, do you mind if I leave as soon as the ladies show off their gowns?" Joshua asked. "I have an appointment at noon with the War Secretary, and given all the carriages that will be headed for the palace, I wouldn't mind getting an early start."

"You can leave now, if you wish."

"And miss seeing Beatrice bedecked in her finery? She'd never forgive me."

The duke regarded him with a pensive look. "Once in a while, I wish Gwyn was as fond of me as Bea clearly is of you."

"No, you don't, trust me. Beatrice is already planning to introduce me to half the women at tonight's ball. When I remind her that I'll be working, she dismisses that with a wave." He snorted. "She never stops matchmaking. Apparently, she thinks it far more important that I find a wife than that I make a living."

"Good God, I can't imagine anything worse than Gwyn trying to pick a wife for me." Thornstock drank some coffee. "By the way, why are you meeting with the War Secretary?"

Used to keeping his affairs close to his chest, he hesitated to reveal that to the duke. After all, the meeting might come to nothing. "It's a minor matter having to do with my half-pay."

"Ah. Of course," the duke said blandly. "I forget that you are still a marine officer."

"Speaking of that, I should go dress. This is an official visit, so they'll expect me to be in uniform."

"Of course, of course." Thornstock pulled out his pocket

watch. "I daresay the ladies won't be down for another hour at least anyway."

Joshua headed upstairs. It didn't take Sheridan's valet long to get him into his uniform, although Joshua noticed his coat was tighter and his pants looser. That was what came of relying on one's arms to compensate for a damaged leg. It was an important reminder that he wasn't like other men. That he never would be.

When he came downstairs, Beatrice and Greycourt had arrived. Greycourt looked much like Thornstock, but Beatrice—

"If you laugh," Beatrice warned Joshua, "I swear I will hit you over the head with my fan."

"You have me shaking in my boots," Joshua teased. "Especially if your fan is as big as that gown and those feathers."

Greycourt chuckled. Beatrice glared at him, and he instantly sobered. "You look like an angel, my love," he said soothingly.

"If an angel's wings were purple and stuck out of the top of her hair," Joshua added, and Thornstock erupted into laughter.

"Well, *you* look like . . . like . . ." Beatrice huffed out a breath. "Blast it, you look quite handsome in your uniform."

"Thank you, ducky. Although to be fair, Thornstock says all ladies find officers in uniform appealing."

"I did not say *all* ladies," Thornstock remarked. "And certainly not all officers appear well in uniform. Prinny, for example, looks like a sausage."

"Because he's not an officer," Joshua said. "More like a royal patron."

"And you lot aren't gentlemen," Aunt Lydia snapped from the staircase. "Shame on you, Joshua. You should be supporting your sister on her big day."

"You're right, of course, Aunt." Joshua turned to Beatrice.

"I'm sorry, ducky. You look beautiful. It's just that . . . well . . . you look even more beautiful when you're not wearing a giant purple sugar puff."

Thornstock and Greycourt howled with laughter, which made Aunt Lydia roll her eyes. Still, it was impossible not to laugh at a dress that had enormous hoop petticoats but the latest high-waisted fashion, so that a woman looked as if she were being devoured from the bottom up by a ball of fabric.

"Ignore him, Beatrice." Gwyn's lilting voice came from the stairs. "We'll be giant sugar puffs together."

"Gwyn!" Beatrice cried as she approached the staircase. "I *told* Grey you would manage to look lovely in spite of everything."

Lovely? She looked magnificent, even with five white ostrich feathers extending into the heavens from her hair. Not to mention a white gown that began under her bosom and ballooned out, hiding what he knew to be the perfect female figure.

She paused on the stairs to stare Joshua down. "Well? Go ahead, Major. Say what you wish so my brothers can laugh at me as well. I know I look ridiculous."

Every eye turned to him, and he scrambled for some compliment he could give her that wouldn't reveal his fervent wish to slip under her skirts and kiss all the bare skin presently hidden from view by her many petticoats. "You look like Luna, goddess of the moon and queen of the stars."

Damn. *That* certainly gave away a bit too much of the effect she had on him.

She flashed him an arch smile. "In other words, I'm big and white and round."

"And you shine at night," Lady Hornsby said as she descended the staircase behind Gwyn, dressed in a similar gown in light green and pink with matching feathers of the same hues. "Both of you do. Or you will, once you change into your much more flattering ball gowns this evening."

"Remember," his aunt put in, "all the other ladies at the palace will be dressed in the same fashion, so it's not as if anyone there will be laughing at you. Besides, you will put them all to shame. You both look quite fetching, my dears."

"She's right, Beatrice," Gwyn said stoutly as she reached her. "To hell with my brothers. And yours."

"Lady Gwyn," Lady Hornsby protested, "please do not say the word 'hell' at the palace."

"I have warned her to watch her language twenty times if I've warned her once," his aunt said, "but she doesn't listen."

"Mama," Gwyn replied, "you know I would never curse in public."

"This *is* public," Lady Hornsby said in obvious exaspera-tion. "And normally I would not mind a bit of saucy language, but this is a debut—you must *attempt* to act like a fresh-faced young woman at the start of her social career."

"Even though I'm closer to the end than the start?" Gwyn said. "Never mind. I understand what you're saying, and I shall heed your advice." She grinned. "At least until I'm married."

Aunt Lydia released a loud sigh, but Lady Hornsby patted Gwyn's arm and said, "That's the spirit. Just hold it in until you marry, and then you can let it all out on your husband."

"So *that's* what Beatrice has been doing," Greycourt said. "All this time I just assumed I was a bad influence."

"You *are*," Beatrice said affectionately. "That's precisely why I love you. We can be bad together."

Joshua turned away to hide the envy sure to be on his face. What his sister had with Greycourt was what he wanted but feared he was destined never to have.

"So what will *you* be doing today while we're at the palace, Mother?" Thornstock asked.

"I'm meeting with Mr. William Bonham, Maurice's man of affairs, because Sheridan is still on his way here, and Mr. Bonham had some questions about your step-father's accounts that couldn't wait. I don't know if any of you have ever met him."

"I did," Greycourt said. "Once, when Sheridan and I were discussing matters of the estate with him. Seemed like a decent enough chap."

"And handsome, too," Lady Hornsby said. "For a man in his sixties anyway." She nudged Aunt Lydia. "Not that Lydia cares."

His aunt cast her a frustrated look. "Stop trying to play matchmaker, Eliza. I'm still in mourning, remember? Besides, I have no wish to marry again."

"And I doubt that Mother wants to marry a man of affairs anyway," Greycourt said.

Joshua stiffened. This was sliding too close to his own situation for comfort. He cleared his throat. "Well, now that I've seen everyone's outrageous attire, I'll be off. I have an appointment."

"With whom?" Beatrice asked.

"Thornstock can explain," Joshua said. "I don't want to be late."

He could lie to the duke about his plans, but he couldn't lie to Beatrice. She would beleaguer him with questions until he either admitted what he was doing or snapped at her. The former would take too much time and the latter would spoil her day, which, for all his teasing, he truly didn't wish to do.

He approached her and took her gloved hand to kiss, because he quite literally couldn't reach her cheek. "You look ravishing, ducky," he said in a soft voice. "And I know you'll impress them all."

His sister beamed at him. "Thank you, dear heart. I'll see you tonight?"

"I wouldn't miss it for the world."

As he turned to leave, he saw a footman whispering in Gwyn's ear. She colored deeply, then said something to the servant and followed him into the nearby parlor.

Joshua made sure to stroll past the parlor door on his way out. A quick glance showed him a young fellow standing and waiting while Gwyn read a note. A messenger? But from whom and regarding what?

He lingered to see if he could find out. With a grim expression, she tucked the message into her reticule and bade the lad wait. Then she went to the writing desk to write a note of her own. A response to the message she'd received? It had to be, because she gave it to the boy and murmured some instructions before handing him a coin.

Joshua considered walking in and demanding to see the message, but there was no reason to believe she would give it to him. She'd been keeping other secrets from him, so why would she divulge this one? And if she didn't, he would have shown his hand.

It might be better to learn what he could in stealth. After all, it might be nothing of importance. Perhaps a friend had fallen ill. Or a family member. No, that couldn't be. They were all here. And if it were Sheridan, she would tell everyone at once.

He walked out the front door to keep from being seen by her. Perhaps he should wait for the messenger to see what he could learn. He had a few minutes before he must leave.

It didn't take long. The lad came out moments later.

A guinea in hand, Joshua accosted him at the bottom of the steps. "Let me see what's in that message you bear, lad, and I will give you this guinea." He was sure Thornstock would be good for it.

The boy's eyes went wide to see Joshua in his undress uniform. It wasn't as impressive as his dress uniform, but its red coat did have gold buttons and epaulettes, his bicorn hat was sufficiently buffed, and his tall boots were polished to a fine sheen.

"Are you in the army, sir?" the lad asked.

"Royal Marines. And the name is Major Wolfe."

"Begging your pardon, Major, but the note is sealed. And if I bring it back to my master unsealed, he'll beat me senseless."

"We wouldn't want that, now, would we?" Joshua said.

But he noticed the lad was still staring at the guinea with a covetous eye.

"I'll tell you what." Joshua held up the guinea. "You answer what questions you can about this exchange of notes, and I'll give you the guinea. All right?"

The lad bobbed his head.

"Who's your master?"

"Mr. Pritchard. Owns a lodging house in Chelsea."

That was not a name Joshua had been expecting. "Why is your master writing notes to Lady Gwyn?"

"Ain't my master writing them. Mr. Pritchard is sending it on behalf of the captain what's staying in his lodging house."

Now *that* was more what Joshua had expected. Or rather, had feared. "What is this captain's name?"

"Don't know. He ain't been staying there long."

"Describe him."

When the boy gave a fairly accurate description of Malet, Joshua's heart sank. Why would Gwyn communicate with the man who wished to abduct her?

He frowned. Unless there was more to the story. Unless she and Malet had a friendship unknown to her brother. After all, her family had traveled back to England from Prussia. They might have met the fellow along the way.

Although she hadn't seemed happy to get the note. And Joshua was almost certain the duke had lied today when questioned about a previous friendship between Gwyn and Malet.

Whatever the reason for their communications, it could not be good. And he hated being right in this instance. Could Gwyn just be flirting with him to keep his suspicions off whatever she and Malet were up to? That possibility tore a hole in him.

"Major?" the lad asked.

"Where is this lodging house exactly?"

The boy rattled off an address, then held out his hand.

"Ah, right. The guinea. Here you go. And thank you."

"You're welcome, sir. And if you ever need a boy in your employ, you just ask for Dick the Quick. Everybody knows I'm the fastest in West London."

"Thank you again. I'll keep that in mind."

He didn't have the heart to tell the lad that the likelihood of Joshua being able to hire a servant was fairly small. Joshua wasn't even sure he could get himself back on the full-pay list.

Speaking of which, he'd better get going. He wouldn't want to miss his appointment. Still, he watched as the boy darted across the street and down the block. If Joshua had time, he would accompany the lad and confront Malet himself.

But he didn't have time. So Malet would have to wait.

# Chapter Eleven

Viscount Castlereagh, Secretary of State for War and the Colonies, was widely reputed to be an intelligent Irishman who ran the War Office with a deft hand. Or that was how he was regarded by soldiers like Joshua.

But something must have occurred to upset the great man's equilibrium, because when Joshua showed up for his appointment, the War Secretary had little to say to him. Despite attempts to moderate Castlereagh's rhetoric by the man's undersecretary, another Irishman named Lucius Fitzgerald, the War Secretary informed Joshua coldly that England needed able-bodied men in this war against Napoleon, not half men on half-pay.

Castlereagh also made it clear that he'd looked into Joshua's situation and had heard about his bouts of temper, which had become a matter for gossip in Sanforth. The War Secretary said that the last thing Joshua should be doing is fighting at war, where ungoverned temper had no place in battle.

By the time Castlereagh was done with his insulting remarks, Joshua was seething. Never had he wanted to throttle a man more, even knowing it wouldn't help his situation. So Joshua uttered a few barely cordial remarks to end the appointment, then marched out into the street, where he hit his cane so hard against a lamppost that it broke.

He instantly regretted that. He would have a hard time finding another sword cane worthy of this one. He stood there staring down at the shattered walking stick and cursing himself. Perhaps Castlereagh was right—he *was* unfit for anything but catching poachers and breeding hunting dogs on his grandfather's estate.

Then, out of nowhere, Fitzgerald, the undersecretary who'd witnessed Joshua's humiliation firsthand, appeared at his side. "Damn. That looks to have been a very useful implement."

Joshua gathered up the pieces, hoping he could somehow repair it. "What do *you* want?" he snarled. "To go in for the kill now that your superior drew first blood?"

Fitzgerald regarded him with a steady blue gaze. "Actually, I want to offer you a position. But not in the Royal Marines. I'd like you to work for *me*."

That flummoxed him. "In what capacity?" Joshua asked warily. "I am no politician, sir, as you might be able to tell."

"Yes, that's painfully obvious." Fitzgerald summoned his coach, which seemed to have been waiting down the street. "The post I'm offering you, however, is more discreet, more . . . behind the scenes, if you will."

Fitzgerald's coach stopped in front of him. "Where to, sir?" the coachman asked.

"Just around the park." Fitzgerald lifted one black brow at Joshua. "Will you ride with me, Major, so we can discuss this further?" When Joshua hesitated, he said, "It can't hurt to hear me out, can it?"

"I suppose not," Joshua said.

Once they were both situated in the coach, Fitzgerald said, "First, allow me to apologize for my superior's insults. Ever since the fiasco at Corunna, he has been difficult to deal with. But he should not have let that govern his behavior."

"No need to apologize," Joshua said. "I'm used to insults."

"Are you really? I think not, given the way you reacted afterward. How often do you lose your temper so spectacularly as to break your cane?"

"This was the first time." Joshua crossed his arms over his chest. "But I *did* break a jug on a man's head because he called me 'Armitage's hobbyhorse' for reporting his poacher offspring to the Armitage estate manager."

Fitzgerald stared at him steadily. "What about your confrontation with that fellow who was kicking a dog? And that other chap who jerked your cane out from under you, causing you to fall? From what I heard, you broke more than a jug for *those*."

Bloody hell, the man had researched him and his bouts of temper quite thoroughly. Joshua wasn't sure what to make of that. "I did indeed. I contend that any man who abuses a dog deserves to have his nose broken. But the fellow who kicked out my cane brought his broken wrist on himself. I fell into him, knocking him over, and he broke his wrist when he tried to brace his fall with his hand. I'd say I wasn't responsible for my actions in either case."

"Perhaps you're right. But I can't have you exploding into a fit of temper for any reason if you are to take the post I'm offering. So I need to know if you can control your anger better than you have in the past."

Nothing like putting a chap on the spot. "The truth is, I'm not sure." Sometimes the anger welled up in him so powerfully that he thought he might strangle on it. In those moments, he had to get away somewhere, be alone, read a book . . . punch a wall.

"Ah." Fitzgerald steepled his fingers. "At least you're honest about it." He mused a moment. "I will be equally honest. I know why you're in London and for whom."

"How the devil—"

"The Duke of Thornstock is a friend of mine. When he was at Brooks's last night, Thorn confided in me about Lionel Malet and needing you to keep the fellow away from Lady Gwyn."

Damnation. If the duke had said this morning that he knew the undersecretary, Joshua would have asked him for an introduction. "What does the post you wish to fill have to do with Malet?"

"I'm looking for someone to spy on the man."

That caught Joshua entirely off guard. "You think Malet is involved with other crimes than just attempting to kidnap Lady Gwyn?"

"Possibly. The man is desperate for money. That's why he's trying to kidnap an heiress to marry. And to hedge his bets, he may also be selling information to the French."

"I'll be damned." Joshua sat back hard. "What kind of information?"

"To be truthful, we're not sure. But we already suspected he was asking around about our troops in the Peninsula. And he's probably finding out quite a bit because he's been questioning soldiers, who see him as a comrade, not as the cashiered and disgraced traitor he is."

"I suppose the news of his being cashiered hasn't filtered down to soldiers in London yet."

"No. And it's the only reason he might get somewhere with his plans. We fear he's trying to gain a copy of Lieutenant-General Wellesley's memorandum to Castlereagh, which proposes that Wellesley use the Portuguese to help lead a campaign against the French. Wellesley is even now on his way to Portugal, but what city he means to set up as his base and how he plans to proceed are secret. If anyone gets their hands on that memorandum—"

"The French could attack Wellesley and his men before they even touch ground. Or right after."

"That's our fear, yes."

Joshua saw Fitzgerald through new eyes. Clever and astute, he was clearly the man behind the throne, who did the hard work while Castlereagh shook hands and brought Fitzgerald's proposals to Parliament.

"That is also where you come in," Fitzgerald said. "We want you to find out who Malet is meeting and what he's trying to sell."

"Why me?"

"Two reasons. One, you still seek to serve your country, despite your battle wounds. That's rare, and—despite what Castlereagh thinks—commendable."

"Ah," Joshua said. "And the other reason?"

"You are still a marine officer with, I've been told, experience in reconnaissance. So you have the skills to shadow Malet without being seen."

"But not if I am 'exploding into a fit of temper.'"

Fitzgerald smiled. "Precisely."

Rubbing his chin, Joshua mused over what the man was proposing.

"And forgive me for being blunt," Fitzgerald went on, "but your lameness is also an asset."

"How do you figure that?" Joshua said with a snort.

"Would you say that people avoid looking at you, acknowledging you?"

"Sometimes."

"That's because we are uncomfortable with our wounded soldiers. The sight of them rouses a deep-seated guilt that we don't do enough to help them. So we tend to look away, to pretend that none of you exist. In many respects, your cane—and your limp—make you invisible to the world."

"But not invisible to Malet," Joshua pointed out. "He knows my face."

"You met him, what, twice? Or so Thorn says."

Joshua blinked. "Perhaps you should hire the *duke* as a spy. He's clearly good at it."

"Or it may just be that your family—*Thornstock's* family—tend to talk about things no one else would."

"That's true, too." Joshua eyed him closely. "Still, both times I saw Malet I was confronting him or his lackey directly. He will not forget my face."

"But he won't expect to see you following him. I daresay he doesn't even realize you're in London."

"I'm afraid you're wrong. He found out from Lady Gwyn's servant that I was with her yesterday."

"That doesn't mean he knows you're serving as her bodyguard. You could be courting her."

*In my dreams, perhaps.*

"In any case," Fitzgerald went on, "the point is moot. As you well know, a soldier skilled at reconnaissance is quite capable of hiding from the enemy, even one who recognizes him. I have utter faith in your ability to shadow Malet without his realizing it. After all, he wasn't the best of soldiers. And now that he's desperate for funds, he'll take reckless chances that a more prudent man might not."

"You could be right."

"Speaking of men needing funds, if you do this for us, we're willing to put you back on full pay, but secretly. And with the condition that you serve as a spy here in London, not a combatant on board a ship."

Joshua mulled that over. It was a good offer. "Does Thornstock know you intend to pay me to follow Malet?"

"No. As I said, this is to be kept secret."

"I understand. But my work for the duke has to come first, because I have already agreed to it."

"I'm sure if I spoke to him, Thorn would be willing to—"

"No." When the undersecretary raised a brow, Joshua said, "I made a promise. I keep my promises. And if breaking this one is what it takes to work for you, I will have to respectfully decline."

Because once he broke his promise to Thornstock, he'd have to move his London lodgings from Armitage House to somewhere else, and he couldn't be sure he could keep an eye on Malet well enough to prevent the arse from getting at Gwyn. He wouldn't risk that.

"Fine," Fitzgerald said, with respect glinting in his eyes. "Do you have any other objections to taking this position? Anything else that might be a hindrance to your doing it adequately?"

Joshua knew he should tell Fitzgerald about his reaction to loud noises. But the man was giving him a rare opportunity to do what he wanted: serve his country. He didn't want to lose this chance.

Besides, ever since he'd been in London, loud noises hadn't seemed to trouble him as much. The clamor in the streets day and night blended into a soothing cacophony, like the roar of ocean waves or the steady sounds of sailors working on board ship.

What's more, in the two nights he'd spent in the City, he'd slept much better than at home. If he proved a real asset to Fitzgerald, he might be able to live here instead of in Lincolnshire. That meant he could see Beatrice often.

And not see Gwyn once the Season was over. That alone made it worth doing. Because seeing her when he couldn't touch her or talk to her was a pain he did not want to endure forever. But if she was in Lincolnshire and he wasn't, or if she was married and in an entirely different part of England . . .

That did not sit well with him either. And the fact that it didn't alarmed him. It also pushed him to make up his mind about one part of Fitzgerald's offer at least.

"I have no other objections. Indeed, I'm happy to spy on a blackguard like Malet if it means getting him locked up in gaol where he belongs." Joshua drew in a deep breath. "But I need time to consider making the post permanent."

"Of course," Fitzgerald said, looking as if he'd expected the answer. "That's probably best anyway. We can determine if you'll meet our requirements."

"And whether I can control my temper," Joshua drawled, fingering the pieces of the shattered sword cane he held in his hand.

Fitzgerald chuckled. "That, too." Without warning, the gentleman took the pieces from Joshua and shoved them under his seat.

"Now see here," Joshua protested, "I was hoping someone could repair that, or perhaps use the blade in a new stick."

"No need." Fitzgerald opened the panel and told the coachman to go back to the office of the War Secretary, then take Joshua to a certain address on Threadneedle Street. "Bennett and Lacy, a sword cutler and gunmaker establishment, will provide you with whatever you need. Just tell them to put it on the War Secretary's account."

Fitzgerald reached under the seat again and pulled out a knobby walking stick. "You can use this for the time being, but Bennett and Lacy can make you a sword cane to your specifications if you find nothing to your liking that's ready-made."

The carriage halted where it had picked them up.

"If you don't mind waiting," Fitzgerald continued, "I'll go inside and write a letter of credit for you."

Well, now. This was something he could get used to. "Sounds as if I'm going to like this post a great deal."

"Good. Because I believe you're perfectly suited to it." Fitzgerald reached inside his pocket and pulled out a slip of paper. "Oh, and before I forget, I tracked Malet to this address, planning to follow him myself, but Castlereagh prefers I work on other things. With England at war—"

"I understand." Joshua took the slip of paper and read it. The address was in Chelsea. Which confirmed that Gwyn had written the note to Malet, damn her. How was he to handle this? "I'll see what I can learn."

"Excellent." Fitzgerald held out his hand. "Glad to have you on board, Major."

Joshua shook his hand. "Glad to be on board, sir. I won't disappoint you."

That was a promise to Fitzgerald *and* to himself. And he intended to keep it, no matter the cost.

Which meant that he must be more careful with Gwyn. If she was indeed involved with Malet, she might be trying to "manage" Joshua's guarding of her the way she seemed to manage everyone else's lives in her orbit. For all Joshua knew, she might even be using him to hide her association with the man she *really* wanted. The thought of her and Malet laughing at him behind his back—

Bloody hell. Joshua didn't want to believe she would do that, but the only way to be sure of her connection to Malet was to go along with her plans until he could figure out exactly what that connection was. Once he did, however, he must be prepared to reveal what he learned not only to her twin, but possibly to Fitzgerald. And that meant not succumbing to his mad urges for her.

# Chapter Twelve

When Gwyn first entered the ballroom of the Greycourt town house, she should have been ecstatic. Her presentation at court had gone better than expected. She hadn't tripped on her train, hadn't said anything stupid to Her Majesty, and had even managed to enjoy her conversations with Thorn.

What's more, Grey had spared no expense for her and Beatrice tonight. His newly purchased Argand lamp chandeliers cast a warm glow about the room, and the scent of fifty or more branches of orange blossoms reminded everyone that it was spring—and that the room was filled with young women hoping to meet their future husbands. A fine orchestra had been hired for the occasion, which was playing exquisitely.

But all she could think of was the note Lionel had sent— right to her home! He'd asked for his money. Again. And he'd said that if she didn't meet with him on the morrow to give it to him, he would go straight to the nearest gossip rag to lay out everything he knew about her. It would mortify her family. Ruin her.

He'd given her no choice but to set up a meeting. That had been risky in itself. She didn't want to meet him anywhere near Mayfair, where her family or their servants might see her. But she'd worked out a plan. She and Mama had already

intended to go shopping tomorrow afternoon, so she'd told
Lionel to meet her around three o'clock in the alley next to
her favorite glover's shop. There she would pay Lionel his
pound of flesh and pray that it sufficed to keep him away
from her forever.

Now all she had to do was get a hundred pounds from
Thorn. And escape Joshua long enough to give it to Lionel
tomorrow.

"Are you having fun yet?"

She jumped, sure that the major had read her mind. But it
was just Thorn.

"You scared me half to death!" she cried, slapping her
twin's hand lightly with her fan. "Don't sneak up on a woman
like that!"

Typical of a brother, he merely laughed. "I came to tell
you I'm leaving."

"But you just got here," she said.

"And I'm already bored to tears." When she lifted a brow
at him, he said, "Come now, Sis, you know I'm not the marriage mart sort. Besides, didn't I do my duty once today by
squiring you through your presentation?"

She softened. "Yes, you did. And I thank you." It dawned
on her that perhaps now was the time to beg him for money,
while he felt marginally guilty for leaving and while Joshua
was halfway across the room talking to Beatrice. "By the
way, Mama and I are going shopping tomorrow, and I need
a hundred pounds."

"For *what*?" He frowned. "I have a line of credit with
every bloody merchant in Bond Street. Just use that. And it's
dangerous for you to be walking around with that much blunt
anyway."

"Isn't that what Joshua is for? In any case, Mama's birthday is next week. It's been a difficult year for her, what with
Papa dying and her worries about the estate and her not being

able to attend my debut activities. So I wish to buy her a very nice gift to cheer her up. But she's shopping with me, so I'll have to be sneaky about it. Which means slipping the merchant some pound notes rather than waiting for him to record the purchase, etcetera, etcetera."

A look of horror crossed Thorn's face. "Oh, God, Mother's birthday. I completely forgot about it."

"Yes, but it's all right. I have it handled. I'll purchase something and say it's from both of us." And she'd use credit for it, so she could give the hundred pounds to Lionel. By the time Thorn learned of it, Lionel would be out of her life for good.

Or that was her plan anyway.

"Thank you, Sis! I'll send the money over first thing tomorrow."

"You're a dear," she said, stretching up to kiss his cheek. When he eyed her suspiciously, she realized she'd done it up a bit brown. "Now go on to whatever house of debauchery you frequent, before I start introducing you to all the young, unattached ladies here."

He didn't wait to see if she really would. He fled.

As soon as he had vanished from her side, a gentleman approached to ask for the first dance. The ball had clearly officially begun. And now that she had the money arranged for Lionel—and an idea for how to escape Joshua tomorrow was forming in her mind—she might as well enjoy herself. Where better to have fun than at a ball in her honor?

But after hours of dancing with scarcely a chance to breathe, she had changed her opinion. She did love the dancing, but the *men* . . . Well, she'd had quite enough of their empty compliments about her eyes being stars and her cheeks peaches. Honestly, did any of these fellows have a single genuine thought in their heads?

What made it worse was, they weren't remotely sincere.

She could tell that by how they quizzed her about her family connections and why she'd waited so long to marry. They merely wanted her fortune. She'd expected that, but it still hurt. Not to mention that it made it harder for her to put up with the arses.

A pity she couldn't take her brothers as partners, but that wasn't allowed. Besides, this *was*, after all, her debut. She was expected to dance with eligible gentlemen. But surely she'd met her quota by now.

Good Lord, but she would never marry a one of them, even if she *could*. After a while, she fled to the refreshments room to avoid them.

In there, a footman offered her a glass of champagne, which she took readily, then sipped as she surveyed the fare. In addition to the champagne, there was fruit punch and tea and negus to drink. All manner of delicious hors d'oeuvres were spread across one table: scotch eggs, brawn, white soup, sliced cold meats and cheeses, and sandwiches, among others. And if sweets were more to one's liking, another table was filled with apricot cakes, lavender shortbread, lemon tarts, Naples biscuits, and such. There were even pyramids of grapes, peaches, and other spring fruits. And this was all to stave off hunger before everyone went in to supper! Grey did nothing by halves.

Still, she wasn't about to eat a peach and risk ruining her debut ball gown, which she'd changed into the second she'd arrived home from the Palace. And where was her bodyguard? She went to stand in the doorway to look. Had she managed to evade Joshua by coming in here? Apparently not, for as soon as the question had entered her mind it was answered by the sight of him leaving his post across the ballroom and making his way through the crowd toward her.

Lord, but he was handsome in his uniform. From his gold epaulettes to his sparkling white trousers and his shining

Hessian boots, he was a fine picture of a man. Gold braid lavishly adorned his red coat and a white cross belt showed him to be an officer, along with the gold officer's gorget that hung about his neck. But as usual he wore a grim expression. The man simply did not know how to enjoy himself properly.

Feeling mischievous, she grabbed another glass of champagne and met him at the door.

"Something bubbly to drink, Joshua?" she asked as she offered him the glass. "Or are you not allowed to imbibe?"

"I don't know why I wouldn't be." He took the glass from her and drank deeply of it. "I may *have* to drink just to endure this night of horrors."

"How wonderful to see Major Grumbler make his debut at *my* debut," she said with a laugh. "Just out of curiosity, what makes it a night of horrors?"

He eyed her askance. "There are too many people of too little intelligence, for one. I daresay none of them has read a book in the past month."

"*I* read a book in the past month," she said teasingly.

"What kind? Wait, don't tell me. A novel. Or some compilation of sentimental poetry about love."

"I'll have you know it was neither. I read *Essays on Gothic Architecture.*"

"Something sensible, then." He sipped more champagne. "I'm astonished."

"Are you?" She ignored the insult to her reading choices. "What book did *you* read in the past month?"

"I read fifteen. Shall I list the titles?"

"Good heavens, no. We'd be here all night."

He narrowed his gaze on her. "Was the book on architecture the only thing you read in the past month?"

"Not in the least. I pored over the latest issue of *La Belle Assemblée*, for one. It was rather thin on information about architecture, but it did have some lovely fashion plates. Those all had titles. Shall I recite them?"

"Do spare me, I beg you."

But she could see the smile tugging at his lips. It always delighted her when she could amuse him. And if she actually got a laugh out of him, she considered it a personal triumph.

She was about to offer a particularly witty bon mot about books when two young ladies approached them. She'd met them earlier at the Palace. What were their names again? Oh, right—Lady Hypatia and Miss Clarke.

"Lady Gwyn," Miss Clarke said with a veiled glance at Joshua. "Lady Hypatia and I were just saying how impressed we were with your presentation to the queen today. You didn't take one step awry. Meanwhile, I nearly dropped my bracelet in Her Majesty's lap, and Lady Hypatia stepped on her own train when she was backing out."

"But I didn't fall," Lady Hypatia put in. She looked at Joshua with blatant curiosity. "I caught myself in time. You, on the other hand, were poise itself, Lady Gwyn."

It was clear they were angling for an introduction to Joshua. That didn't amuse Gwyn quite as much as she would have thought, probably because women had been asking her about him all evening. It had become rather annoying.

She considered letting these two dangle a bit longer, but that seemed cruel. So she introduced them to Joshua, who managed something very nearly *like* a smile, about the best any stranger could hope for from him.

"Aren't you dancing this evening, Major?" Lady Hypatia asked.

Gwyn caught her breath. What was wrong with the chit? Didn't she realize how rude her question was? The only men allowed to have canes or walking sticks in a ballroom were those who actually needed them. Obviously, Joshua qualified.

"Afraid not," he said tightly. "I'm on duty." He leaned

pointedly on his cane, but the two ladies were apparently too smitten by his good looks and fine uniform—or too heedless of what the cane must mean—to notice anything else.

"On duty!" Miss Clarke surveyed the supper room, then lowered her voice. "Are you guarding someone in here?"

He briefly looked taken aback. Then a sly glint appeared in his eyes as he met Gwyn's gaze. "I am indeed."

Gwyn glared at him. Surely he wouldn't *dare* say who. If word got out that she had a bodyguard, tongues would wag and Mama would be most unhappy.

"Can you say who it is?" Lady Hypatia asked, furtively looking around the room. "It must be someone very important. One of the dukes perhaps?"

"Perhaps," he echoed.

Miss Clarke eyed him suspiciously. "I think you're bamming us. You're not on duty at all, are you, Major?"

"I can neither confirm nor deny it," he said.

Lady Hypatia leaned in. "Tell us this, then. Have you fought in very many battles?"

"Quite a few, actually. The Battle of Berlin, the Battle of Prussia, and the Battle of Constantinople, among others."

Gwyn lifted her gaze heavenward. How he managed to keep a straight face while spewing such balderdash was anyone's guess.

"Were they bloody?" Lady Hypatia asked, wide-eyed.

"Oh yes." Joshua finished his champagne. "I saw the enemy rip out the heart of one of our Royal Marines and eat it right there."

The two ladies gasped.

That only seemed to encourage him. "There was death as far as the eye could see. The ocean reeked of blood."

"How awful!" Miss Clarke said in a tone that said she found it fascinating.

Already annoyed that the ladies were looking at him

worshipfully, Gwyn decided she'd had enough. "Pay Major Wolfe no mind. He's making all of that up. There are no such battles, and certainly not any that included the Royal Marines."

Joshua flashed her a look of mock outrage. "You *doubt* me, Lady Gwyn? I am deeply hurt."

"Hurt in the head, perhaps," she shot back. "Because Berlin is landlocked, which makes it impossible for you to have fought a maritime engagement there. Prussia is an entire country, so that battle would have been sizable indeed."

His lips twitched again. Clearly, he was fighting a smile. "And Constantinople? Are you claiming there wasn't a Battle of Constantinople?"

"Not at all. But it took place over six hundred years ago. So unless you've found the secret to immortality, you couldn't have fought in it. As Miss Clarke said, you *are* bamming us. I dare you to deny it."

"And if I don't? What shall you do then?" His eyes were twinkling now. "Court-martial me? Have me thrown in gaol?"

"I'll have you thrown in the coat closet until you sober up," Gwyn said. "Because only a man who's foxed would tell such blatant lies."

He laughed outright. "No one can fool you, can they, Lady Gwyn?"

"Not many can, I confess, and certainly no officers. I learned early on not to trust them. They tend to exaggerate."

That seemed to sober him. Apparently, he'd caught on that she meant Lionel. Or rather Hazlehurst, who was serving as the substitute for the younger version of Lionel.

The two ladies looked disappointed. They'd swallowed every word of his tales, and now clearly felt foolish. Given that this whole thing had started when they'd rudely asked him about dancing, Gwyn wasn't inclined to make things easier for them.

It wasn't because she was jealous. Certainly not. They

could have him. One of them might be more successful at capturing his heart. If he even possessed such a thing.

Fortunately, two gentlemen approached just then who *were* interested in dancing with Lady Hypatia and Miss Clarke. The ladies were more than happy to oblige, leaving Gwyn still standing with Joshua.

As soon as they were gone, she turned on him. "You are almost as incorrigible as Thorn! The Battle of Berlin indeed." She shook her head. "I would never have thought it of you."

With a shrug, he let the footman take his empty glass. "I had to get rid of them somehow. They wouldn't leave. But I confess, I didn't expect them to be quite so gullible."

She planted her hands on her hips. "And why were you eager to escape them anyway? They were flirting with you. You'd think you'd find that flattering."

He steadied his glittering gaze on her. "Trying to marry me off, are you, my lady? Are you and Beatrice working together now to arrange my future happiness?"

The supper room suddenly seemed far too quiet. "Not with either of those two. As you say, they aren't very bright. You deserve someone more intelligent." She forced herself to say the next words. "And there are plenty of clever women here. Women who've asked me about you."

That seemed to catch him by surprise. "Who's bamming whom now?"

"I mean it. They want to know if you're eligible and why you look so serious and whether you intend to marry." An acid note crept into her voice, try as she might to restrain it. "Oh, and they're curious about why you keep watching me. They worry that it's because you and I have an understanding."

"And what did you tell them?"

"I told them that as the grandson of a duke you're eminently eligible, that you look so serious because you're a serious fellow, and that you only intend to marry if you find a woman who suits you." Which *she* obviously did not.

"I meant," he said sharply, "what did you tell them about our 'understanding'?"

"Oh. The truth, of course. That we have none."

He cocked one brow. "So how did you explain why I keep watching you?"

She fought to keep a straight face. "I told them you were madly in love with me . . . but it was unrequited, of course."

"Of course," he said coldly.

Irritated that he could believe she'd lie about such a thing, she decided to spin out the tale further just to see how long it took before he caught on. "I told them you are sure that if you follow me around like a lapdog, I will one day— Damn!"

"You will one day damn who?" he asked.

"That coxcomb coming our way. Sorry, but I need to escape. He hasn't seen me yet." She walked toward the far end of the supper room, where stood a set of French doors.

Joshua kept pace with her. "Wherever you go, I go. Especially if it's outdoors, where it would be easier for Malet to snatch you."

"Fine. But only if you don't alert that coxcomb to where I'm headed. We can hide in the gardens until he tires of looking for me and returns to the ballroom."

They slipped through the doors and out onto the terrace. Beyond it were the gardens, reachable by a few steps down. She walked toward them.

Joshua followed, taking in the gardens with a careful eye. "Greycourt certainly knows how to spend his money well. I've never seen a property as large as this in London."

"It's Grey's forte—buying properties and turning them into something greater, with judicious management and good investing." She lifted her skirts as she descended the steps. "Your sister married well."

"Trust me, I'm aware of that." He went down the steps after her, though at a slower pace. "And he must really love her. It's the only way I can see him choosing to marry a woman with no prospects."

"He doesn't care about her prospects. He only cares about *her.*"

As if realizing they were veering into subjects he never wanted to discuss, he asked, "Why are you trying to avoid this coxcomb anyway?"

"Because he fancies himself a wit and keeps going on and on about my rosy cheeks and my golden locks."

Joshua blinked. "Your hair is red."

"I know! To be fair, it's a bit hard to tell colors by candle-light—"

"Not *that* hard. Good God, what's wrong with the fellow?"

"Apparently, the same thing that has been wrong with *all* my dance partners this evening." She paused to gaze back at the French doors, but she didn't see the coxcomb, thank God. "Judging from the balderdash they were spouting, they have brains made of cheese."

Joshua laughed.

"Shh! I don't want him to hear us." Though she hated to stifle Joshua. She'd had two laughs in one night out of him. "He'll come down here and ask me to dance, and you know the rules—I'm not allowed to say no unless I mean to sit out the rest of the evening. Then again, that might not be such a bad idea. My family keeps tossing dance partners at me in hopes that one of them will stick, but they all have terrible taste in men."

"I'll tell you what—if the coxcomb finds us out here, I'll say that you've already promised *me* the next set."

She paused in scanning the terrace to stare at Joshua. "You would dance with me?"

"Don't be absurd. I'd make a fool of myself. But if he's as unobservant as Lady Hypatia and Miss Clarke—and he sounds as if he is—he might not realize I can't dance with a bad leg and a cane."

The idea of his dancing with her took hold. She didn't want to examine too closely why. "You could manage the minuet, I daresay. It's slow and requires a man to put his hands out anyway, so you could use your cane without it looking *too* odd."

"Thank you, but I'd rather not hobble around the floor for all the world to see. Besides, they've already danced the minuet, and if I remember right, it's only danced once at a ball."

She cocked her head. "Did you used to dance, before you were wounded?"

"I did, though I had few opportunities. There aren't many women aboard a man-of-war. I could only dance while we were in port."

"Did you enjoy it?"

"For the most part. After being cooped up on a ship for weeks with a lot of foul-smelling sailors and marines, it was wonderful to kick up one's heels with a sweet-scented woman." His gaze on her turned suspicious. "Why do you ask?"

"Because now that you've mentioned the possibility of your dancing, I consider it a challenge to see you do so. After all, we're alone out here, so no one will care if you aren't perfect at it."

"Gwyn—" he began in a warning tone.

"I'm thinking the waltz might work," she said, tapping her finger against her chin.

"What the hell is a waltz?"

"It's a dance in three-quarter time that's quite popular in Berlin and Vienna. And unlike so many English dances, it allows you to hold on to your partner with both hands for the entire time. That would be the best of the dance choices, I think, though not out here on uneven ground."

Taking his hand in hers, she began to walk along a path through the gardens that lay parallel to the house. "Come with me, if you dare. I'm going to teach you to waltz."

# Chapter Thirteen

What the devil was she up to? As she wound through the gardens, Joshua prayed she wasn't trying to leave the grounds. Given the note she'd sent Malet earlier in the day, Joshua would have to put his foot down about her heading anywhere beyond Greycourt's property. And right now he didn't want to get into an argument with her.

She was holding his hand. She was complaining about her suitors. He liked both things better than he should, especially after an evening of being forced to watch her dance with every fool in creation. Of fighting to keep his jealousy under control when all he wanted was to punch her partners in the face.

And thus prove to Fitzgerald that he was unequal to the task of spying on anyone.

Damnation! He had sworn not to become besotted with her. What was wrong with him? He *knew* better. He had to be careful, had to not let her manipulate him into going along with her plans, whatever those were. It may not seem like it sometimes, but *she* was not his employer. Thornstock was. And Fitzgerald, hopefully.

"Where are we heading?" he asked her, more gruffly than he'd intended.

"To the orangery."

Relief coursed through him. He'd forgotten Beatrice's mention of Greycourt's orangery, a separate building that could be entered from the garden or the house.

"There, we can have both privacy and a nice stone floor on which to dance," Gwyn added.

He groaned. The last thing he needed was privacy around her. His record on that score hadn't been good so far. He didn't know which was worse: being alone with her while taking her in his arms, or attempting to dance and falling flat on his face at her feet.

Still, God save him, the prospect of holding her for an entire dance tantalized him. Even knowing she was secretly corresponding with Malet didn't keep him from wanting her. So he'd have to use their privacy to his advantage.

After all, two could play her game. She wanted to lull him into letting her do whatever she pleased? Fine. He would let her. It might be the only way to get to the bottom of what was going on between her and Malet. If he asked her flat out, she wouldn't tell him. She'd already had ample chance today to tell him that Malet had corresponded with her. But if he strengthened their intimacy, she might begin to trust him enough to confide in him.

He snorted. Now he was lying to himself. Forget strengthening their intimacy—what he really wanted was to *be* intimate with her. Even the thought of it made him hard.

Damn, they'd better reach that orangery soon, before they ran into one of her many suitors—or worse yet, one of her brothers—who might take note of the decided bulge in his breeches.

He needed to take his mind off desiring her. "So tell me, what are some of the other pieces of 'balderdash' gentlemen have 'spouted' at you this evening?"

"Oh, you know, the usual. My eyes are like emeralds—"

"They are."

"And my lips are like cherries—"

"Once again, they are. So far, I cannot fault your suitors' flatteries, which sound more like compliments."

"Come now." She eyed him askance. "You can't tell me you would blather such unimaginative observations."

"No, I would merely call you something 'big and white and round.'"

"What are you talking about?"

He raised a brow. "This morning? When I called you Luna, goddess of the moon and queen of the stars? That was your response."

She winced. "Oh, dear, that was very bad of me. And once I thought about it and realized you weren't comparing me to the moon itself, I rather liked it. No woman should complain about being called a goddess and a queen." Her voice turned acid. "It's certainly better than being told I have lovely, child-bearing hips."

"Someone actually said that to you?" he asked, incredulous.

"While he was dancing with me. I swear it."

He shook his head. "Even I have the good sense not to say something like that when trying to woo a woman."

"I should hope so," she said with a smile.

Her smile would melt stone, and he was not as immune to it as he should be.

They had reached the orangery now. She let them in by the garden door and hurried over to the stove that made the orangery cozy and warm even on a chilly spring night. Igniting a piece of kindling off the stove fire, she went around lighting candles. He would have preferred to be in the dark with her, but he didn't want to alarm her by saying so.

Clearly nervous, she was chattering about the architectural wonders of the orangery—how Greycourt had replaced the slate roof with glazed glass and how he used stoves for heating it in winter rather than open fires because it was better for the oranges.

He barely heard the rest. He was too busy drinking his fill of her in a gown that was probably a bit fast for an eighteen-year-old but suited a woman of her age perfectly. Despite the virginal white, the bodice was seductive as hell, cut low enough to show the swells of her bosom. And it had this line of gold ribbon or embroidery or something that swept from just below her right breast—where the high waist was—down diagonally to end at the left hem of the gown, where it then circled the hem a couple of times.

It looked like a Christmas gift wrapped in white paper and sealed with gold ribbon, where all one had to do was undo the ribbon to have the present open like a flower and reveal all sorts of good things inside. That was what he wished to do: unwrap every inch of her to see what lay beneath.

"Shall we begin?" she asked, her throaty tone merely enhancing his pleasant fantasy.

*She's talking about the dancing, you fool, not fulfilling your fantasy. Get your mind out of the gutter.*

"I warn you," he said as she came toward him, "this may not work."

"All we can do is try," she said lightly.

There was a white wicker settee piled with cushions next to where he stood, so she took his cane and propped it there. Then she paused to gaze down at it. "That's a new cane."

He was surprised she'd noticed. "A friend gave it to me after I broke mine earlier today."

She caught her breath. "What friend?"

"The Undersecretary of War."

"Oh, right. I forgot you had an appointment there today. Did it go well?"

"Well enough."

He certainly couldn't complain about the sword cane he'd

found ready-made at Bennett & Lacy, along with the pair of travelers' pistols that would serve him better than the duke's ornate one. And the gunsmith was making him a cane with a pistol to hide in the handle, too, although it wouldn't be ready for a week.

"This cane seems quite a bit stouter than your other one," she said. "Does it have a sword in it, too?"

"It does. Why? Are you wanting lessons in swordplay now?" When delight leaped in her eyes, he said hastily, "That was a joke."

"We could trade lessons," she said with a minxish smile. "I'll teach you to waltz and you can teach me to use a sword."

"Let's not get ahead of ourselves. I'm not even sure I *can* waltz."

"Right." She came up to him. "For the first position—"

"Wait a minute." He already felt unsteady without his cane. "How many positions are there?"

She avoided his gaze as she removed her gloves, then tossed them onto the cushions. "Only nine."

"*Nine!* Are you daft?"

"Just try the first one, all right?"

"If you insist." But if she was taking off her gloves, he was removing his, too.

Moving to stand next to him, she put her left arm across his back and his right arm across hers. That steadied him a bit. Perhaps he *could* do this.

Then she said, "Now you keep your left foot facing forward while you put your right one perpendicular to it. Like this."

He stared at the perfect V her feet made and felt defeat swamp him. "I'm sorry, dearling, but my right calf and foot won't move that way."

"Of course they will, if you just—" She caught herself. "Oh. You mean they *can't* move that way."

"Exactly. They're pretty much frozen in their present position."

She lifted her gaze to him, her cheeks stained scarlet. "I didn't realize . . . that is, practically every step of the waltz requires both the man and the woman to put their feet like that or point them or some such. So the waltz definitely won't work. I am so very sorry."

"I'm not." Relieved that he hadn't had to fall flat on his face to prove he couldn't dance, he pivoted to pull her fully into his arms. "It allows me to hold you without having to watch my step and count off the beat."

"We could try . . . another dance," she breathed, though she readily put her arms about his waist.

"Must we?" He brushed a kiss to her brow. "Holding you is something I rather enjoy."

She nuzzled his neck. "Do you, now? It's very scandalous, you know."

"Not nearly as scandalous as some things we've done." He began to kiss his way along her forehead. "And definitely less scandalous than I intend to be."

That made her tremble a bit, yet he could feel the wild beat of her heart against his lips at her temple. Nor was she pulling away. So surely she must want *him* a little herself.

She took a shallow breath. "Earlier, you told me . . . you knew better than to say certain things while wooing a woman." Her voice grew husky. "What *would* you say? If, for example, you were trying to woo me?"

"Hmm." He thought a moment as he continued scattering kisses down to her pretty ears. "I'd say you have eyes as green as forest pools, the kind a man could lose himself in. That you have a lemony scent all your own, both tart and sweet, which somehow makes it more delectable."

Her breath feathered past his cheek, quickening as he tongued her ear. "*Now* who's been reading sentimental poetry?"

"Shall I go on?" he asked.

"There's more?"

"Ah, dearling," he said, "there always seems to be more to enjoy with you. More wit, more surprises . . . more of *this*."

And with that, he covered her mouth with his. He couldn't seem to help himself. She was so giving and eager, as if she'd been waiting for him to come along and open her wrapping paper.

Their kiss rapidly grew heated until all he could think about was touching her. But he couldn't do it while also holding on to her for support. So he dropped onto the settee next to his cane, pulling her down and onto his lap.

She gave a little squeak, but threw her arms about his neck all the same. "I'm not hurting you, am I?"

"God, no. And even if you were, I would endure it just for the chance to hold you like this."

He leaned her back so he could kiss the soft swells of her breasts, which he'd been coveting a taste of since he'd first seen her in the ballroom. He knew he didn't dare undo her gown enough to suck them the way he wanted. They both had to return to the ballroom eventually, and he wasn't entirely certain he could get it all back properly.

But there was something else equally pleasurable that he could do, and it would hardly dislodge her gown at all. Sliding up her skirts a bit, he reached beneath them to run his hands up her thighs—her sweet, silky thighs—above her garters. She dragged in a shuddering breath that only inflamed him more.

"So soft," he rasped as he caressed her. "Your skin is as delicate and smooth as the finest satin. It makes me want to do this."

He lifted her off his lap to set her on the settee next to him. Then, after moving to the other end, he spread her legs apart so that one was on the settee and the other on the floor. From there, all he had to do was push up her skirts in order to bare all to his gaze.

"Joshua! What are you—"

He bent to kiss her thigh.

"Oh. Good. Heavens. This is insanity."

Yet her hands grabbed at his shoulders as if to hold him close, and she made no effort to close her legs. He took that as a definite sign of encouragement.

With his heart thundering in his chest, he kissed and tongued his way up her thigh to the prize he was more than eager to gain—the thatch of curls at the juncture between her legs that hid the tender flesh he wanted to suck.

He could already smell her arousal. God save him, how it drove him out of his mind!

"Are you . . . trying to seduce me . . . sir?" There was a hint of alarm in her voice now.

"I want to pleasure you," he said honestly. "If you'll let me. Will you?"

He could barely see her eyes in the candlelight, but he would have sworn they glittered with anticipation. Though he told himself he was doing this as part of his campaign to make her confide in him, in his heart he knew it was more than that. He wanted her, was holding his breath as he awaited her answer.

Then she smiled like a cat in the cream. "Please do."

That was all he needed to hear.

# Chapter Fourteen

Despite giving him permission to do this, Gwyn hadn't expected him to stare at her *there*. She ought to find it embarrassing. Instead, she thought it the most . . . most *carnal* thing she'd ever experienced! Her blood roared in her ears, and she couldn't help squirming under his eager gaze.

She squirmed even more when he delved through her curls with his thumbs to unearth the flesh beneath. "You're wet for me, dearling. Wet and warm and fragrant, like a spring flower opening to the sun after a rainstorm."

There was that endearment again. And more sweet words, too. Who would have guessed that Joshua had a gift for the poetic?

Then . . . *then* came something even more surprising. He bent to kiss her. *Down there!* And given the way he went on to flick and lick and tease her flesh . . . well, it seemed obvious he was enjoying it as much as she.

She couldn't imagine how, because she was enjoying it beyond anything. Fire raced through her veins, and Joshua stoked it higher with every lash of his tongue. He might not have romantic feelings for her, but he certainly desired her. Surely no man would do this . . . odd thing to a woman without desiring her.

Nor had she ever experienced such an incredibly sensual

bombardment. Joshua's mouth and tongue and fingers aroused her where she least expected it, and the feeling . . .

Oh, it was *incredible*. She heard herself making moans and gasps that sounded as if they were coming from someone else. Because surely she couldn't make such noises.

"Joshua . . . I haven't ever . . . This is so . . . Good *Lord*!"
She'd had no idea such wonderful sensations existed! Clearly, she'd taken leave of her senses. Then Joshua started thrusting his tongue inside her, and her heart nearly failed her. It was . . . *exquisite*. No other word sufficed.

Catching his head in her hands, she pressed him into her to gain more of the ecstasy she craved, and he gave a triumphant chuckle.

She didn't care if he triumphed, as long as he kept . . . doing . . . kept doing . . . oh, Lord, *that*! Exactly that. Because now he was delving in and out of her with his tongue in a rhythm that seemed both familiar and exotic. It tugged her up and up, like Jack's mythical beanstalk growing toward the sky.

Soon Joshua's tongue was stroking more deeply, and his thumbs were stroking, too, but in an incredibly sensitive spot that made her want everything he could give her. She could hardly breathe for the excitement rising down there, carrying her on to greater heights . . . into the clouds and beyond to magic worlds . . . that unfurled as if . . . in a dream.

"Joshua . . ." she begged, not quite knowing what she was begging for. And then whatever it was found her, like a bolt of lightning. "Joshua!" she screamed, clutching him to her as she shattered into a million pieces, all at once.

As waves of pure, decadent pleasure shook her, she collapsed against the settee's back. "Ohhh, *Joshua*."

He kissed her thigh, then drew down her shift so he could wipe his mouth on it.

"That was . . . amazing," she whispered. "I never dreamed

it could be like that with a man. It was the perfect end to my debut ball."

"Has it ended?" he asked in a ragged tone. "What a shame, now that I am finally beginning to enjoy it."

"No, you're right. It can't be over." She pushed herself up to sit beside him once more. "You . . . haven't . . . found *your* pleasure yet."

He pulled down her skirts to hide her legs. "I had enjoyment enough in pleasing you."

She arched a brow. She knew exactly how men found their pleasure, and it wasn't like this.

"Besides," he continued, "someone is bound to have missed us by now, and we'll soon have them all gossiping if we stay out here too long. You *are*, after all, one of two guests of honor at this ball."

She found her gloves crammed between the cushions and drew them on. "I suppose you're right."

That he could go so easily from giving her the greatest pleasure she'd ever known to thinking rationally about hiding their illicit encounter was upsetting. But then, that was Joshua's way, wasn't it? Pretend he didn't care, that it didn't matter. Or perhaps he wasn't pretending. Perhaps he was a less-obvious version of Lionel, still wanting to take advantage of her without marriage being part of it.

Feeling an acute pain in her chest at that possibility, she stood and roamed the room, hunting for her reticule. She found it on the floor near the settee. Then she heard Joshua's cane clicking on the stone floor as he came up behind her.

"I do not regret one moment of what we did," he murmured. "It was . . ."

When he faltered in describing it, she said, "Magical. For me, it was magical. Thank you for that." She struggled to hide her hurt. "But don't worry. I won't assume that it means anything. After all—"

"So this is where you two got off to," a hard voice said from the door that led to the house proper. "I did wonder."

Gwyn whirled to find Beatrice standing there, glaring at Joshua. Heat rose in Gwyn's cheeks. How long had his sister been standing there? What had she seen?

Oh, Lord, if she'd seen Joshua pleasuring her, Gwyn would just die.

"They're asking for you in the ballroom, Gwyn," Beatrice said, though her gaze never moved from her brother. "Grey wants to make a toast to both of us, and I told him I'd find you."

Gwyn swallowed. "I–I wanted to show Joshua your orangery. He seemed rather keen to see it."

Beatrice snorted. Gwyn risked a look at Joshua only to find him wearing that bland expression he wore when he didn't want anyone delving beneath his surface.

"Well, then," Joshua said, coming up to offer Gwyn his arm. "I suppose we'd best return to the ballroom."

"Gwyn," Beatrice said, "if you could please go in and give me and my brother a few moments alone? Tell Grey I'll be there shortly."

Joshua dropped his arm, and half in a trance, Gwyn hurried out. Oh, she would never live this down. Never! She hoped that Beatrice had been the only one to notice that both Gwyn and Joshua were gone.

Otherwise, Gwyn's debut had just gone from magical to disastrous.


Joshua didn't say a word as Gwyn fled. Or after, for that matter. Because judging from the look on his sister's face, she was about to do all the talking, and it would not be pleasant.

"Are you trying to ruin her?" Beatrice asked bluntly.

"Ruin her? We merely came out here to see the orangery. And Lady Gwyn had some odd notion she could teach me to waltz, but of course that didn't work."

"I am not a fool," Beatrice said calmly. "I know what I saw."

*Saw*? Bloody, bloody hell.

Then he remembered that his sister could be sly when she wanted. "What could you possibly have seen but us talking?"

Beatrice stuck out her chin mutinously. "I saw her hunting for her reticule."

"Which she dropped while we were attempting the waltz."

"And she looked rather . . . disheveled."

"That happened while I was hobbling about, trying to dance."

It was no use. As Beatrice had said, she was no fool. She stared him down. "I thought you were a gentleman, Joshua, but clearly I was wrong. So help me, if you harm one hair on my friend's head—"

"I would never harm her," he said earnestly. "Not as long as I live and breathe."

His sister seemed taken aback by that statement. Damn, he shouldn't have admitted as much, especially to Gwyn's bosom friend. But he wasn't going to take it back. Let Beatrice make what she would of it. It was true.

He went over to straighten the cushions on the settee, and she followed him. "You harm her by walking out into the gardens with her and staying gone for half an hour or more."

He raised a brow. "Have you been spying on me? Because I seriously doubt anyone else in that ballroom noticed."

"That the guest of honor and the only man in uniform in

the room disappeared at the same time? I assure you *someone* noticed."

"Who?" he demanded.

"We probably won't know that until the gossip rags start circulating tomorrow morning."

"*If* that happens, and *if* the gossip looks as if it might in any way ruin her reputation, I will do right by her, I swear."

"You will marry her."

"Not that she would have me, but yes." Although before he did, he would demand to know what the devil was going on between her and Malet.

His sister planted her hands on her hips. "Why *wouldn't* she have you? You're a wonderful fellow when you wish to be. But when people edge too close, you always start pushing them away, and then, of course, you end up alone. So you blame it on your wounds instead of your fear, and on and on it goes."

"Thank you for that fine assessment of my flawed character," he snapped. "Now, may we go in?"

She gave a heavy sigh. "*We* aren't going anywhere. I am returning to the ball and *you* are leaving."

"The hell I am." He walked up to loom over her. "I'm her bodyguard. I do not leave her side." Especially with things between them so unsettled.

"Thorn told Grey all about the arrangement you made with him, and Grey told me. But I assure you, she is safe with us. Thorn might have left, but Sheridan and Heywood are here now. And Grey will accompany her and Lady Hornsby home whenever they're ready to leave. But if you go back inside with me, anyone might guess I found you two alone together. I won't risk it. This way, if someone asks where you are, I can say you left hours ago. That you hate balls or some such."

Her plan made sense. But it still chafed him that his sister was treating him the way he'd treated Greycourt last year, when Joshua had found the duke in her bed. Joshua hadn't even gone as far as Greycourt, for God's sake, and Beatrice was treating him like a scoundrel.

Or an untrained hound who needed to be schooled in proper behavior.

As always, his sister could tell when he was angry, for she placed a hand on his arm. "Dear heart, I don't know exactly what lies between you and Gwyn, but I know what she'll suffer from the gossips if they figure it out. This is best and you know it." She ventured a smile. "And you don't enjoy balls anyway; admit it. You were glowering at everyone all evening. While the family knows that's typical for you, our guests may not."

He could hardly tell her the truth—that watching Gwyn play the social butterfly was difficult, knowing how quickly men would be calling on her after tonight. Would then be giving her offers. Perhaps already had. It wasn't as if Gwyn would tell *him* about it.

"Fine," he said. "I'll go. I'll probably see you tomorrow."

"No, you won't. Don't you remember? Shortly after the four of you came in this evening, Gwyn mentioned that she's planning on taking Aunt Lydia shopping tomorrow, which I assume means you're going, too."

"Of course." He had forgotten, mostly because while Gwyn had been talking about it, he'd been too busy scanning the room for Malet to pay attention to what she was saying. A shopping trip. Damnation. "I should have put my foot down the moment she mentioned it. It's too dangerous."

"Nonsense. Surely the man won't attempt a kidnapping in broad daylight on Bond Street."

It did seem unlikely. "Are you going, too?" Even his

hoyden sister enjoyed the occasional day on Bond Street, according to Greycourt. "Or Heywood's new wife? What's her name again?"

"Cassandra. She and Heywood had a long trip and are fairly exhausted. As am I. So I intend to be asleep. *Gwyn* is only going because she has to. Aunt Lydia's birthday is next week, and our social schedule is so crowded that tomorrow was the only day she could buy a present for her mother. She would have preferred not bringing her mother along at all, but Aunt Lydia insisted, because the two of them have scarcely had any time together."

And ladies did like to shop. It seemed to be the female equivalent of hunting. He would simply have to be on his guard the whole time they were out to make sure Malet didn't "accidentally" show up at one of the places they went.

That reminded him: he still had work to do this evening. "You'd better go on in, before Greycourt comes looking for you and realizes I was out here alone with his half sister."

She blinked. "You're right! I hadn't thought of that. He's a bit irrational when it comes to the possibility of you and Gwyn together." She kissed his cheek. "Thank you for understanding. I probably will see you often at various social gatherings in the coming weeks." She turned away, then paused. "Promise me you'll think about what I said."

"Which part?" he countered, though he knew which one.

"Never mind. You never listen to me anyway."

"Damn it, Beatrice—"

But she was already hurrying off, and as he watched her go, he felt a lump in his throat. She had grown up so well, his ducky. And with very little help from him, too. One day, he would have to find a way to repay her for the months upon months she'd spent nursing him back to health after he'd come home so badly wounded.

For how often he gave her pain.

Wincing, he went to check the settee and the area around the stove to make sure neither he nor Gwyn had left anything incriminating. Then he spotted his gloves, half hidden under the settee. Damn. Had Beatrice seen them, too, or worse yet, noticed he wasn't wearing them? God, he hoped not.

After putting them on and making sure his attire was presentable, he strode off across the garden to the entrance gate. With so many people at the party, the hackney coaches lay thick upon the ground, so he had no trouble finding one to take him to the address in Chelsea.

He was spoiling for a fight after the discussion he'd just had with his sister, and the best candidate as sparring partner was that damned Malet. If Gwyn wouldn't reveal what was going on between them, Joshua would get the information from the man himself.

Unfortunately, he was to be denied that as well. When he arrived at the address Fitzgerald had given him, the landlord, Pritchard, informed him that "Captain" Malet was out on the town.

That chilled Joshua. "Where?"

Pritchard shrugged. "How the devil should I know? You officers do as you please."

Joshua pulled out a sovereign and held it up. "Can you at least tell me what part of town he's in tonight?" Because if it was Mayfair, Joshua was going to throttle the man when he found him.

Pritchard's eyes widened. "Covent Garden, of course. No doubt he went to find a soiled dove or two to spend his money on. God forbid he should pay for his lodgings."

Thank God it wasn't Mayfair.

When Pritchard reached for the coin, Joshua pulled it

back. "Not until you answer all my questions. How long has he been living here?"

"Nigh on to five months now. Owes me two months' rent. But he did say as how he was coming into a great deal of money soon, and he'd pay his rent then."

"Did he say why he was coming into money?"

"No. And I don't care how he gets it neither. Long as he pays his rent."

It was a damned shame the man didn't know more. Was Malet counting on the money he'd get by marrying Gwyn, either by kidnapping her or some mutual arrangement? The latter made Joshua grit his teeth, but he had to consider it.

Or was Malet sure of getting money because he was selling information to the French? That possibility appealed more to Joshua, because it meant Gwyn wasn't involved. Then again, if Malet was expecting to get paid by the French, that didn't explain why Gwyn was communicating with him, a man who was supposedly a stranger to her.

"Have you ever seen Malet with any Frenchmen?" Joshua asked Pritchard.

"Not here. I'm not letting any frogs into my place. If he's got dealings with the French, he's taking them elsewhere."

Interesting. Where would Malet go to carry off such delicate negotiations? Clearly, the landlord had no answer for that.

Having run out of pertinent questions, Joshua gave the landlord the guinea. "One more thing: Don't let Captain Malet know anyone was asking about him."

Pritchard's eyes gleamed with avarice. "It'll cost you another guinea to keep me quiet."

"Fine." Joshua handed him another.

At the rate he was going, he would run out of hard cash

soon. But Fitzgerald would pay him back for this one, and if he didn't, Thornstock would.

Joshua considered hanging about a while longer, but if Malet had gone to Covent Garden, the arse might not return until morning. Meanwhile, Gwyn's shopping trip was tomorrow, and Joshua fully intended to accompany her for that. So he'd better return to Armitage House.

He wouldn't put it past her to try to sneak out without him.

# Chapter Fifteen

Unfortunately for Joshua, the next day dawned clear and bright. After coming back from Chelsea last night, he'd drunk an ungodly amount of brandy, only to awaken near ten with an aching head. Bloody hell. He rarely drank like that, and this was why. He'd better get himself presentable before the shopping trip or the ladies might try to leave without him, and he'd have to fight them. He wasn't in the mood today for any battles.

It took a cold bath and some cups of coffee to have him feeling almost human again. And just in the nick of time, too, for his cousin Sheridan came into the morning room at eleven to help himself to some toast.

Usually his green eyes were dark with worry and his light brown hair was disheveled from the many times he'd raked his fingers through it. After all, he had the weight of the dukedom on his shoulders, and the dukedom was ailing.

But this morning, Sheridan appeared damned cheerful. "You look like hell."

"Thanks," Joshua muttered. "I feel like hell."

Sheridan chuckled. "I should have warned you about our brandy." Sheridan sat down opposite Joshua and poured himself some tea. "It's fairly potent."

"That's an understatement." Joshua looked at his cousin. "Wait, how did you know I'd indulged in brandy last night?"

"We use the same valet, remember? And I'm afraid he's a bit of a gossip."

With a groan, Joshua made a mental note not to use the valet for anything when he was cropsick.

Sheridan perused the papers, letting Joshua drink his coffee in peace for a while. When he finished eating his buttered toast, he rose. "I have to meet with William Bonham, Father's solicitor." He headed for the door, then paused to grin at Joshua. "Enjoy your shopping trip with the ladies."

As he walked out, Joshua gritted his teeth. "Thanks for your support, Coz," he muttered under his breath.

At least he had a little more respite to fight with his queasy stomach. Then the ladies entered the morning room around noon, chattering like magpies. The noise reverberated.

He grimaced. Perhaps he could use yet another cup of coffee. A few more hours of sleep.

A new post.

"You don't have to go with us, you know, Joshua." To his surprise, it was his aunt who'd spoken. "We already have a footman coming along to carry packages."

"*One* footman?" he joked feebly. "I doubt that will suffice. Besides, I've been wanting to shop for a hat and haven't had the chance. I can't imagine a more pleasant way to do so than in the company of you two ladies. And as you both can probably tell, I could use a pair of females to help me make sure my new hat will pass muster with the fashionable sort."

His aunt laughed. "You've come to the right place, then. We are both quite good at being fashionable." She glanced at Gwyn, who wore a day gown as vivid a purple as the sky at sunset. "And I know my daughter would enjoy having your company."

"But only if you feel up to it." It was Gwyn's turn to smirk at him. "I understand you drank a great deal of brandy last night."

"Gwyn!" her mother said.

"Well, he did. My maid told me so. She had it from your maid, Mama, who had it from Joshua's valet. So we know it's true. Servant gossip is always the most reliable."

"All right, you termagant." Damn it all to hell, did the entire *family* know how he'd spent last evening? Joshua swallowed the last of his coffee and rose. At least he was steadier on his feet than before. "Now you force me to prove I can hold my liquor."

Gwyn chuckled. And off they went.

With the day so pleasant and Bond Street only two miles from Armitage House, they decided to walk. After a while, he began to feel like himself again, especially with Gwyn's hand on his arm. As they neared the corner of Hyde Park, a loud clap sounded near them, and Joshua tensed. He probably would have done more if Gwyn hadn't held on to his right arm with both hands.

It was nothing, of course—a workman who'd started pounding a piece of ironwork into place with a large hammer—but it left him shaken enough to wonder how he would have reacted if Gwyn hadn't been next to him.

"Thank you," he bit out under his breath.

"You're welcome," she said softly, turning his insides to putty.

Or perhaps that was just the lingering effects of being cropsick. Regardless, he was careful to watch for Malet as they walked. Nor did he relax his vigilance once they began shopping. Whenever Gwyn separated from her mother, he made sure to go with Gwyn; the footman always went with Aunt Lydia anyway.

Oddly enough, his story for why he had to shop with them

proved useful. He actually did need a hat, and the ladies were eager to help him find one: a handsome beaver top hat he could wear whenever he didn't wear one of his uniforms . . . or his old clothes as a gamekeeper. It certainly looked better than the one of rabbit felt he'd been donning.

What's more, Gwyn insisted that he charge his purchase to Thornstock's account. While her mother was examining the straw hats for ladies, Gwyn murmured, "If not for Thorn, you wouldn't even have needed a tale for why you must shop with us. Let him pay. He can well afford it."

"You merely wish to get some of your own back on him by spending his money."

Her eyes twinkled. "That, too."

"Fine," he said. "But I'll tell him to take it out of my pay."

She huffed out a breath. "You suck the fun out of everything."

"I can think of a few things I didn't suck the fun out of for you last night."

Her cheeks turned a lovely pink that made him wish he had the right to kiss her in the middle of a hatter's shop.

Damnation. Best not to think of that.

The next shop they went to was a glover's. "I shall see if they have any gloves for ladies doing archery," Gwyn said. "You ought to get better gloves yourself, Joshua. The ones you had a few days ago were showing signs of wear."

With a nod, he went over to the counter where men's gloves were laid out, but he watched her furtively while he pretended to look at them. She appeared agitated and kept glancing up at the clock on the wall.

Her mother said she was heading to a shop across the street in search of a new watch for Thorn, and that seemed to relieve Gwyn, which only made Joshua pay more attention. But subtly. If she was expecting a note from Malet or, worse yet, expecting the man himself, Joshua wanted her to continue with her plans so he could actually catch him in the act.

He had just finished paying for a pair of gloves in Yorkshire tan when he noticed her drape her shawl oh-so-casually over a chair tucked away in a corner, where it wouldn't easily be seen by the clerk.

Joshua was fairly certain it wasn't accidental. But was it a signal of some kind? If so, he couldn't figure out what. When Gwyn said she was ready to go and made no move to pick up the shawl, he *knew* it meant something. But it was better to keep quiet and see what happened.

With a thank-you to the clerk, Joshua thrust his new gloves into his greatcoat. Then he and Gwyn walked out to the street and found her mother and the footman waiting for them. The four of them were halfway down that block, when Gwyn said, "Oh, Mama, we should have ices at Gunter's. It's right down here."

"Ices, my dear? Truly? I still find it a bit chilly for that, don't you?"

"Balderdash," Gwyn said. "I've heard they have a new elderflower flavor, and I know how much you like elderflower wine, Mama."

"Well," her mother said, "now that you mention it . . ."

But no sooner were they in Gunter's than Gwyn said, "Oh, dear, I left my shawl in the glover's shop. I shall just run back and get it while you order. Do make sure you order an ice for me, too."

She turned to go, and Joshua hurried to her side. "I'll go with you."

"Please don't," she whispered. "I have to purchase Mama's birthday gift there. It's a darling pair of gloves made of gray kid, which she can actually wear throughout her half-mourning. But I need you to keep her occupied so she doesn't find out what I'm doing."

"Very well," he said, watching closely for her reaction.

She looked inordinately relieved, and that convinced him that he was right—this subterfuge had more to do with her note to Malet than with her mother's birthday. He let her leave and gave her time to reach the glover's shop. Then he walked out and scanned the street. He was just in time to see her dart right past the shop and then disappear.

He walked as swiftly as he could to the glover's shop, then heard raised voices coming from the alley that ran next to it. Halting at the end near the street, he hid himself to eavesdrop on their conversation. Gwyn was definitely arguing with Malet. Joshua recognized the bastard's voice from before. And what he heard chilled him.

"You asked for fifty pounds, Lionel, and I agreed," Gwyn said.

*Lionel?* She called Malet by his given name? Damn it, she *had* known the fellow before their recent encounter! And what was this about her giving the scoundrel money?

"Then you doubled it," she went on, "so I've brought you a hundred pounds. Now you wish to have *more*? Do you know what I had to do to get this to you? How many lies I had to tell, how many subterfuges I had to arrange?"

"And who were you lying to, dearest Gwyn?" Malet said, his very voice a sneer. "That cripple of an officer, Wolfe?"

Joshua nearly bit through his tongue trying to keep his anger in check.

"Don't call him that!" Gwyn cried.

"Ah. So you have a tendre for the oafish major, do you?"

"You're being ridiculous," Gwyn said, sounding desperate now.

Or was that just his wishful thinking?

"I wonder, is he aware of how sweet your lips are or how tender your tits? I wonder how much you would pay to keep *him* from knowing about—"

THE BACHELOR
167

"This has naught to do with him!" Her voice hardened. "I have paid you all I intend to pay. Go ahead, tell the world whatever you wish."

Blackmail? Was the woman paying for Malet's silence? But for what?

"Just remember that Thorn will have your head if you say a word," she went on. "He gave you a fortune ten years ago to leave me be. So if you renege on your bargain with him, he will call you out."

The conversation in the carriage on the way to London leaped into Joshua's mind. But she'd said that the fellow Thornstock had paid off was named Hazlehurst.

No. Her *mother* had said it. Gwyn had merely gone along. It had to be Malet, unless Thornstock had paid off *two* of her suitors. And what was Malet holding over her head that necessitated her giving the scoundrel more money?

Joshua had a sickening feeling he knew the answer to that.

"I'm not afraid of your brother, dear girl," Malet said. "I'll fight a duel with him any day of the week."

"No!" she cried. "You will not. I will turn you both in to the magistrate before I allow it. You have your hundred pounds, so we are done, I tell you. Done! And if you don't like it, you can go to hell."

"We are not remotely done, my sweet."

"Let go of me, Lionel!" she cried. "Stop it!"

Time to intervene. Joshua would have preferred to preserve her secret by not letting her know what he'd heard, but clearly that had become impossible. He headed down the alley toward them, fire erupting in his blood as he saw that Malet had her pinned against a wall and was fighting to kiss her. She shoved at him and tried to hit him, but was clearly losing the battle.

The bastard! How dared he?

An unholy fury overtaking him, Joshua rushed up to hit

Malet with his cane. The devil howled and pushed away from her to come at Joshua, but Joshua braced his bad foot against a barrel and started striking Malet with his cane, over and over—in the head, the chest, whatever he could hit. Malet attempted to defend himself and got in a punch or two, but no one was a match for Joshua in a temper.

Joshua struck Malet until the man dropped to his knees and started shielding himself with his hands. Blood ran down Malet's face from an open wound on his head, and even that did not keep Joshua from his course.

Then Joshua felt Gwyn pulling on his arm and heard her screaming, "Stop! Stop! *Stop!* You'll kill him!"

He rounded on her, still holding his cane like a cudgel. "Do you care?" he snarled.

Fear leaped in her eyes. "About *him*?" she choked out. "No. But I very much care that you not hang for murder, especially when it's committed on my behalf."

The words were a bucket of ice water thrown in his face. They brought back to him some semblance of control, of rational thought. They cooled his fevered blood to the extent that he was able to lower his cane.

Then shame set in. Once again, she'd seen him behave like an ungoverned arse. A savage animal. What she must think of him! Now that she'd witnessed him at his worst, she feared him. It was his only regret. Because he sure as hell didn't regret beating Malet. Joshua only wished he'd thought to pull out the blade of his cane and kill the bastard.

"Are you all right?" he asked her. "He didn't hurt you, did he?"

She shook her head. "He didn't have time, thanks to you."

Meanwhile, Malet was wiping blood from his eyes. "You damned whoreson! What is wrong with you?" He tried to get up and had to brace himself against the wall to do so.

"Gwyn," Joshua said, "go join your mother."

"I'm not leaving without you."

To Joshua's surprise, worry etched lines in her face as she pulled out her handkerchief and dabbed at his cheek. Apparently, some of Malet's blood had sprayed onto him.

Malet made a grab for her and nearly fell flat on his face, which seemed to infuriate the man further. Struggling to get up off his knees, he growled, "I see you've got quite the gallant protector, Gwyn. So the cripple yearns for you, does he?"

Anger fairly choked Joshua. "You're the one trying to force yourself on her. You're the one yearning, it seems to me."

"For *her*?" Malet wiped blood from his eye with the back of his glove. "I had her years ago, in Prussia. And a sweet piece she was, too. I'd happily take her to bed again, but yearn for her? Never."

Joshua looked over to find Gwyn's face reddening with humiliation, which told him all he needed to know. That Malet spoke the truth. That this was what the arse had been blackmailing her over: her seduction . . . possibly her rape. Malet wouldn't make a distinction between the two.

Nor would anyone else in society, sadly enough. If news of either got out, *she* would be the one ruined, not Malet.

And the thought that the arse had tried to make *money* off her past . . . infuriated Joshua all over again. It reminded him of Uncle Armie trying to blackmail Beatrice into becoming his mistress.

"Please, Joshua," Gwyn whispered, "can we just go?"

"In a moment. I have a few more things to say to this scoundrel."

He reached down to snatch Malet's purse out of his greatcoat pocket, then remove the hundred pounds and hand those to Gwyn.

"Hey!" Malet cried.

Joshua pushed the button on his cane, which allowed him to pull the blade from its "scabbard," then pressed the point of the sword to Malet's carotid artery. "Come near her again, and I will thrust this so deep that you'll bleed to death within moments. This is the end of your blackmailing her, do you hear me?"

Malet turned white as chalk.

Joshua went on. "It had also better be the end of your trying to tamper with Thornstock's carriage. You could have killed us all in your attempt to . . . to . . ." It dawned on him that it made no sense for Malet to try waylaying their carriage if he'd simply been blackmailing Gwyn.

And Malet's face showed nothing but confusion. "I've never tried to tamper with anyone's carriage. You can blame that on someone else." Then his voice turned sullen. "I'm only guilty of trying to get some money for myself. Which I deserve, damn it. Gwyn's family has done nothing but try to ruin my life. Between Colonel Lord Heywood and Gwyn's damned brother—"

"Her 'damned brother' did the right thing, and I intend to continue in his footsteps. Just to make sure you don't forget, let this be a warning to you . . ." Joshua dragged the point of his blade over Malet's cheek, taking grim satisfaction from the line of blood it left behind. "Approach her again and you die."

Joshua sheathed his blade in his cane, then turned to usher Gwyn to the entrance to the alley.

Malet cried out behind them, "I will tell the world all your secrets, Gwyn. I don't have to come near you to ruin you, you little harlot!"

She flinched, and Joshua felt his anger swell all over again.

Looking back at the bastard, Joshua said, "Go ahead. I dare you. The day you spout your lies, the newspapers will hear the truth about your leaving the army—how you seduced an orphan girl of fifteen and refused to marry her. How she died as a result of your cruelty. How you were cashiered for it. Then I will announce my own engagement to Gwyn, making your accusations sound like so many sour grapes over losing her."

Gwyn gasped, but Joshua wasn't done with Malet. "Once all the gossip has died down and Gwyn and I are wed, you'll wake up one day to find my blade at your throat. And not a soul will know—or care—who murdered you. I'll make sure of that."

It wasn't entirely an idle threat. If there were any way to wipe Malet off the earth without Gwyn suffering further scandal, Joshua would find it. Indeed, he prayed he could prove Malet a traitor. Because then the man would hang, and Joshua wouldn't even have to dirty his own hands to kill him. Although it was possible that the money Malet's landlord said he was expecting was simply the blackmail money. A hundred pounds would buy lodgings for quite some time.

They left the alley then, with Malet cursing behind them. It was a good thing that not many people were shopping just then, so they'd had no witnesses to the confrontation. Or none that wished to acknowledge it, apparently.

Joshua started to walk toward Gunter's, but Gwyn stopped him. She took his right hand in hers. "Your glove is ruined."

He looked down to see that his right glove had split during his beating of Malet.

She stripped it off. "Oh, dear. You'll have to keep your hand in your pocket."

"Can't. I have to use this hand to hold the cane when I walk."

"Oh. Of course." She looked anxious. "But Mama will wonder—"

"I have a new pair of gloves." He took them out of his pocket. "I'll just wear these, all right?"

As he removed his old ones and pulled on the new ones,

she frowned. "They're a different color. Mama will notice. She always notices such things." She lowered her voice. "Though I suppose we can tell her that your old ones were too ragged to salvage, so we discarded them at the glover's."

He nodded. "I'll let you handle your mother. You've had far more experience doing it than I." Something else occurred to him. "Where's your shawl?"

"Oh, Lord, it's still in the glover's shop. Let me just fetch it."

When she came out with it and they began to walk again, she glanced down at his cane. "I hope you didn't ruin it by beating Lionel with it."

"I don't care. Just as I don't regret what I did to him in the alley."

Her gaze shot to him, and a blush stained her cheeks when she saw how intently he was looking at her. "Later, you and I will talk, I promise," she whispered. "But right now, we must join Mama before she comes looking for us and happens to see Malet in the alley. Or worse, stumbling out."

Joshua had so many questions, so many matters he wanted to clarify. But she was right—here and now was not the time.

"Whatever you wish," he said. "I place myself in your hands." He stared hard at her. "Until we can be alone."

# Chapter Sixteen

*Until we can be alone.*

Gwyn sighed. There would be a reckoning once they were, and she supposed she deserved one, given that she'd put Joshua in the untenable position of fighting her battles.

Though, at the moment, she was grateful for his interference. Who knew what might have happened if Joshua hadn't shown up when he had?

Still, the fact that he'd had to listen to . . . to Lionel's insinuations and make his own conclusions . . . She couldn't stand his knowing the truth about her. It was worse even than having Thorn—or Mama—know. How would she explain it to him? Joshua seemed so rigid most of the time.

Not to mention, prone to violence. The episode with Lionel still sparked fear in her. It was alarming how much trouble Joshua had controlling himself. The only thing that gave her solace was that she'd been able to bring him back from the brink. Today anyway.

By the time they got back to Gunter's, the knot in Gwyn's stomach was so tight, she had to halt outside to calm herself. She looked up at Joshua. "Mama must never know what just occurred. It will upset her terribly, and given her present fragile state—"

"Your mother isn't as fragile as you think." He glanced

away. "But no, I don't want to tell her that I nearly killed Malet. Or why."

"Thank you." Bad enough to realize that Joshua knew the reason. She certainly wasn't ready for Mama to know. There was no way of being sure how she'd react. "Mama doesn't need to have such ugliness in her head."

"Does she know about you and Malet at all?"

Gwyn nodded. "She knows we courted. Remember when she and I were talking about Hazlehurst in the carriage? That's whom we really meant. It was so long ago, Mama didn't remember the name, probably because she doesn't know any of what I told you concerning Thorn and Lionel."

"Ah. And you didn't correct her because you didn't want me to—"

The door to Gunter's opened, and Mama came out with two glass bowls and spoons in hand, effectively ending their intimate conversation. "It's about time you two returned. Your ices are melting. Why, I've already finished mine. And Joshua, why on earth did you go running off? One minute I'm ordering an ice for Gwyn and the next I'm looking around for you both. I had to guess what to order for you."

"I'm sure whatever you chose is fine." He took the bowl from her, as did Gwyn with hers, then added, "Do we eat them here in the street or . . ."

"We go over to the square to eat them," she said. "That's what everyone else does."

They walked over to the Berkeley Square gardens, where Gwyn deliberately chose to sit on a bench facing away from the alley. As Mama sat beside her, Joshua leaned his cane—and then himself—against a tree so he could eat, his gaze darting across to the alley every few moments.

Lord, but he was a gorgeous specimen of a man. Yes, his leg seemed a bit . . . twisted beneath his buff trousers, but his chest strained at the buttons of his old-fashioned, figured waistcoat and his shoulders filled out his blue coat quite pleasingly.

He caught her staring at him, and, misunderstanding her purpose for gawking at him, flashed her a reassuring smile that made her breathing quicken. He had an amazing smile when he let himself use it. And when she lifted a spoonful of her ice to her mouth, a heat flared in his eyes that she half-expected to melt *his* ice. And hers. And anyone else's in the vicinity.

Unfortunately, Mama caught her and Joshua eyeing each other with something akin to lust and got a speculative look on her face.

Her gaze narrowed on Gwyn. "Where *did* the two of you go off to anyway?"

When Gwyn started and didn't answer, Joshua stepped in.

"I forgot about needing new gloves," Joshua said smoothly, as if he'd been lying to Mama his whole life. "So I returned to the glover's after Gwyn went that way. And she helped me pick a new pair."

"The ones you're wearing now? Oh, dear, you should take them off while you eat. You'll stain them."

"Don't worry about me. Gwyn picked a pair that specifically repels ice cream."

Mama gaped at him, then laughed. "Sometimes you surprise me, Nephew. Just when I think you don't even know how to joke, you say something like that." Aunt Lydia patted Gwyn's arm. "But you're right about Gwyn. She is quite helpful at choosing items for gentlemen."

When Joshua lifted a brow, Gwyn wanted to sink under the bench. "Mama, you make it sound as if I'm buying things for men all the time."

"Don't be silly," her mother said. "My nephew knows I'm speaking of your brothers. Don't you, Joshua?"

"Of course," he said, his gaze locking with Gwyn's.

"Although surely she has helped a beau or two with such choices occasionally."

"Not that I can recall." Mama stared off across the park. "The only one I remember her helping was that fellow Hazlehurst. But she was so young then. What were you, Gwyn? Nineteen?"

"Twenty," Gwyn said wearily. And right then, she was in no mood to continue the subterfuge. "You're thinking of Ensign Malet, Mama. I think you've mixed up those two gentlemen."

"Malet! Good Lord, you're right. I should have remembered that. He had such an odd name. But then, Hazlehurst is an odd name, too."

"It is indeed," Joshua said blandly.

Gwyn glared at him as she ate her ice.

"So which one was Thorn nasty to?" Mama asked.

"Both of them, actually. Thorn was nasty to all my suitors." And that was the truth. "He never thought any of them worthy of me. My social life got considerably better when he left for England."

"Is that why you refused to return with him?" her mother asked.

Gwyn could feel Joshua's gaze boring into her like a carpenter's drill. "That was part of it. Part of it was my not wanting to leave you and Papa." She smiled at Mama. "And given Papa's untimely death, I'm very glad I had those years with you both." Papa might actually have been her stepfather, but he was the only father she'd ever known.

Her mother smiled and took her hand. "*I'm* very glad you made that decision, although at the time I thought it might have been better for you to go with Thorn."

That startled her. "Why?"

"Because of your age. I had no idea when we'd be returning to England, and I thought coming here with Thorn might give you a better chance at finding a husband. If you'll recall, eligible gentlemen were fairly thin on the ground in Berlin, unless you wanted to marry a German. And then we wouldn't have been able to see you once *we* returned to England, which we would have done eventually."

Gwyn should reveal the truth to Mama about what had happened between her and Thorn. She'd kept it hidden long enough. She could never tell Mama about why Thorn's actions had nearly proved disastrous for her later on, but at least if she explained *some* of why she'd been angry, her family could stop speculating on it. Because whatever she told Mama was going to be passed on to the rest of them eventually. Mama had never been good at keeping secrets.

"Actually, Mama, Thorn wasn't just nasty to Ensign Malet; Thorn paid the man quite a bit of money to go away. Thorn was convinced that the ensign was a fortune hunter, so he offered the man funds just to see what he would do. Once the scoundrel took the money, it proved that Thorn was right about Ensign Malet's character."

And it proved she had been *wrong* about it. That still stung, even after all these years. Even after Lionel had turned into a blackmailer. Because she really hated that she hadn't noticed what an arse he was until it was too late.

"Why, that arrogant rascal!" Mama said.

Gwyn blinked. "Who? Ensign Malet? Or Thorn?"

"Both, I suppose. Though I was really speaking of your brother. As you said in the carriage the other day—Thorn had no business running anyone off. It's not as if you were a child. You were perfectly capable of making your own decisions in such matters. I don't blame you for being angry with him."

"Even though he turned out to be right about Malet?" Joshua put in.

Mama sniffed. "Yes. Because he could have handled it better. He could have told her why he believed Ensign

Malet to be a fortune hunter and let her come to her own conclusions."

Her mother had hit the nail on the head. That was what had made her so furious with him at the time. Thorn had decided she was incapable of listening to reasonable arguments concerning any fellow courting her, and then had taken steps to handle the matter without her knowledge or consent.

Mama looked at Gwyn. "I assume that Thorn had evidence of Malet's eagerness to marry an heiress?"

Gwyn blinked. "I–I don't know. I never asked, and he never offered. I just assumed that Thorn had turned into an overbearing arse as he approached his coming of age."

Mama chuckled. "He *was* a bit full of himself back then, wasn't he?"

"Still is," she muttered.

"Not quite *as* full of himself, I think. But perhaps you should ask him what made him pay Ensign Malet off. And if his reasoning was sound, and he wasn't just being his usual overbearing self, you might want to consider . . . letting bygones be bygones?"

"I might," Gwyn said. Mama had made her curious now. She had never spoken with Thorn about it because of everything else going on in her life after Lionel left. Then Thorn was gone, without their mending their rift, and their relationship had suffered.

Not for the first time, she wondered what her life would have been like if she'd married Lionel. Miserable, probably, given the kind of devil he'd proven to be. And she could only imagine how awful he might have been to their children.

The knot in her belly tightened even more. No, she wasn't going to think about that. It hurt too much, even after so much time had gone by.

"Wait a minute," Mama said. "Isn't Malet also the name of that fellow who tried to kidnap Heywood's wife and her cousin at Christmas?"

"Yes," she said blandly. "Turns out he's actually the same fellow."

"Well, if anything proves he was a scoundrel from the beginning, that does." Mama breathed deeply. "Now that you've both finished your ices, we should probably head home, don't you think? You may wish to rest before attending the opera this evening."

"We're attending the opera?" Joshua asked, looking as if someone had just threatened to kill the hunting dogs at Armitage Hall.

"You don't have to go," Mama said. "I'm sure Grey wouldn't mind accompanying Gwyn. I daresay Eliza would be grateful for any night she doesn't have to chaperone."

"Does *Grey* enjoy the opera?" Joshua asked skeptically.

"Who doesn't enjoy the opera?" Mama said.

Joshua snorted. "Beatrice told me that the only thing she dislikes about London is the opera. And from what I understand, Grey doesn't enjoy going anywhere in society unless my sister goes with him."

"Yes, those two are still madly in love," Gwyn said, trying to squelch her envy of that. "To be honest, Mama, I may not be up to going either." It depended on her talk with Joshua. "Although I do have the most fetching opera gown . . ."

Joshua stared at her. "You would go to the opera to wear a new gown?"

"Of course not." She forced a lightness into her voice that she didn't feel. "I would go to the opera to be *seen* wearing my new gown."

When that got a laugh from him, the knot in her stomach loosened a bit, for the first time all day. If she could still make him laugh, he might not be *too* angry with her.

Though it wasn't his anger she dreaded. It was his contempt for her as an unchaste woman. Not that she thought she deserved it, but if he turned out to be the sort of fellow who believed that she did, she didn't know how she would bear it.

Mama rose and took their bowls, then handed them to the footman with a request that he also fetch them a hackney coach. As the footman hurried across the road, Mama said, "I hope you don't mind, but I do not relish the walk back. You're welcome to walk, however, with the footman."

"We'll ride with you, Mama," Gwyn said. Because if she and Joshua walked back, he would wish to talk, and she didn't want to talk about Lionel in public.

As Mama nodded, then headed toward the street, Joshua offered Gwyn his arm, and she took it. He slowed his pace so that they fell a bit behind Mama. She knew it was deliberate, because even with his bad leg, he seemed able to keep up with them most of the time.

"Do you know that suite of rooms on the third floor that is closed up just now?" he murmured.

"The Tapestry Suite?" she asked.

"Is that what it's called?"

"Given that every wall has a tapestry? Yes."

He cast her a searching glance. "We need to talk. Privately. That seems as good a place as any. Meet me up there as soon as you can get away from your mother when we arrive back at Armitage House."

"Very well."

Her stomach sank. Now came the reckoning. He had sort of offered marriage, but that had just been his way to shut Lionel up. Still, after everything the two of them had done together, she supposed he might actually want . . .

She sighed. She had no idea what to expect from him. She would simply have to brace herself for whatever it was.

Though if he condemned her for her past, she wasn't sure she could ever forgive him.

# Chapter Seventeen

As Joshua paced the drugget-covered carpet of the Tapestry Suite's bedchamber, the largest of the rooms, he began to wonder if Gwyn would actually come. He'd been waiting quite a while, and the longer he waited, the more questions he had. And the angrier he grew.

She'd repeatedly lied to him about Malet. And considering that her brother had paid the arse off ten years ago, Thornstock had lied to him as well, both about her prior connection to Malet and the nature of the threat he posed to Gwyn.

How much did Thornstock know about her past with Malet anyway? For that matter, could Joshua even believe what Malet had accused her of?

He had to. Otherwise, Malet had no reason to blackmail her.

"I'm sorry it took me so long." Gwyn walked in and closed the door behind her, then locked it, to his surprise. "I had a difficult time getting rid of Mama. She *finally* went up to take a nap, after I refused to talk about . . . us."

"Why refuse?"

"She was hoping we might marry," Gwyn said bluntly. "But don't worry. I squelched that idea."

Damnation. Part of him had begun to hope that himself.

Which just showed what a fool he was. "You mean, because you would never wed me."

"Don't be silly. If things were different—" A weary sigh escaped her. "But they're not. And I'm not daft enough to hold you to the promise—threat—you made to Lionel: that if he sought to ruin me publicly, you'd save my reputation by marrying me. For one thing, I know you were just trying to protect me. For another, you deserve to have the sort of wife you actually want."

That caught him entirely off guard. "What sort of wife would *that* be?"

"You know," she said with a vague wave of her hand, "a wife above reproach, who doesn't . . . have a checkered past."

"Yes," he said sarcastically, "because I'm so far above reproach myself that I must needs have a wife who is equally so. Never mind that I can't walk properly, that I jump at loud noises, that I have trouble controlling my temper . . . That I nearly beat a man to death in a fit of anger earlier today."

"On my behalf!" When he lifted a brow, she walked over to stare blindly out the room's one window. "Don't think I'm unaware of *why* you were so angry at him. You realized I was . . . not the chaste innocent you'd assumed, and you blamed it on Lionel." Her back was as straight as a ramrod. "And to a certain extent, on *me*."

"*What?* That wasn't why I was angry, for God's sake. It was because Malet was threatening you, trying to line his pockets by holding your past association with him over your head. Any man who does that isn't worth the ground he slithers on."

Her breathing grew ragged, as if she were on the verge of tears, and she still wouldn't look at him. "You don't understand."

"I understand perfectly. The bastard took advantage of

you in your youth, was paid off by your brother to put an end to it, and then tried to come back and take advantage of you all over again in a different fashion." He approached her. "He's the sort who preys on women. Heywood told me that much. And hearing how he acted with you, how he's acting now, merely confirmed it."

Her gaze swung to him, so dark and uncertain that seeing it cut him to the bone. "You seem to be operating under the assumption that he forced me into his bed. But he didn't. I *let* him seduce me."

That gave him pause. But then he realized— "It doesn't matter. He knew what he was doing. You did not. He had an unequal advantage. Just like—" He caught himself before he revealed Beatrice's secret about their Uncle Armie. "I've seen how scoundrels like him work. Hell, if your brother hadn't married Beatrice, I would have had his head for daring to take advantage of her, duke or no duke. I certainly wouldn't have blamed *her* for it."

Frustration knit her brow. "You still don't understand. At the time, I genuinely fancied myself in love with Lionel."

He ignored the pang those words gave him. "I assumed as much. The only thing that matters is whether you fancy yourself in love with him *now*. And I gather that you don't."

She blinked, as if that were a silly remark. "Of course I don't. Once he took Thorn's money to leave, his mask was ripped off and I saw him for what he truly was—the worst sort of blackguard. Although by the time I realized it, he was long gone, leaving me . . . no longer chaste. Indeed, it was some months after his disappearance that I even learned of Thorn's meddling and what it meant."

"Is that why you're still so angry at what Thorn did?"

"Partly."

When she said nothing about any other reasons, he bit back an oath. It rankled that she still didn't completely trust him with her secrets, but he could hardly blame her. Malet had taught her not to trust men. In some respects, her twin had taught her that, too.

"There's one thing I don't understand about all this," he said. "When your brother paid Malet off, did he *know* that the man had seduced you?"

"I doubt it, or he wouldn't have given Lionel a penny. And even after Lionel mysteriously vanished, I didn't tell Thorn, for fear he would challenge Lionel to a duel upon his return. You see, I didn't realize that Lionel was gone for good. I—I thought he'd been posted elsewhere or—" She shook her head. "I didn't know what to think, frankly. I just kept waiting for a letter or a visit that didn't come."

God, it was worse than Joshua had thought. No wonder she was angry with Thornstock. The duke had left his twin to dangle in the wind. Granted, Thornstock had thought he was doing the right thing, but . . .

"After Thorn revealed everything," she went on, "which he did only because I was pining away for Lionel, I continued to keep my physical relationship with Lionel secret because I dared not risk Thorn's hunting Lionel down to duel with him."

"Thornstock probably would have won, judging from what I've heard about his prowess with a dueling pistol."

"I couldn't be sure. And though I didn't want Thorn to die, I was just as worried he might ruin his own life by killing Lionel. After all, not even the stepson of a British ambassador on foreign soil can murder a British soldier with impunity. What's more, our stepfather wasn't expected ever to become duke, so—"

"It would also have ruined *his* future in diplomacy."

"Exactly."

Another question occurred to him. "So, does Thornstock *still* not know that Malet seduced you?"

"He does not. And I prefer to keep it that way."

Joshua remembered her threatening to turn in both Malet and her brother if Malet initiated a duel. "Then should I assume you also didn't tell Thornstock about the blackmail?"

She looked at Joshua as if he'd gone mad. "I would have had to tell him the reason for it."

"And once again, you were worried he'd fight Malet."

"Yes."

"So what *did* you tell him about why Malet was on the estate a week ago?"

"That Lionel had asked me to meet to renew our acquaintance, and I'd gone there in person to make sure he understood I was no longer interested. Then Lionel had attempted to kidnap me."

Joshua gaped at her. "Your brother *believed* that 'balderdash,' to use your favorite word?"

She nodded. "That's when he decided I needed a bodyguard." Interlacing her fingers over her stomach, she smiled faintly. "I think he just felt so . . . guilty over sending Lionel away years ago that he didn't pry too much into whether I was telling the whole truth."

Anger swelled up in Joshua again. "That means both you and your brother lied to me about my purpose here. If even one of you had told me the truth about the blackmail—"

"*I* didn't tell you because you would have gone straight to Thorn. He's the one who pays you, after all." She tipped up her chin. "And Thorn didn't tell you because he doesn't trust anyone, even me. Thorn figured it was best for us to focus on what he believed to be true—that Lionel was trying to kidnap me."

"What about once we got to London? If you'd told us about the blackmail then—"

"You both would have known I'm . . . what Lionel called me." She straightened her shoulders. "A harlot."

Joshua snorted. "Neither of us would consider you a harlot."

"No? Trust me, sometimes Thorn can be quite prudish. And you don't strike me as the . . . sort of fellow to condone fornication."

It was beginning to dawn on Joshua what was at the root of all this. And why Malet, clever devil that he was, had stumbled on the one thing she feared most of all, the one thing that had kept her silent. Like the torn ligatures and muscles in Joshua's leg that still ached after five years, her wound was hidden, and no one except Malet could see it. What was worse, the bastard knew exactly how to press on it to cause her pain.

"You're afraid to find out what your twin might think about you and Malet." Joshua walked closer, his heart pounding in his ears. He was on the verge of really understanding her. "You're afraid to find out what *I* think. That's why you've chosen the strategy of not telling anyone the truth. Of rejecting me before I can propose marriage. That's why you've drummed up this nonsense about my deserving a different sort of wife."

"You do."

"I don't know what I deserve. But I know what I want." He stared into her lovely face. "And I'm not stupid enough to base it on anything Malet said. Long before he appeared in our lives, I'd already formed an opinion of you, based on what I'd witnessed of you and your family, what I'd *heard* about you and your family from Beatrice. I paid attention to every detail, especially about you."

For a moment, her eyes widened and her features softened. "Did you really? Because you mostly seemed to ignore me."

"I will concede that. It was my attempt at self-preservation. I could already tell how dangerous you were."

"Me! I'm not dangerous."

"You're more dangerous than you know, at least to my peace of mind. Because although I denied it to myself, I knew you had the capacity to wreak havoc on my carefully manufactured life."

She stiffened. "How? By exposing you to my harlotry?"

"You are not—" He huffed out a breath. "Are you aware what a major in the Royal Marines does, Gwyn?"

"Fights?"

"Leads men. Not just men, but thousands of men. To get to that position, I had to learn how to assess situations. Strategize. Most importantly, I had to pay attention to the qualities of the soldiers and junior officers under me. I had to know who had proved worthy of their rank, who could best handle a landing party, who was well-versed in the art of war. I had to be a good judge of character, and I was, which is why I was promoted to major so young."

"Precisely," she said in a defeated tone of voice. "And why you are considered a hero. It's also why you deserve a wife who's above reproach."

"You mean, a wife who's not a 'harlot.'"

She thrust out her chin. "Yes."

Her stubbornness on the subject was starting to irritate him. "With all my experience at judging people, I should hope to hell I can tell the difference between a woman who was led astray and a 'harlot.' Tell me, Gwyn. How many times did you share Malet's bed?"

"Only once, I'll have you know!"

It didn't matter to him, although he was surprised it was only the one time. But he believed her. She looked so adorably outraged that he couldn't do otherwise.

He wanted to laugh at that, but somehow, he knew she

wouldn't take it well. "And how many other men's beds have you shared?"

"None. But it's not really a matter of quantity to men, is it? Or to good society. Once a woman loses her virginity—"

"You're not a harlot!" He shook his head. "If anything, Malet is the harlot."

"A man can't be a harlot, more's the pity," she said mutinously.

"I don't see why not. From what I understand, Malet has bedded plenty of women, and he was paid a great deal of money by your brother after bedding you. If that's not the definition of a harlot, I don't know what is."

"Someone should tell *him* that." She crossed her arms over her chest.

"Take it from me, dearling—if you accept every insult or slur hurled at you, you will spend all your days dodging them. Some people's opinions aren't worth worrying over. And yes, I'm still trying to learn that. But I'm doing better."

"Except in certain situations."

He gave her a ghost of a smile. "True."

"The point is, now that you know I'm not the sort of woman you wish to wed—"

"You have no idea what sort of woman I wish to wed." He strode up to her, and, when she looked as if she would back away, caught her about the waist to pull her close. "I don't care about Malet or what you did with him. Do you think *I've* been chaste my entire life? I assure you, I have not."

She glared at him. "It's different for men, and you know it."

"It shouldn't be."

"You don't believe that."

"I do. The world would be a better place if there were more gentlemen in it who treated women as ladies."

She lifted her hands to his shoulders. "Now you sound like a prude, which I know quite well you are not."

"Not around you anyway." When she looked stricken, he added hastily, "And it has naught to do with some secret 'harlotry' in your makeup. It has far more to do with the fact that I can't resist you. I've fought hard to do so for the past several months, and all it did was make me want you more."

She cast him a sad smile. "That's why you have this mad idea that you must marry me to save me from Lionel. Because your rules as a gentleman dictate that it's the only way you can make love to me. But it's not. You don't have to worry about deflowering me, about 'ruining' me. You *want* me, don't you?"

Bloody hell, the very idea of having her destroyed his resistance. "Gwyn—"

She placed a finger to his lips. "The only way to satisfy that need is to take me to bed. Here. Now." She looked behind him. "And, conveniently, there's already a bed in this room. How clever of you to arrange matters that way."

"*Gwyn—*"

"You can have me, Joshua, now that you know I am not the chaste innocent you assumed. So assuage your desire for me, and see how you feel once that's done. It's the only way I will take seriously any proposal of marriage from you."

"I don't want you sacrificing yourself in some bizarre attempt to prove me a scoundrel, Gwyn. Just because Malet abandoned you after bedding you doesn't mean I would. Not to mention—"

He caught himself before he could point out that she might find herself enceinte as a result. As long as she *wanted* to marry him, her finding herself with child would work in his favor by convincing her to do what she already wanted.

And the thought of her, heavy with his child, made him even more eager to have her in his bed.

She was staring at him. "Not to mention what?"

"Never mind. Of course, if you happen to desire me—"

"Did you think I was *pretending* to desire you last night? Because surely you could tell I was not."

He groaned. She had a point. And if she desired him, that was an entirely different matter. "You are no harlot," he rasped. "But you're definitely a seductress, a siren, an irresistible and enchanting—"

She kissed him. So sweetly. So erotically.

Damn it all to hell. He wanted her, and she wanted him. And if, in the process of taking her to bed, he proved to her he truly *did* wish to marry her, that would be all the better.

# Chapter Eighteen

When he drew back to tug her mobcap off her head, Gwyn began to untie his cravat. She knew Joshua meant well. He truly thought he didn't care about what she'd done with Lionel. But he did, of course.

She didn't wish for Joshua to commit to some fruitlessly noble act that might result in an unhappy marriage when he merely wanted her in his bed. Besides, she wanted him in *her* bed, too. By following her desires and his, she'd assuage his burning need once and for all, while also having a chance to . . . to find out what swiving was like with the only man she'd cared for in the past ten years.

So she drew off his cravat and gave herself up to his next highly enticing kiss. He'd already taught her that he was very good at kisses. Particularly the sort that went beyond her ken—like the ones he'd lavished on her inner thighs and privates last night.

Just the thought of *those* kisses made her pulse do a mad dance.

As if he could read her mind—he seemed to do that a *lot*—he dragged his mouth from hers to murmur, "You said there was a bed in this room."

Her blood caught fire. "There is." Taking him by the hand, she drew him to the four-poster bed with its curtains drawn.

She pulled open the curtains, relieved that the bed had linens on it. She didn't fancy having her first—possibly her *only*—time with Joshua take place on a bare mattress.

Then she felt Joshua unfastening her gown. Why, Lionel hadn't even bothered to undress her—he'd just thrown up her skirts and gone right to it.

But Joshua . . . well! He neither hurried things himself nor rushed *her* along. And his slow motions gave her body time to prepare, time to hunger for him. Not that she needed it. She was already more than eager to have him.

He spread open the back of her gown and undid the ties of her stays to loosen them. Then he kissed along the nape of her neck.

Good *Lord*. The faint scrape of his evening beard against her skin was *so* delicious. Who could have known that a mere kiss there would make her wish to tear off her clothes and throw herself into his arms?

"Are you sure your mother won't come looking for you?" he asked.

"I told her I didn't feel well." When he nipped her earlobe, she gasped. "That . . . that I was going to lie down . . . so I would feel better in time to . . . go to the opera tonight. And I told . . . my maid not to . . . bother me."

"Will she listen?" he asked in a ragged murmur. "Or will I have to spirit you off?"

"What an intriguing . . . idea . . ."

The man knew just what to say to make her melt. And ache. *Everywhere*. Who would have thought it of the gruff major?

Then he slipped his hands inside her gown and around to the front so he could tug her stays down to free her breasts for his fondling. She got decidedly warm down below, even though he was caressing her through her shift. And when he thumbed her nipples erect? The thrill of it had her sighing aloud.

"I honestly don't understand why some gentleman hasn't snapped you up before now," he whispered in her ear. "Don't think I didn't see that pile of visiting cards when we came in this afternoon. I'm not surprised. You looked like a goddess last night." His voice hardened. "I daresay by the end of the week, half the eligible bachelors in London will be offering for you."

She caught her breath, unsure whether to exult in his being jealous or to wonder at the way he put it, as if he half-expected her to take one of those offers. She waited for him to mention her inheritance, as he had that day at Cambridge, as if it were all she had in her favor. If he did, she would walk right out of the room.

"I hated every fellow who danced with you when I could not," he said, "who got to talk to you and smell your lovely scent." He nuzzled her hair. "You smell like lemons and honey, like a fresh summer rain, and your silky skin makes me want to rub you all over myself." He paused. "That sounds odd, doesn't it? I'm not very poetic, I'm afraid."

Perhaps not, but sometimes he could be downright sweet. Though she didn't think she'd better say that. Men didn't like to be considered "sweet."

The most important thing was that he desired *her,* not her money. "Oh, I've heard you be poetic a time or two. Though it's not poetry I want from you just now." She covered one of his hands and urged it down to the place between her thighs that yearned and burned for him. "I want *this*—you touching me in the most intimate ways. You inside me."

He moaned. "God save me, dearling, don't say things like that or I may finish before I've begun. I'm damned well about to perish just from holding you like this." He pressed his stiffening flesh against her bottom. "Can you feel what you do to me? I'm desperate to be inside you already."

"Then what's stopping you?" she rasped.

"My determination to make you as mad for me as I am for you. To make you understand how badly I wish to marry you."

When he rubbed her between her legs, she gasped. "Marriage . . . and desire are two different things." Or a woman should keep them separate anyway. Otherwise, she could end up in serious trouble.

"How would you know? You haven't married. Yet." Joshua moved his other hand from her breast, but only so he could tug gently on her coiffure to dislodge her hairpins.

As he spread her long, unruly locks down her back, his voice roughened. "Your hair's like liquid fire. You have no idea how long I've been waiting to run my fingers through it."

"Then you should have tried sooner," she teased, almost giddy with the confirmation that it wasn't her fortune he was after.

"I doubt your family would have approved." He stroked her hair so tenderly that a lump formed in her throat. "Probably still wouldn't."

She turned to face him. "So we won't tell them."

"At least not until you accept my offer of marriage."

"Exactly," she lied, his earlier words still stuck in her head: *Just because Malet abandoned you after bedding you doesn't mean I would.*

There he went, being noble. She didn't want him doing that. Besides, his proposal probably wouldn't be forthcoming once she told him the rest of her secrets, but there was no point in bringing up any of that right now. Because before she did, she meant to have him in her bed.

She pulled at his coat, trying fruitlessly to get it off, until he took over and shrugged out of it. Running her hands down his sleeves, she marveled at the muscles she could feel bunching beneath her fingers. "This is what *I've* been wanting to do: touch you, caress you, know every part of you."

"Hell, Gwyn, you have a way of seducing a man with words." He pulled on the sleeves of her gown until he had the whole thing pooling on the floor.

"Is that what I'm doing? Seducing you?" She sucked in a sharp breath when he untied her shift, then brought both that and her stays down in one quick motion, leaving her in only her stockings and shoes. "Because it surely seems as if you're seducing *me*."

"I'm flattered you noticed." He stepped back to look her over, and the already noticeable bulge in his trousers grew. "You are so damned beautiful. And funny and clever and kind. Malet must have been out of his mind to take mere money instead of you."

The words shattered once and for all the hard kernel of betrayal that had lain inside her for years, that she'd barely even realized was there until Joshua took a hammer to it.

And now he seemed determined to replace it with a heat that soaked into her everywhere. He came close to cup her between her legs, making her shiver deliciously, and his voice grew ragged. "I love the feel of your damp curls and your soft, warm mons. It makes me half mad for you."

Her breath had begun to quicken, as had his. Frantic to see him as naked as she, she unbuttoned his waistcoat and the few buttons of his shirt, and then tore both off, leaving his chest bared for her eager gaze.

Just as she'd imagined, it was magnificent. Though scars appeared here and there that looked as if they might have come from swordplay, they didn't detract from his well-wrought muscles. Dark curls dotted his upper chest, then trickled down the center to his belly until they petered out at his navel.

She spread her hands over that glorious expanse of male flesh and gave him a coquettish look. "My, my, Major Wolfe, what fine muscles you have."

"The better to hold you with," he rasped.

But when she reached for his trouser buttons, he stayed her hand. "Don't," he said firmly. "I have a great many uglier scars than the ones on my chest."

"Do I strike you as a woman who would grow faint to see them?"

"You wouldn't be the first." When she frowned, he hobbled to the bed and sat down heavily on it so he could take off his boots. "As I told you, I haven't been chaste all these years. Although the only time I tried to lie with a woman after I was wounded, she was . . . shocked enough by my scars to beg me to . . . er . . . leave."

Gwyn was outraged on his behalf. "Who *was* this woman?"

He thrust his bad leg out in front of him. "A merry widow in Leicester."

"Well, that is ridiculous! Clearly, she had never been privy to your . . . skills at lovemaking, or she wouldn't have been so squeamish."

He smiled faintly. "Don't say that. You still haven't seen my scars."

She kicked off her shoes, but when she started to untie her garters, he said, "Leave them on. The sight of you in your stockings drives me out of my mind."

"The thought of driving you out of your mind drives me out of *mine*," she said with a laugh. She walked up to where he still sat on the bed, and he caught her to him so he could suck her breasts, which he did with great enthusiasm. Without leaving the bed, he unbuttoned his trousers and drawers, then shoved them down just enough to expose his thrusting member. But before she could even get a good look at it, he pulled her onto his lap.

"What are you doing?" she asked. "I want to see your—"

"Later," he clipped out.

"But surely my sitting here makes your leg ache."

"Do I look as if I'm in pain?" he rasped, and began caressing her breasts with great skill.

So she gave in. If he didn't want her to see his damaged leg, she would acquiesce. She didn't want him flinching at every touch or reading too much into her curiosity. She wanted him making love to her the way she knew instinctively he could.

"Straddle me," he ordered her, his face lit with anticipation. "Please."

The idea caught her in its snare, thrilling the part of her that must surely be a harlot, no matter what he said. She wasn't entirely certain how straddling him would work, but Lord help her, she wanted to find out.

He held her by the waist and guided her into position until she was kneeling on the bed on either side of his hips, with her bottom resting on his upper thighs. Then it dawned on her what he was aiming for.

Heavens. She'd never imagined such a thing until this moment.

"Come down on me," he ordered, in that low rumble of a voice that seduced her every time, "I need to be inside you."

She hesitated. "You're sure I won't hurt you?"

"If you don't stop asking about whether you're hurting me, I swear—" He broke off when he saw her flinch. "My bad leg is stretched out—you're not putting any weight on the part that might hurt. And honestly, you'll hurt me more if you *don't* take me inside you."

So she did. And the feeling of it was exquisite. He filled her up so completely that she thought she might melt all over him. "Oh, Joshua . . ." She wriggled a bit, seeking to fit herself better on him.

He groaned. "God save me. You're so tight and warm . . . I may not survive this."

"I *am* hurting you!" she cried.

"Absolutely not," he growled, and held her still when she tried to rise off him. "But if you can move up like that and then down . . . Yes, that's it, dearling. Move . . . exactly like that. For God's sake, do it . . . again . . . before I lose my mind."

"Ohhh . . . *right* . . ." She was such a fool. It might have been years since she'd been bedded, but she did remember the moving part.

And as she started to slide up and down on him, he closed his eyes in an expression of unadulterated pleasure. "Yes, ride me," he said hoarsely. "Like that, yes. You have no idea how long I've . . . imagined having you atop me like this."

She flashed him a tremulous smile. "You certainly hid it well enough."

"I'm not . . . hiding it now, am I? God, it feels . . . good."

"Probably . . . as good as it . . . feels for me," she said.

It was the truth. There was none of the embarrassment or discomfort or awkwardness she'd experienced before—just a wild energy driving her on until she really *was* riding him, clasping his shoulders and undulating on him in search of the same carnal explosion she'd felt last night.

He must be searching for it, too, judging from his low moans and the way he clutched her waist to urge her on. And now she felt the slow build of sensation again, like last night, only this time she could control it, could hold on to it . . . a little longer . . . long enough for it to head higher . . . hotter . . . harder into . . . into . . .

Heaven.

"Yes!" He thrust deep and spilled himself inside her. "Yes, dearling, yes!"

Definitely *yes*. As her body quaked around him, she held on to him for dear life, relishing the ecstasy, trying to eke out every last drop.

She collapsed on top of him, and he kissed her neck, her hair, her ears, whatever he could reach.

Lord help her. This was better than anything she'd known. And now that she'd experienced it with him, she didn't want to give it up. She didn't want to give *him* up. Perhaps he would agree to be her lover.

No, somehow she doubted that. But if she told him everything and he then refused to marry her . . .

She didn't know how she would bear it.

# Chapter Nineteen

It had been five years or more since he'd shared a woman's bed, but he was fairly certain nothing before that had compared to this. To having Gwyn in his arms, on his lap. To being inside her. Oddly enough, the waning of his erection made him only more eager to have her again.

He would never have guessed she wasn't an innocent. She'd been so tight and, sometimes, so incredibly naïve. Then again, she practically *was* a virgin, having shared Malet's bed only once.

She squirmed a bit, and his cock slipped from her.

"Are you all right?" he murmured.

What he really wanted to ask was how he compared to Malet in bed, but even if she was truthful about it, he wasn't sure he wanted to know. After all, he had practically run roughshod over her in his eagerness to make her his.

But she gave a contented sigh. "I honestly don't know. It was . . . amazing."

Thank God. "For me, too. Then again, unlike you, I knew it would be."

She kissed his temple. "Are you that sure of me?" she asked coyly.

"Hardly."

But he wanted to be, which meant proposing marriage. It

was the only way to prove that bedding her didn't change what he wanted.

Still, now that the time had come to make an offer, an odd panic filled him. What if she turned him down? She'd been reluctant to consider marriage earlier. She'd said it was because he deserved a different kind of wife, but what if that wasn't the real reason?

Perhaps he should just pray that he had put a babe in her belly. That would solve everything. She would have to marry him then. She wouldn't dare not.

He dragged in a heavy breath. That was not the way to a woman's heart, he was fairly certain.

He nuzzled her neck, and she sighed. "I daresay I could sit here on top of you for . . . days."

"That would become uncomfortable very fast, I would imagine," he said dryly.

"Oh, dear, your leg!" she cried and slid off his lap.

"My leg is fine, Gwyn," he snapped.

He was starting to get irritated by her insistence on thinking of him as one step from being an invalid, a man who was only half a man, an object of pity. A man who didn't deserve her. Perhaps *that* was why she had refused to accept the idea of his marrying her. Perhaps it wasn't her shame over her past, after all.

God save him, what if she didn't want him for anything but *this*?

Rising from the bed, he buttoned up his drawers before she could glimpse the worst of his disfigurement.

"Wait, I wanted to see—"

"What? The scars that make me unsuitable for marriage to a duke's daughter? So you can pity the poor cripple?"

The look of shock on her face made him instantly regret the harsh words.

"Don't call yourself that!" she cried.

"Why not? It's what I am."

"You are so much more than that, if you could only see it." Her brow furrowed as she rose. She found her shift and put it on. "But before we can marry and have any kind of meaningful future together, I should think you would *want* to share yourself with me, so I could know you fully, in every aspect of your life."

In other words, she wanted him to bare his soul, to relive all the painful moments with her. No, thank you.

*But when people edge too close, you always start pushing them away, and then, of course, you end up alone.*

Damn Beatrice. She was wrong. He had a perfectly legitimate reason not to let Gwyn see his scars. After all, at least one woman had already recoiled from them. The very idea of Gwyn recoiling . . .

No, he wasn't ready for that.

"Joshua," she said softly, "you can trust me."

"The way you trusted *me*?" he shot back. "Sneaking around, amassing your blackmail money, sending notes to 'Lionel,' and arranging secret meetings with him? You could have confided in me, but instead—"

"How did you know I sent Lionel a note?"

One look at her pale face and he groaned. A body would think he'd have learned by now not to speak when he was in a temper. Because this was what happened. He said things he shouldn't.

He shrugged and started trying to dig himself out of the hole. "Well . . . you did send him a note, didn't you?"

Her expression hardened. "The only way you could have known that was by spying on me. Following me. You say I don't trust you? You're as bad as Thorn. Neither of you trusts *me*."

"With good reason, apparently," he said, having learned

in the marines that the best defense of one's actions was to attack.

But perhaps not so much with ladies, judging from the cold glint in her eyes.

Hastily, he seized on something else Gwyn had said. "You said, 'Before we can marry.' Does that mean you're agreeing to my offer?"

"What offer?" She ducked her head to tie her shift with angry jerks of her fingers. "You haven't actually made an offer of marriage." Now she was concentrating on wriggling into her stays, but it was clear she couldn't tighten them herself.

He went over to help her. "Haven't I?" he said, though he knew he really hadn't. He finished with her stays, then waited while she pulled on her gown. That would need buttoning up, too. "I could have sworn I did."

"You did not. We talked around it, about it, over it." When he buttoned up her gown, she added, "You told Lionel that if he revealed anything about my past, you would announce our engagement. But you never actually asked."

"Perhaps not, but you knew what I meant. What I wanted."

She whirled to face him, her eyes those deep forest pools he could drown in. *Was* drowning in.

"Because now I read your mind?" she said in a clipped voice. "You offering to announce our engagement was a threat that was conditional upon Lionel's bad behavior. It didn't involve actually *asking* me. Or are you having second thoughts about marrying me now that you've bedded me?" She picked up her mobcap and stuffed her hair up inside it. "Is that why you're choosing to fight with me?"

"I am not choosing to fight with you. I am merely pointing out—"

"And in case you were wondering," she went on, "the only person pitying you, Joshua, is *you.*"

She marched toward the door.

He followed her, his temper rising. "Even if I did offer for you in the exact way you wish me to, you wouldn't accept me, would you?"

She turned to look back at him. "You would never lower your pride enough to risk my saying no, so I guess we'll never know, will we?"

Then she walked out, shutting the door behind her.

He stood there speechless, his hands curling into fists. She was making him insane! Choosing to fight, indeed. The only person choosing to fight was *her*. Clearly she desired him, and clearly she had enjoyed their lovemaking. What more did she want from him?

*But when people edge too close, you always start pushing them away, and then, of course, you end up alone.*

"Shut up, Beatrice!" he cried into the rafters.

The sound of servants running brought him up short. He'd yelled loudly enough to be heard?

Bloody hell. He'd better be fully dressed before they descended on him. He hobbled around to pick up articles of clothing, then finished dressing. By the time a maid and two footmen burst in, he was headed for the door, cane in hand.

"Sir, are you all right?" the maid asked. "We heard screaming."

"I was looking for something up here and couldn't find it. Please forgive my frustration. I . . . um . . . tend to talk to myself."

One of the footmen stepped forward. "If you tell us what you're looking for, Major, perhaps we could . . ."

But Joshua had already pushed past them and out into the hall. Let them wonder. People always wondered about him anyway. Might as well give them a better reason for it than his battle wounds.

*The only person pitying you, Joshua, is* you.

Wonderful. Now he had both Beatrice *and* Gwyn in his head. Time to drown out their voices. And he had the perfect place to do it, too.

It was high time he gave the Duke of Thornstock a piece of his mind.


Gwyn had barely reached her bedchamber on the second floor when she heard Joshua yelling something upstairs. A pox on him! He would bring all the servants running.

She hurried inside, praying that her maid wasn't there. Thankfully, the room was empty, which was a good thing because she feared she was about to cry. And she *never* cried. Blast it all! She dared not let anyone see her. She'd never be able to tell the truth about why she was upset.

Tearing off her mobcap, she threw herself across the bed and began to sob. What a coward she was! Instead of being determined to have the last word in their argument, she should have told Joshua she would marry him. But what if she had, and then, when she told him the rest of what had happened between her and Malet, he'd changed his mind? She knew Joshua—he would marry her anyway once she accepted his . . . his *non*proposal. It was the gentlemanly thing to do.

That started her crying again, so hard that at first she didn't hear the firm knocking at her door. But when it was coupled with Beatrice's voice . . .

Oh, no, she couldn't let Beatrice see her like this! Beatrice would guess who had caused her distress, and then she would either defend her brother or go give him a lecture. Then again, perhaps he could use a lecture from someone other than her.

She was still trying to decide what to do when Beatrice said, more softly, "Dearest, I'm coming in unless you say otherwise."

Perhaps talking to Beatrice was a good idea. She might know more about why Joshua was so maddening. She would certainly know if Gwyn had a chance with him, given the peculiarities of her situation.

Gwyn sat up to pull her handkerchief out of her pocket, then saw the blood on it from when she'd wiped Lionel's blood off Joshua's face. That started her crying all over again.

The door opened and Beatrice peeked in, then said, "Oh, my dear, what has happened?" She slipped inside and closed the door. "Can I help?"

Gwyn was still staring at her bloody handkerchief through her tears.

When Beatrice hurried over and saw it, she started. "You've hurt yourself! Shall I fetch your mother?"

"No!" Gwyn said. "It's not my blood. And Mama can't know."

"All right." Beatrice whisked the bloody handkerchief from her and placed her own clean one in Gwyn's hand. "There. I know you don't want to wipe your nose with a bloody one."

Gwyn cast her a grateful smile as she dabbed at her eyes and blew her nose. Then she sat there staring down at Beatrice's nicely embroidered handkerchief.

Beatrice took a seat on the bed next to her. "Dare I ask whose blood it is?"

"Do you swear not to tell Mama or Grey if I tell you?"

"That sounds ominous." Beatrice pondered the request for a moment. "I don't mind keeping secrets from your mother if you think it will hurt her. But Grey . . ."

"Will quite possibly commit murder if he learns what I tell you."

Beatrice blinked. "He'd murder Joshua?"

"Not Joshua. Well, probably not Joshua. But he might murder Lionel Malet. Actually, he'd have to get in line behind Joshua and Thorn, if they knew the whole story."

Taking Gwyn's hand, Beatrice pressed a kiss to it. "Then it sounds as if we should keep them from hearing about it. I don't fancy seeing either my brother, my brother-in-law, or my husband in gaol."

Gwyn sighed and squeezed Beatrice's hand. "That's the trouble. I have to tell Joshua. Or rather, I don't have the right to keep it from him if I mean to marry him."

Beatrice gaped at her, then hugged her. "Oh, my dear, that's wonderful! I *knew* the two of you would end up married. We could all tell you were falling in love with each other."

"Well, I don't know about that," Gwyn said dully. "So far, we haven't really talked about love."

And why was that? Probably because they both professed to be cynical about it. And with good reason.

She stiffened. Those were the very words Joshua had used. It still riled her. "We've barely talked about marriage. And I don't know if he'll marry me once he knows that . . ."

She burst into tears again. Good Lord, when had she turned into such a watering pot? Just look at what the man was doing to her!

Beatrice held her close, patting her back and saying comforting things.

When Gwyn could stop crying, she said, "I do so . . . love having a . . . sister even if . . . you're only a half sister-in-law." She blotted her eyes again. "Is that what you are? Is that even a . . . sort of relation?"

Beatrice smiled. "It counts, as far as I'm concerned. Besides, when you marry Joshua—"

"*If* I marry Joshua. Which looks more unlikely by the

moment. Too bad you weren't around when I met Lionel Malet. You would have given me good advice, and then I wouldn't be in this . . . this *pickle*."

Beatrice drew back to stare at her. "Lionel Malet? *Captain* Malet? The one who tried to kidnap Heywood's fiancée and you?"

"The very one." Gwyn slumped. "It's a long story."

"I have plenty of time to listen." Beatrice rubbed her back. "Your mother sent me up to see how you were, but she's enjoying her visit with Grey so much, I doubt she'll notice if I take a while."

Gwyn sighed. She needed to tell all this to *someone* who would give her good advice. Or at least keep her from throttling Joshua. Or begging him to marry her. "It all began ten years ago . . ."

She proceeded to tell Beatrice the entire shameful story— about falling for Lionel, being seduced by him, and then being betrayed by him . . . and Thorn.

Beatrice looked more and more shocked as Gwyn's tale went on, and Gwyn began to worry that perhaps she shouldn't have revealed quite so much to her friend.

Then Beatrice shook her head. "I swear, men can be absolutely impossible! Thorn paid Mr. Malet off to abandon you? Mr. Malet *blackmailed* you? The bastard! I hope Thorn gave him what for!"

"No. Joshua did." She pointed to the bloody handkerchief still sitting on Beatrice's lap. "That's Lionel's blood."

Beatrice blinked. "How much does my brother know?"

"Nearly all of it." So Gwyn told her what she'd told Joshua and how he'd reacted—leaving out the part about sharing his bed, of course. She didn't want her friend knowing she was *that* much of a harlot.

*You're not a harlot!*

Well, that was one thing Joshua had seemed doggedly

determined to impress upon her. And she was even beginning to believe it.

When Gwyn finished her tale, Beatrice hugged her. "Oh, my friend, I am *so* sorry you're going through this. Leave it to Joshua to make matters harder for you."

"Well, at least I don't think Lionel will be trying to blackmail me anymore. Joshua made sure of that."

Beatrice eyed her closely. "And then he proposed."

"Sort of. Not really. We left things up in the air. He lost his temper, so I lost mine, and we said things we shouldn't have." She twisted the handkerchief in her hand.

"If it helps, I can reassure you that Joshua is surly to everyone, including me. It's not that unusual for him to lose his temper."

"Trust me, I know that only too well." Gwyn ventured a smile. "At the same time, he can be so thoughtful when he wants." Like lacing up her gown even as they were arguing and without being asked. "And he does say the loveliest things sometimes."

Beatrice lifted a brow. "We *are* still talking about my brother, aren't we? The cranky fellow who snarls at anyone who gets near?"

"He's not as bad as all that. He was very kind about my past involvement with Lionel. He took my side. Why, he came near to killing Lionel when the man was trying to . . . er . . . renew our acquaintance."

"That last does sound more like my brother."

"The thing is, there's something I haven't told him. And I can't consider marrying him until I'm sure how he . . . feels about it. So I was thinking that perhaps because you are already married, and you're Joshua's sister . . . Well, you could help me figure out how to tell him and how he might react."

"You have a right to your secrets, you know."

"This one involves him, too." Gwyn dropped her gaze

to her hands. "You see, it's quite possible that I . . . can't have children."

Beatrice looked stunned. "Good heavens, what makes you say that?"

Now came the hard part. "It has to do with the fact that after my one time with Lionel, I ended up enceinte."

"Oh, Gwyn." To her credit, Beatrice didn't look shocked at all as she took Gwyn's hand. "And that made everything worse than it already was, I suppose."

"It did. I actually wouldn't have known it until much later, if not for my maid. Having been in service with another woman before coming to my family, she recognized the signs—my morning sickness, my two missed courses, my tender breasts. We had endless discussions about what to do—whether to tell Mama and Papa, whether to tell only Thorn and get him to spirit me away somewhere until I had the baby, whether to go to the nearest army officer in an attempt to find Lionel. I was frantic, as you might imagine."

"I'm sure you were terrified."

"Lionel had been missing for months, and I didn't yet know why. I . . . I didn't dare tell anyone about the child until I knew." Just thinking of that time made Gwyn sick to her stomach. "Then I started bleeding badly one morning, and my maid sneaked in a midwife friend to see me, and the midwife told me that I'd indeed been pregnant and had lost the child."

"Given that Lionel had already gone," Beatrice said gently, "I suppose that was something of a blessing."

"That's what I thought at the time. But later I got to thinking . . . perhaps I caused it in all my terror of bearing a bastard. Perhaps if I had been calmer or had made a better decision or—"

"Dearest, you did not cause it."

"I don't know." She folded her arms about her waist,

wishing she could magically heal whatever might have gone wrong there. "The midwife who examined me and took note of the bloody . . . stuff that came out of me said I had the sort of womb that meant I would never be able to bear a child. If that's true, it was nothing I did that caused me to miscarry. Although that's little consolation when you consider that it also means I'm made the wrong way for bearing children."

"Hmm," Beatrice said, sounding skeptical. "So, until now, no one except your maid and her friend knew about your miscarriage."

Gwyn nodded, her throat feeling raw. "She and my maid had a heated argument about why I lost the babe, because my maid didn't agree with her friend's assessment. But what if the midwife was right?"

"And what if she wasn't? Perhaps it was merely an accident of nature, and no one's fault at all. There's no way to know for sure. Although I'm not the best person to consult about that, because I don't have children yet." Beatrice mused for a moment. "Have you been to any London doctors to ask?"

"How am I to do that? My old maid didn't travel with us from Prussia, so I would have to find a physician on my own or tell Mama. And I don't know what physician to trust with such a secret." She shot Beatrice an anxious look. "If this got out, I wouldn't be the only one to suffer from the gossip. The whole family would have to endure it."

"True." Beatrice eyed her with concern. "I know you don't want to hear this, but you really *should* talk to your mother about it. She's had five children by three different husbands. If anyone knows how birthing works, it's her."

"But then I'd have to reveal what I did with Lionel." Despair crept over Gwyn. "She would be horrified."

"I doubt it. Your mother strikes me as being far more resilient and practical than that."

How interesting that Joshua had said the same thing. "I don't know."

"You ought to at least talk to her before you talk to Joshua."

"Right. Joshua." She choked back tears. "How can I tell him I may never be able to give him a child?"

Beatrice put her arm about Gwyn's shoulders. "If he loves you, it won't matter to him."

"Or he'll say it doesn't matter to him, but he won't mean it."

A skeptical expression crossed Beatrice's face. "Have you ever known my brother to say one thing but mean another? The man has trouble with the concept of keeping one's opinion to oneself."

When Gwyn eyed Beatrice askance, Beatrice said, "I know, I know, it's our family curse. But Joshua is the most shining—or horrifying, depending on how you look at it— example of it. He says what he thinks. Believe me, if your being unable to have children bothers him, he'll tell you."

"I hope you're right." Though she was no longer sure about anything concerning Joshua.

"Do you love him?" Beatrice asked.

The question caught Gwyn completely off guard.

"I mean," Beatrice went on hastily, "I know you said you haven't talked about it, but—"

"Honestly, I'm not sure how I feel. If wanting to hold him close one minute and strangle him the next is love—"

"It sure as the devil is part of it." Beatrice glanced away. "But mostly it's about trust . . . trusting someone enough to know that no matter what you tell them, they'll be on your side, and it won't change how they feel about you.

That's why you should never give your heart to someone you don't trust."

Despite everything, Gwyn *did* trust Joshua. Or she did *now* anyway. She was just afraid she'd lose him once he found out that she might be childless for life. If she'd ever really had him.

"I'm going to tell you something I probably shouldn't," Beatrice said, "because my brother said it to me privately, although not in confidence. But I love him enough to want what's best for him, and I think you're what's best for him."

Gwyn said nothing, just looked at Beatrice expectantly.

"The night I caught you two together," Beatrice went on, "I threatened him if he ever harmed you, and he said, 'I would never harm her. Not as long as I live and breathe.' Those are strong words for Joshua. And though I think he was embarrassed afterward to have shown so much of his true feelings, I also think he meant them."

Shock rippled through Gwyn. They *were* strong words, so strong that she could hardly imagine him saying them. But Beatrice wouldn't lie about something like that. Gwyn knew it, as surely as she knew that Joshua wouldn't hurt her in one of his rages. Not physically anyway.

Would he hurt her in other ways? Next time they argued, would he accuse her of having been with another man before marriage? And if they were unable to have children, would he throw that back at her, too?

She didn't think so, but she wasn't sure.

Beatrice squeezed her shoulder. "The thing about love is, it's like drinking fire and trusting it not to burn you, though it seems to burn everyone else. It means trusting someone when by all accounts you shouldn't. Because you know, somewhere deep in your heart, that the person you're trusting is worthy of that."

"I trusted Lionel," she ventured.

"Did you? Truly? Or was there an annoying voice in your head that said he would hurt you in the end?"

Gwyn tried to put herself in her younger self's shoes. She remembered how she'd felt when Lionel had flirted with other women in Berlin. She remembered being unsure, even then, of whether he wanted her for herself or for her fortune. Lionel had managed to assuage that fear with his fawning flatteries and his pointed attentions, but only barely.

Meanwhile, her present self knew, beyond a shadow of a doubt, that Joshua had never wanted her for her fortune. Odd, how completely she believed it.

"There's a certain amount of risk in falling in love," Beatrice said. "What you have to ask yourself is, would being with Joshua be worth the risk?"

*Yes.*

Gwyn would endure any pain, any scandal, any risk, to be with him.

Now if only she could convince *him* of that.

# Chapter Twenty

At Thornhill, Joshua was ushered into the inner sanctum—the duke's study—which was more spacious than the entire downstairs of the dowager house Joshua rented on the Armitage estate. It was sobering, to say the least. But it didn't change what he'd come to say.

With a smile, Thornstock rose to greet him. "What brings you here, Major?" Critically, he scanned Joshua's rough-looking attire. "I thought you were accompanying Lady Hornsby and Gwyn to the opera tonight. But you're damned well not doing it dressed like *that*."

"It was never settled whether they'd decided to go for certain. Or whether Grey might be the one to go with them." He shrugged. "It doesn't really matter. Either way, they won't have to worry about Malet ruining their evening because I intend to beard the lion in his den as soon as I leave here. Hence my deliberately ragged clothes. No point in ruining a perfectly good suit."

It was high time Joshua commenced with his work for Fitzgerald, and tonight seemed as good a time as any. It would keep his mind off the beautiful woman he'd managed to insult earlier.

"Of course," Joshua went on, "I could have done a much better job of keeping your sister safe in London if you had told me the truth about Malet in the first place, instead of hiring me under false pretenses."

Thornstock's expression showed nothing. "I don't know what you mean."

"You should have informed me that Lionel Malet pursued your sister ten years ago. That he didn't just begin going after her a few months ago because he wanted to kidnap and marry an heiress as revenge upon your half brother."

The duke dropped heavily into the chair behind his desk. "How did you find out?"

"Your sister told me."

"Recently?"

Joshua crossed his arms over his chest. "Today, as a matter of fact. So I'm fully aware that you and she both lied to keep me from realizing what was going on. And yes, I'm also aware that when the two of you spoke of Hazlehurst, you really meant Lionel Malet."

"Damn." Thornstock slumped in his chair. "You might as well sit down, Wolfe." When Joshua did so, the duke asked warily, "What exactly did my sister tell you?"

Joshua drew in a steadying breath. "That you paid Malet to leave her alone ten years ago. And that you told him you would cut her and him off if he tried to elope with her."

"Oh. So, pretty much everything."

"'Pretty much?' Is there something she left out?"

The worry knitting Thornstock's brow demonstrated that the man did care about his sister. "Only things she doesn't know."

That surprised Joshua. "Like what?"

"For one thing, how much I paid him. I didn't want her to realize . . ." He dragged one hand through his hair. "How insultingly little it required to buy him off. I told her years ago it was a vast sum. I hope you will not . . . well . . . tell her the truth."

"I would never tell her anything that might wound her." And what was wrong with Malet anyway? Gwyn was worth her weight in gold. How could the idiot not see that?

Joshua groaned. How could *he* not see it? He had run her off when all she'd wanted was *him*, apparently. While that proved that the woman was mad, she wasn't nearly as mad as Joshua was for not recognizing that she was the best thing ever to happen to him.

"I know that she and I both lied to you," Thornstock said, "but—"

"She had her reasons, embarrassment being primary among them. But what were yours? Why deceive me about your true purpose for hiring me as her bodyguard? Why lie straight to my face—only yesterday, mind you—about the fact that you both knew Malet from before? I could have better handled my task if I'd had that bit of crucial information."

"It seems to me you've handled it perfectly well so far. And if I'd told you the truth, would you have taken the post?"

That was a good question, one that Joshua wasn't sure how to answer. "I might have."

"Or not. And I knew that if Malet had the chance to spirit her off, he'd make sure that he ruined her this time. I couldn't take the chance."

If anything proved to Joshua that Thornstock was unaware of Gwyn's true relationship to Malet, it was that.

"Besides," Thornstock went on, "she told me she didn't want *me* squiring her everywhere. But I thought she might tolerate you."

God, he hoped she was doing better than merely "tolerating" him.

"Why has this come up now anyway?" Thornstock asked. "The last time I spoke with her privately, before we left Lincolnshire, she and I were in agreement about how much to say. What changed?"

Malet and his blackmail.

Joshua wanted to tell her twin about that so badly he could taste it. But if he did, he'd be doing exactly what Gwyn had been worried about all these years—ensuring that Thornstock went off to duel with Malet. And though Joshua sincerely believed Thornstock would get the better of Malet in any such fight, Gwyn would never forgive Joshua for risking it. Or for putting her brother in a situation in which he might be charged with murder.

If Joshua cared about her, if he wanted her as his wife, he had to respect her wishes. It was as simple as that. And he did want her as his wife. Of that, he was certain. No one else suited him as well as she.

So what he had to do now was figure out how to gain her hand.

Thornstock asked again, "Major? What changed?"

"I saw Malet lurking about while we were shopping today, and when I confronted him, he made some remarks about his past with your sister. That's why I questioned her later on the subject. But don't worry: I mean to make short work of him once I get him alone. I daresay he won't bother her anymore after I'm done with him."

With any luck, Malet would be hanging from the gibbet for treason once Joshua was done with him.

"Did Gwyn hear what he said when you confronted him?"

"She did."

Thornstock looked ill. "Did she indicate whether she still had . . . er . . . feelings for the devil?"

"I don't think you have to worry on that score. She makes no bones about the fact that she despises the man."

"Good. She told me as much at the estate, but I wasn't certain whether to believe her. At least she's seen his true colors at last." The duke picked up a pencil on his desk and tapped it idly. "Though . . . um . . . I suppose she's still angry with me for paying Malet to leave."

"You'll have to ask her. Whatever problems you have with your sister, you will have to work out on your own." Joshua rose. "I won't spy on her for you anymore."

That seemed to startle Thornstock. Then he narrowed his gaze. "Are you smitten by my sister, Major? Will I have to buy *you* off as well?"

The words sparked Joshua's temper. He leaned over the desk and lowered his voice to a threatening murmur. "You're welcome to try, Your Grace. But I don't think you'll like the outcome." He reached into his greatcoat pocket. "Oh, and that reminds me. Here's your pistol back." He set it on the desk. "I've acquired weapons of my own, so I won't be needing yours."

"What do you mean?" Thornstock asked in alarm. "That's supposed to be your compensation for the job. Malet is still out there!"

"And I intend to protect her from him. I just won't require any payment for it. Not from you anyway."

Leaving the duke gaping after him, Joshua walked out the door.


Night had already fallen by the time the hackney reached Chelsea. Thornstock's remarks about Malet had nagged at Joshua the whole way. Malet *was* still out there. And now that the man had lost the blackmail money he'd counted on, he would be infinitely more dangerous—that was, *if* Fitzgerald was correct about what Malet hoped to sell.

There was only one way to find out: slip into the fellow's rooms at the lodging house and search for whatever documents he might have stowed away. That was assuming Malet

*Sabrina Jeffries*

was off nursing his wounds in Covent Garden. If he were at the lodging house, Joshua might have to wait a while.

Then again, a desperate Malet would surely not spend his time in the stews. He needed money and had promised the landlord some. If he left the place, it might be to meet with his French associate to sell whatever he had. Joshua would have to remain flexible on this mission.

The driver let him out in front of the lodging house and Joshua handed him his payment. But before he could even enter, he spotted Dick the Quick loitering in front of the place.

At first, the lad didn't recognize him out of uniform. That wasn't surprising; Joshua had worn his old greatcoat and a floppy hat he'd bought off a coal heaver after Fitzgerald had commissioned him to spy on Malet.

But as Joshua neared the lad, Dick narrowed his gaze on him, then came running up. "Major? What brings you here? And dressed like that, too!"

Joshua pulled the lad aside. "I'm not here as the major, so don't call me that. There's a crown in it for you if you can keep my secret, all right?"

Dick bobbed his head.

"And there's two shillings more if you can tell me whether Captain Malet is inside."

"He is, sir. Shall I fetch him?"

"No. I'm going to sit by the window inside that tavern across the way. If you'll stand inside the lodging house and hurry outside to signal to me when Malet is about to leave, you'll get another couple of shillings."

"Yes, sir! I'll be on the lookout for him."

"Just don't alert him to my presence."

Joshua started to walk across to the tavern and then thought of something else. "One more thing, lad. And it pays

much better than the rest, if you can manage it. Assuming
that it's necessary."

"Oh, sir, I can manage anything. I told you, I'm your
man."

"Well, then, here's what I'd like you to do. If I head off
down the street . . ." He explained everything as he kept an
eye on the lodging house door. When he was done, Dick
assured him that he could carry out the tasks exactly as
Joshua commanded.

Joshua went into the tavern and found a seat by the
window. If he planned to be doing this sort of work for a
while, he would need assistants—lads like Dick the Quick.
What better time to make sure the boy could be trusted?

He ordered an ale and sat there nursing it for a good hour
at least. Then Dick appeared at the door to the lodging house
and nodded toward him.

Pulling down the brim of his floppy hat, Joshua slipped
out into the street just in time to see Malet leave the lodging
house. Joshua hesitated only a moment. The way Malet was
scanning the road told him that the man wasn't just headed
off to Covent Garden for an entertaining evening.

No, the only reason Malet would be careful not to be followed was if he were off to commit some villainous act,
either treason or the kidnapping of Gwyn. Either way, Joshua
wasn't going to waste time searching the man's room and risk
missing Malet's rendezvous with the enemy . . . or Gwyn.
Better to follow the bastard.

As Joshua made his deliberately slow way behind Malet
along the road, he paused to tell Dick, "Here's the first part
of your pay, lad," and press a guinea into the boy's hand. "You
know what you have to do for the second part." Then Joshua
continued on.

He was careful not to follow Malet too closely. The man
was definitely behaving suspiciously—stopping every block

or so to glance around as if looking for anyone after him. Fortunately, it was dark in the streets of Chelsea.

Besides which, Malet had a way of hunching his shoulders as he was about to stop that warned Joshua to duck out of sight or pretend to be looking in a shop window just as the bastard looked back.

Nor did it hurt that they were within a stone's throw of the Royal Hospital, where aging and severely wounded veterans were housed as in-pensioners or treated on an out-pensioner basis. Chelsea pensioners were everywhere, making the sight of a man using a cane even more common than usual.

Eventually, Malet halted at a tavern and went in. Joshua looked through a window just in time to see the fellow take a seat at a table with another man. Joshua went inside and found a table next to theirs that was empty. Then he held up one finger to the barmaid, who nodded and brought him a mug of ale.

As he hunched over it, he strained to hear the conversation at the next table.

"What happened to you?" the stranger asked Malet. His accent was faint, but unmistakable. French, for certain.

Excitement rose in Joshua's blood. Fitzgerald had been right, after all.

"Got into a fight earlier today," Malet said offhandedly. "Had to show a fellow I wouldn't tolerate his nonsense."

Joshua downed some ale to keep from snorting.

"Judging from your black eye and badly swollen cheek, you were on the worse end of that fight," the Frenchman said.

"Do you have my money?" Malet asked in an icy voice.

"If you've brought what I asked for."

"I have. But it took some blunt to get Wellesley's memorandum. I had to pay off servants in two households."

*Two* households? Castlereagh and Wellesley's, no doubt.

The Frenchman slid a purse across the table. "There is

plenty in here to compensate you for whatever expenses you incurred."

Malet picked it up and looked inside, then smiled as he tucked the purse into his coat pocket. He removed a thin sheaf of papers from his other coat pocket and set them in the center of the table. "Then this is for you, monsieur."

"Don't call me that, you imbecile." The Frenchman cast a look about the tavern, then leaned forward to hiss, "I don't need a mob of angry Englishmen chasing me down the street."

That was Joshua's cue. He rose and took a few steps to the empty chair between them at their table. As they looked up, startled, he sat down and said, "I hope you'll settle for one angry Englishman, sir. Mobs are so unwieldy."

Malet gaped at him. "Wolfe? What the—"

"Happy to see you, too, Malet." While he still had the element of surprise, Joshua pulled both his loaded pistols out of his greatcoat pockets, pushed the barrel of one against the Frenchman's knee and the barrel of the other against Malet's.

Smiling the whole while, he said, "Now, you gentlemen have one of two choices. The first is that Malet retrieves that purse from his coat and passes it to me, while you, monsieur, slide that sheaf of papers to me. The second is that I, in an instant, make you both as much invalids as the pensioners hereabouts, and then scoop up the documents and money on my way out while you're both writhing on the floor. A fate you both richly deserve, by the way."

The Frenchman glared at Malet. "You damned imbecile. You were followed!"

"Personally," Joshua continued, "given the treasonous nature of your transaction, I would prefer the latter choice. But the ball might go through one of you and hit an innocent individual, which would be troublesome for me. So I'll leave the choice up to you."

Malet glowered at him. "You wouldn't *dare,* Major."

Joshua fixed a deadly gaze on Malet. "I believe I've already proved once today that I will dare a great many things."

The Frenchman reached inside his coat. Without even turning his head from Malet, Joshua half-cocked the pistol he held to the Frenchman's knee. "That would be unwise, monsieur."

Hearing the sound, the fellow blanched and pulled his hand out empty. "*This* was the fellow you fought with? A *major?*" the Frenchman hissed at Malet. "Gah! You have to be the most incompetent English soldier I've ever met. No wonder you were cashiered!"

"Ticktock, gentlemen," Joshua said. "Either make the decision now or I will make it for you." And to emphasize his determination, he half-cocked the pistol aimed at Malet's knee.

Joshua was itching to shoot Malet, and not in the knee either. But he figured that Fitzgerald wouldn't approve of that method of settling the situation. And Joshua really did wish to prove himself worthy of the post Fitzgerald was offering him.

So he shifted his gaze to the Frenchman. "The document, sir. Give it to me now, and I will let you leave."

Not that it mattered. If Dick the Quick was as fast as his name attested, he was somewhere in the tavern waiting for this to be resolved so he could follow the Frenchman. Joshua knew he couldn't keep control over two men in a public place, but he didn't have to. Malet was the traitor.

Still, that didn't mean he wanted to watch the French spy go free. And that was where Dick came in. He could tell Joshua exactly where the man was residing, and Joshua would pass that information on to Fitzgerald.

The Frenchman sighed, then shoved the sheaf of papers at Joshua.

"Go on, then," Joshua said, but didn't move his pistol until the spy rose and headed for the door.

Then he slipped it into his coat pocket and steadied his other pistol between Malet's legs. "I suggest, sir, that you hand me the purse and come with me. Or you will have a very unhappy future."

Malet looked fit to be tied, but he handed over the purse, which Joshua slid into his coat pocket. And when Joshua rose and stood behind him with his pistol against the man's neck, Malet knew he had no choice but to stand and go with Joshua.

No one could see the gun Joshua held on Malet, and even if they could, they wouldn't care. Malet had obviously chosen a rather low tavern so that no one would notice what he was up to with some Frenchman. That worked in Joshua's favor. He could use his cane to walk with one hand while holding the pistol in Malet's back with the other.

"Where are you taking me?" Malet asked.

"To a friend of mine, who will be delighted to hear that I've caught a traitor."

"You don't even know what's in those papers," Malet said as they walked out into the night.

"Actually, I do. And anyway, it doesn't matter. I caught you selling them to the French. That's all that counts. You will hang for treason, which is no less than you deserve."

Malet got quiet as Joshua steered him toward the nearest coach stand. They were nearly there when Malet kicked Joshua's cane out from under him, pushed him into the waterman for the stand, and ran.

Cursing a blue streak, Joshua quickly righted himself, but the streets were crowded and Malet seemed to have disappeared.

"Damnation!" Joshua cried.

It was a miracle neither of his pistols had gone off. But

they were new enough that the half-cock notches had done their job and kept them from firing. Before anyone could see the one in his hand, he shoved it into his greatcoat pocket.

"Are you all right, sir?" The waterman stood and brushed himself off. "That bloody arse was in a hurry, he was."

"He was, indeed. And I'm fine, thank you," Joshua said as he scanned the streets. He felt like an utter fool, and clumsy to boot. He also couldn't see the bastard anywhere.

He should never have taunted Malet with the fact that he would hang for treason. He should have waited to get the arse into the hackney first.

"Looks like you're bleeding, sir," the waterman said. "Probably banged your head on my bucket."

"What?" Joshua touched his hand to his forehead. Sure enough, he *was* bleeding, but he didn't care. He'd lost Malet.

For the next hour he questioned the hackney coachmen and roamed up and down Chelsea. But it was no use. Malet had escaped. Damn his soul to hell. At least Joshua still had the papers Malet had tried to sell and the money he'd expected to get for them. Joshua would have to be content with that.

He hired a hackney, meaning to go to Fitzgerald's, when something dawned on him. Malet was a vengeful sort. In his anger, he might try to kidnap Gwyn, either for revenge or ransom or to trade her for the papers.

Joshua scowled. Not on *his* watch. That man was not going near Gwyn ever again. Joshua could report to Fitzgerald in the morning. Tonight he had to make sure Gwyn was safe.

So he told the driver to take him back to Armitage House. Even if Joshua knew which opera Gwyn and the rest had been planning to attend and whether they'd even decided to go, he couldn't head there in his present attire.

On the way, he very carefully restored each pistol to its uncocked position. He started to return them to his greatcoat pockets, but it occurred to him that if there were any chance he might encounter Malet at the house, he should be prepared for it.

So he put only one pistol into his greatcoat pocket. He had the perfect hiding place for the other. He pulled out the cloth he generally used to stuff the boot of his bad leg so he could wear it. Plenty of room in there without the fabric, sadly enough. Good to know that he could keep items in there if he needed to.

As he slid the pistol inside his boot, a hollow fear built in the pit of his stomach. What if Gwyn and the others *hadn't* gone to the opera or had already returned? The more he thought about Malet possibly hurting Gwyn, the more likely it seemed. Bloody hell, he shouldn't have lingered so long looking for the bastard.

Because if he lost Gwyn . . .

He couldn't lose her, simple as that. He had to make things right between them. If she didn't want to marry him, so be it, but he had to *try*. The idea of not having her in his life was . . . was . . .

Unthinkable. He had to do whatever he could to keep her in it.

# Chapter Twenty-One

Joshua waited impatiently for the hackney to reach Armitage House. After it arrived, he practically threw money at the driver before climbing the steps as quickly as any man with a cane and a bad leg could.

He had just made it inside and was trying to keep the footman from taking his greatcoat, which still had his pistol in it, when Gwyn came running down the stairs, her expression anxious. "Where the devil have you been? And why are you dressed like that?"

"I'll tell you later. But first, has Malet been here?"

"Malet! Why would he be here?"

She looked genuinely confused. Thank God she was safe. For the moment anyway. Even now Malet might be making his way here.

Joshua forced a calm into his voice that he didn't feel. "I thought you were at the opera."

"Lady Hornsby and I waited for you to accompany us there, and when time went on and you didn't show up, we realized you weren't going to. She went home. Even Mama gave up and retired for the night. But *I* have been waiting for you ever since, sure that something awful had happened to you!"

She was worried about *him*? That was . . . faintly amusing. And gratifying, especially because she was dressed like a queen in the new opera gown she'd spoken of earlier. The quintessential white gown was cut quite low for evening, and only a bit of blue lace kept it from being outrageous.

Damnation. It showed far more of her breasts than anything should. Not that he wasn't enjoying it. "Forgive me. I didn't mean to worry you. I thought Lady Hornsby wasn't going to the opera, so Grey and Beatrice were taking you."

Reminding him a bit of his sister, she fussed over him and tried to take off his coat. "Just as you told me and Mama earlier, Beatrice doesn't like the opera and Grey wasn't going without her. But Lady Hornsby was quite keen on attending. Apparently, Mama was wrong about *that*. Lady Hornsby was very disgruntled when you didn't show up."

He brushed Gwyn's hands away and removed his coat himself, then draped it over his arm. "And you? Were *you* eager to go?"

"That hardly matters now."

"It matters to *me*. To be honest, I don't care how Lady Hornsby felt about it. But I would sincerely regret having kept you from any activity you enjoyed."

That seemed to catch her by surprise. Damn, how was it that he always shocked her when he complimented her? Was he really so bad at showing the woman how he felt?

Apparently so.

Eager now to get her alone, he took off his hat unthinkingly and handed it to the footman.

Gwyn gave a little cry. "Something awful *did* happen to you!" She reached up to touch the cut on his forehead, which had already scabbed over. "Does it hurt?"

"No. In truth, I forgot all about it." Though his pulse was quickening at just the thought of her concern for him.

With an eye at the footman, she whispered, "Did Lionel do this?"

"In a manner of speaking."

Her eyes widened. "Well, I should put some salve on it to make it heal faster. Give your coat to John and come with me to the kitchen."

"I'd rather hold on to my coat, actually."

"Don't be silly," she said, and grabbed it from his arm. "My word, it's heavy!"

He took it back from her and urged her down the hall, away from the prying eyes of the footman.

"Good Lord, what is in your pockets?" she asked.

"A pistol, for one thing." When she looked startled, he added, "As I said, a long story. But first, let's go look for your salve."

Not in the kitchen, however. He wanted privacy, and he wouldn't find it there. Fortunately, on the way, they passed the back parlor, which would do nicely. After glancing back to make sure the footman couldn't see them, he murmured, "In here," and guided her inside.

The minute they went through the door, Joshua closed and locked it.

"You can't do that!" she cried. "Not if you wish to preserve my reputation."

"First of all, no one knows we're in here." He laid his coat over the nearest chair. "And second, because I am still hoping you will marry me, I doubt anyone will protest for long. Except perhaps your twin."

"Thorn! What's he got to do with it?"

"As far as I'm concerned? Nothing." Taking her by surprise, he backed her against the door. Then he steadied himself against it with his forearm and kissed her. Hard. Thoroughly. Had it really only been half a day since he'd seen her?

It felt like forever.

It must have felt like it to her, too, because she threw her arms about his neck and kissed him back rather enthusiastically. She let him plunder her mouth for several wonderful moments.

Until she came to her senses and pushed at him. He drew back just enough to stare at her. "What?"

"I'm supposed to be getting you salve."

"I don't need it." He kissed her forehead, her temple, her cheek. "What I need is *you*."

She cupped his head in her hands, forcing him back. He was shocked to see tears welling in her eyes.

"I need you, too. I need you not to be running around London after that arse Lionel. I need you not to get yourself killed for no reason other than male pride."

"It's not what you think. Trust me, I wasn't in any real danger tonight. I had everything under control." Mostly.

Of course, being Gwyn, she fixed on the wrong part. "You weren't in 'real danger tonight'? I didn't know you were going to be in any danger at all! And you got that wound on your head *somehow*."

"I did. You're right." Shoving away from the door, he took his cane in one hand and her hand in the other and led her over to the settee.

He should probably tell her *something*. Fitzgerald hadn't forbidden it, although Joshua would imagine the man didn't wish him to reveal all to her either. But if they were to marry, she had a right to know what her husband had decided to do with his future. *Their* future.

She sat down warily. "Does this have to do with the pistol in your coat?"

"It does." He rubbed his chin, trying to figure out how much to say. "You see, I've been offered a post with the War Office that doesn't involve going back into battle."

"That's wonderful!" she exclaimed. "I mean, it is, isn't it?"

"It is."

"But how . . . when . . ."

That part was tricky. "I suppose I should have said something to you before, but I didn't come to London just to be your bodyguard." He told her what his plans had been, and how the War Secretary had thwarted them.

To his surprise, she was irate on his behalf. "Not that I would wish you to return to the war, but he was wrong about your capabilities. You are as capable as any man I know, if not more so."

He smiled. When was the last time any woman had championed him, *believed* in him, other than his sister? "As it happens, the undersecretary agrees with you. Mr. Fitzgerald has offered me a position that . . . well . . . makes more use of my brain than my brawn."

She turned skeptical. "Then how did you get hurt?"

"It turned out that I needed to use my brawn to get out of a situation that my brain got me into." He began pacing. "In any case, this post means I'd be living in London most of the time from now on. How would you feel about that? If we married, I mean."

"I would love it. Most of my family is here, and eventually Mama might prefer to be here. Besides which, I grew up in Berlin. I'm more comfortable in cities than in the country." She cocked her head. "But wouldn't London be difficult for you, with all the noise and bustle?"

"Believe it or not, no." He strove to figure out how to put everything into words. "It's odd, really. I always thought that because loud noises sparked my . . . memories of the war, I should live somewhere quiet and secluded, where I wasn't likely to encounter them."

"Like Sanforth."

"Exactly." He faced her. "But I think I was wrong. The

constant noise of London actually *masks* the kind of sounds to which I generally react."

She smiled. "Like this afternoon, when that hammering made you jump, but not react nearly as dramatically as in Cambridge."

"Today was a different matter entirely. That was all you, dearling. You . . . calmed me somehow."

"Yes, but I assume your new post means I can't always be with you," she said anxiously.

"That's true. But I am calmer just knowing you are there for me at the end of the day. And I'm hopeful that . . . my re-actions will lessen now that I'm to live somewhere, well, for lack of a better word, noisy. All I can do is try."

"Right." She gazed down at her hands. "So, um, this post had something to do with why you were hurt tonight?"

"Yes."

"Then why did you say it involved Lionel?"

"Because it did. It does." He dragged in a heavy breath. "He's up to more mischief than anyone realized, though my employer recognized it and sent me . . . after him. But I can't tell you more than that."

Lifting her gaze to him, she sighed. "So this post will re-quire a great deal of secrecy, I assume."

"I'm afraid so. Just know that it allows me to work on behalf of my country. I'll tell you however much the War Office allows, but I may not always be able to reveal the whole matter. You won't be able to let anyone know for whom I work. I probably shouldn't even be telling *you*, but I figure if any woman can hold her own secrets for as many years as you have, you won't have any trouble keeping mine."

He sat down next to her on the settee. "The good part of this, however, is that the post will put me back on full pay and enable me—*us*—to live more comfortably than we might on the Armitage estate."

She eyed him askance. "I should hope that my *dowry* will enable us to live comfortably." When he narrowed his gaze on her, she added hastily, "Assuming that we *do* end up married, which is by no means certain."

"Right." But he took heart in the fact that she was talking about it as if it might happen. "Whatever you wish to do with your dowry is fine with me. You can dictate what you want for the settlement. If you'd prefer to keep your money and use it for our children—"

"And if we don't have children?" she whispered.

"Then you can spend it however you please."

She nodded, her mind clearly wandering elsewhere. After a moment, she noticed he was watching her closely, and she forced a smile. "So . . . exactly how dangerous will this post be?"

"Honestly, I'm not sure yet." He took her hand in his. "But I can almost certainly say it was nothing to what I went through on the battlefield."

"How would I know?" she said.

In that moment, he realized he would never have her in his life if he didn't *let* her into his life. He might not be able to tell her about the spying, but there were things she wanted to know that he *could* reveal.

"You *wouldn't* know. Which is why I'm going to tell you how I was wounded in the marines. And then *show* you how I was wounded in the marines. If you think you can stomach it."

She looked startled, then earnest. "I can, I swear." She brought his hand up to her lips and kissed it. "You can trust me."

When she'd said that earlier, he'd had trouble believing her. But now he stared at her, his heart in his throat. "I know."

# Chapter Twenty-Two

Did he truly? Because if he did know, then she had to be equally honest with him. Trust *him*. And that frightened the very devil out of her.

He sat down beside her and thrust his bad leg out in front of him. "I was wounded aboard the *Amphion* during the Battle of Cape Santa Maria in October 1804."

She shifted a bit so she could look at his face. "I don't know that battle."

"Probably because it wasn't much of one. Spain hadn't yet declared war on Great Britain."

"Oh, wait, I *do* remember! That was the battle where three Spanish treasure ships were captured and brought back to England before they could reach France. And *then* Spain declared war on us."

"Exactly."

She stared at him. "But I didn't think anyone on our side was wounded in that battle."

"There weren't many—four on the *Lively*, though they had two deaths as well. And only three of us wounded on the *Amphion*." His jaw flexed. "My wounds were the worst."

"Tell me," she said as she took his hand and laid it in her lap.

He looked at her with a tortured gaze. "I've never told

anyone what happened, you know. Not even Beatrice, and she was the one who fought to keep me from dying."

"You can trust me," she said again. It was the only thing she could think of to say. It was true, but she wished there was a way to ease his pain. "But if it hurts too much to talk about it—"

"No. I want to tell you. I *need* to tell you. You see, I was barely conscious for the first year after I was wounded, living in a fog of laudanum. By the time I *could* tell anyone, I didn't want to." He shot her a faint smile. "But I think I must now. How else am I to stop reliving it?"

Her throat was raw with unshed tears. "I'm not sure you will ever stop reliving it," she said. "It's part of who you are. But perhaps sharing the burden will make it a little lighter? That's what I hope anyway."

He reached up to cup her cheek. "Always the optimist, eh?"

"For other people, yes. For myself, not as much as I'd like." She squeezed his hand. "But I plan to be an optimist for you."

"Good. Beatrice could use someone to take over her job. Although, to be honest, I wasn't much of a sunny-natured fellow even before I was wounded."

"Really?" she said sarcastically. "What a shock."

He smiled and chucked her under the chin. "You always make me laugh."

"I try." She shot him an arch smile. "Though I'm still waiting for you to tell me how you were wounded."

He nodded. "It's not a very interesting story, to be honest. Without going into too much detail about strategies and such, our four navy ships waylaid four Spanish ships. One of them, the *Mercedes,* fired broadside at my ship, the *Amphion.* We returned fire. Somehow we hit the magazine of the

*Mercedes,* which exploded while we were very close to the ship. I was up on the forecastle, and near enough that the lower right side of my body was raked by the explosion. It seared my right thigh, and severed some muscles of my right calf."

His eyes grew haunted. "It wasn't just that either. For the next hour it was hell on earth around us. I had seen some pretty awful sights during my years in battle, but mostly the results of hand-to-hand combat or cannon. This was the worst. In the explosion of the *Mercedes,* all but forty of its two-hundred-and-eighty crewmen died—two-hundred-and-forty men screaming, drowning, parts of bodies raining down—"

He caught himself. "Sorry. You don't need to hear all the grisly details. Suffice it to say, the battle was over very quickly. The *Mercedes* sank. Two of the other ships surrendered. The last ship tried to escape but was captured."

"And I imagine you weren't conscious for most of it."

"Actually, I was in a great deal of pain for most of it, but I was lucky in that I was treated more swiftly than most because of my rank." He took her hand. "I narrowly escaped having my leg amputated. Fortunately, our ship's surgeon didn't believe amputation should be a first resort."

"Is that unusual?"

"Sadly, yes. Many a sailor has found himself under the saw, whether he wished it or not." He squeezed her hand so hard that she thought he might break it, but she didn't let on.

He released her hand. "I was fairly delirious from the pain, but I was still capable of protesting such an action. And thanks to the surgeon's feelings on the subject, I was spared."

"Show me," she said gently. "You told me that I wasn't hurting you this afternoon, but I can't really believe that without seeing the damage." When his face clouded over, she added hastily, "But only if you wish."

"I do wish."

As he removed his Hessians, she rose to light a candle from the coals in the fireplace, then went around the room, lighting candles so she could see. Meanwhile, he stood to dispense with his trousers and drawers. His shirt was long enough to cover his privates, and she noticed as she went back to sit on the settee that he'd kept on his stockings.

But there was still plenty to see.

She trailed her fingers over a long swath of his thigh where it looked as if his skin had been mauled and later healed into a mass of raised flesh. When she ran her fingers lightly over it, he sucked in a breath.

"I warned you," he said in a tense voice. His apprehensive expression fairly broke her heart.

"Yes, you did," she said, purposely adopting a matter-of-fact tone.

Even though she ached inside for what he must have suffered, she realized now that she had to hide it. When she had unwittingly let her pity show this afternoon, he hadn't handled that well. Perhaps, in time, he wouldn't mind so much, but for now she had to be careful.

She returned her attention to his thigh. "I assume that this is the part that was burned?"

"Yes."

She couldn't look at him, couldn't let him see how deeply his wounds affected her. "It seems pretty bad. Does it still hurt?"

"No," he said in a clipped voice.

Reaching for the garter on his injured leg, she glanced up at him. "May I?"

He nodded tightly. As she untied it and drew down his stocking, he talked, as if to keep his mind off what she was doing. "Aside from the woman I told you about, the one who recoiled when she saw this, the only people who have seen my wounds are Beatrice and a handful of doctors."

She gazed at the withered leg as she unveiled it, realizing that he wasn't putting his weight on it, which was why he could stand there without needing his cane. "Would you rather sit?"

"Yes, thank you." He sat down and lifted his bad leg so she could pull off the stocking.

What she saw was truly sobering. There were long dents in the skin where the muscle had wasted away, scars upon scars, and burned flesh that had healed, leaving shiny, mis-shapen areas.

"How did you survive this?" she said, choking back tears. "You must be very strong-willed. Otherwise, you would have died in the hospital."

"I daresay I survived because I was only in a hospital for a week. When our ship docked in Gosport, a letter was sent back to Armitage Hall about my injuries, and Beatrice and MacTilly, our Master of Hounds, showed up to transport me home. Beatrice said there was no way in hell she was leaving me in a hospital. And in truth, the doctors had already done everything they could do for me anyway."

"I've always liked your sister." Gwyn smiled at him. "And now I like her even more."

"She was fearless. She got me through infections and fever and God knows what else. I was only half-conscious for most of the year I was in her care, so I don't remember much. Between the laudanum and the whisky she poured into—and onto—me, she did whatever she had to do with me. And whatever she did worked. Though it's a miracle I didn't develop a craving for opium when it was all past me."

"Why didn't you?"

"I wasn't about to let her sacrifice go for naught. Not that she would have let me. There was no fighting her. She was determined to see me survive, and in the best possible situation she could manage."

Gwyn struggled to contain her tears. "Then I owe her a debt of gratitude."

"So do I," he said hoarsely. "Because without her, I wouldn't have lived to meet you."

He leaned over to kiss her, so sweetly that it nearly broke her heart all over again. Then he drew back to pin her with a yearning look. "Gwyn, I know I'm not what you probably want, and I know that you would probably prefer a husband who lacks my difficulties, but . . ." He took a steadying breath. "Will you marry me? Take me as your husband with all my flaws? Have my children?"

Those last words were a sword cutting through all her happiness. "The problem is, well . . . I'm not sure I can *have* children."

She wasn't entirely surprised when he eyed her with astonishment. "Why in God's name would you think that?"

Oh, Lord, this was so hard. It had been easier telling Beatrice. "Because in addition to seducing me years ago, Lionel also got me with child."

"You bore that arse a child?" Joshua said in a hollow voice.

Her stomach roiled at the thought of telling him all this. But she had to. If he truly wanted to marry her, he needed to know. "I didn't *bear* the child. I lost it when I was four months along. And the midwife who secretly cared for me afterward said she didn't think I'd be able to have any more." She cast him a wan smile. "That's the other reason I haven't married. Because every man wants a son to carry on his name. And I don't know if I can provide one."

A muscle worked in his jaw. "I don't understand. Why on earth would you think you can't have a son?"

"Not just a son. Any child." With a sigh, she began to tell him everything she'd told Beatrice. He asked questions and made comments that showed he was thoroughly unfamiliar with the inner workings of women.

"So," he said, "if I'm understanding you correctly, you think you can't have children because of what one midwife said about your womb."

"And because I lost my first child. My *only* child so far."

"That's not saying much, because you've only shared a man's bed twice. And it's too early to know about that second time." He lifted a brow. "I hear that the fellow who bedded you has his own problems."

"Joshua, do be serious," she chided him.

"I'm trying, honestly. But—" He scrubbed his face with one hand. "You said that your maid didn't agree with her friend's assessment? That means there's a good chance that the midwife is wrong."

"And an equally good chance that she's right."

"True. Personally, I agree with my sister. Before you decide what the future might hold in that regard, you should talk to your mother. She has a wealth of experience in having children."

"Yes, but then I'd have to tell her that I gave my innocence to Lionel. That isn't something I relish revealing."

He rubbed his chin. "All right. Then tell her you're asking for a friend. Perhaps Beatrice. Say that you want to know if one miscarriage is a sign that there will be more."

"Beatrice might not appreciate my dragging her into it."

"Very well," he said, obviously getting more annoyed by the moment. "Then perhaps you could see another doctor, who could examine you to determine if the midwife was correct. Or perhaps you could see another midwife."

It was just as she'd feared—learning of her inability to have his child was changing everything. "Or perhaps you

will simply have to accept that I might never have children."
When he said nothing, she said, "It's not my fault, you know.
It's just the way my body is made."

"Of course. I wouldn't blame you for that. It's just that—"

"You were hoping for children."

His gaze swung to her. "I was hoping for children with
*you.*" He took her hands in his. "And I'm not entirely convinced it's impossible."

"I didn't say it was." She arched one brow. "But I could
find myself with child, endure weeks of anticipation, then
*still* lose the babe."

She looked away, not wanting him to see how much the
memory of her first loss still hurt, even though it wasn't
convenient, even though it had proved providential in many
respects. "Given what I went through the first time, I'm not
sure I want to go through it again."

"*That* is the real reason you haven't married before now,
isn't it?"

She slumped her shoulders. "Yes. Losing a babe . . . you
can't know how difficult it is. It was hard enough when I
wasn't certain what had happened to the baby's father and
whether I would ever see him again." Her gaze met his. "But
to have it happen to a child I *wanted*—"

"If you prefer not to have children, that's fine." He eyed
her closely and dragged in a rough breath. "We won't have
them. We'll take steps not to."

She knew such steps existed, but she doubted any of them
were particularly enjoyed by men. "You don't mean that."

"I do. I'll endure anything if it means having you in my
life." He caught her by the chin. "Because you are the most
important part of this equation. You and me. Us."

He brushed a kiss to her lips. "Besides, there are other
possibilities. We could take in foundlings. There's a hospital

full of them here in London, I'm told. Surely we could find *one* in the whole place that suits us."

That made her smile, as he'd probably meant it to do.

"I don't care what we do as long as we do it together," he went on. "If you don't want to take a chance on having our own child, I am happy to oblige. And I can prove it, too."

"You can't prove how you will feel in five or ten years." She stood and hurried to the door, then unlocked it.

But before she could open it, he rose and came up behind her. She could hear the tapping of his cane and swung around to stare hopelessly at him. Catching her about the waist, he lifted her with one of his incredibly strong arms and set her on the console table beside the door. "I can prove how bereft I would be without you."

"Joshua . . ."

He kissed her with a desperation she understood only too well, because she felt it, too. She would be bereft without him, too.

And what would it hurt, one more time with him? She had already been with him today, had already risked having a child with him and losing it. What was one more time? Let him prove himself if he could.

Because after this, there might be no more.

# Chapter Twenty-Three

Joshua would *not* let her give up on them. They belonged together. She just needed to be reassured that he would take the necessary steps to keep her safe from pain. And he would.

Or he hoped he would anyway. Because just holding her again, touching her again was turning him into that ungovernable beast he kept trying to restrain. The one that desired her more than life.

Apparently, she was rather ungovernable herself, for she took his hand and pressed it to one of her breasts, urging him to fondle it.

He broke the kiss to murmur, "Steady, dearling. We have all the time in the world."

"You don't think anyone will come looking for us?" she whispered. "Because my maid is bound to wonder where I am."

"In that case . . ."

He tugged up her skirts, then caught his breath as she wriggled her bottom so she could hike them up to her waist. Just the sight of her in her silk stockings, with the satiny skin above them, made him hard as stone.

But he had to see her bountiful breasts with their nipples

he color of ripe peaches. He craved a taste of those nipples, which would tighten into pebbles the minute he caressed them with his mouth. And thankfully, her daring evening gown, which already showed half of them, made it simple to ease the bodice down to give him what he craved.

"Yes," she whispered as he bared her breasts. She shuddered when he bent to lick one nipple. "Oh, Joshua, yes. One day, sir, I swear I'm going to see both halves of you undressed. But not tonight."

"No, not tonight." He took each breast in his mouth in turn, already about to explode with need for her. Her nipples hardened, and his cock did the same. "Gwyn," he said hoarsely. "You unman me, I swear."

"I rather think I do the opposite." She parted her legs and gripped his arms to bring him in closer. "You seem quite thoroughly . . . manned."

He choked out a laugh. "And you, dearling, are a teasing wench." The kind of wench he could spend the rest of his life with.

Urging her bottom closer to the table edge, he found the pearl between her nether lips and rubbed it, determined to show her that he could hold back his own needs long enough to arouse her no matter how hard he was or how badly he wished to make love to her.

"Joshua!" she cried. "Now who's the tease?"

The words made him ache to take her. He flicked his tongue over her nipple one more time, then straightened. The pleasure was simply too much. He had to be inside her. He couldn't wait.

"Come into me, my love," she choked out as she pulled on his arms. "Please. *Please.*"

The fact that she wanted him as much as he wanted her nearly made him come right there. Which would hardly prove his point.

What point was that? Ah, yes, that he could take measures to keep her from becoming pregnant with his child. He could do it. He *could*. If that was what it took to have Gwyn as his wife, he could give up anything.

He entered her slowly, his cock stiffening even more from just the tight, hot, velvety feel of her. "I'm not hurting you, am I?"

"No. Oh . . . that feels so . . . so . . ."

"Amazing?" he said hoarsely. "Because that's how it feels for me."

"I was . . . going to say . . . incredible, but . . . amazing is good, too."

"Thank God." He drove into her up to the hilt, his body tensing with the effort of trying not to come too soon. He wanted to feel her quaking around him first, pulsing and squeezing him in her release. Only then did he mean to pull out.

Finding her pearl once more with his fingers, he pressed it and thrilled to the gasp she gave. She was his, damn it. If he had to go childless the rest of his days, he would. Because he wanted her as his wife.

As his love.

She shifted her position, and he nearly went out of his mind.

"Dearling," he murmured as he thrust deep, over and over. "My sweet dearling . . . my love . . ."

"My *love*," she echoed, her eyes dark green pools of pleasure.

The words struck him to the heart, bringing him to the edge of coming. He loved her. He did. And he would do anything for her.

Now was his chance to prove it. He shifted her until his thrusts thrummed her pleasure spot with every stroke. Over and over he drove into her until she erupted. He could see it in her eyes, feel it on his cock.

And when she cried, "Oh . . . my . . . *Lord, Joshua*!" in the throes of her release, it was enough to bring him right to the edge of coming. Swiftly, he jerked his cock out of her, which damned near killed him, and spilled his seed on her thigh.

"What . . . are you doing?" she asked hoarsely.

He held her close as he came. God, how he loved her. He loved her unabashed enjoyment of making love, her sense of humor, her loyalty to those she loved. He could do this. He must. Because losing her over something like her ability to have children was intolerable.

Kissing her hair, her forehead, her temple, he waited for them both to stop quaking. She was his now. He would make sure of it.

"Joshua." She drew back to gaze up at him. "Why did you—"

"So I could prove I was willing to keep from getting you with child. What I just did is how I can do it."

She gaped at him. "But . . . but you didn't—"

"Oh, trust me, I did. Just not inside you."

She swallowed. "And that doesn't . . . frustrate you?"

"A little." He kissed the tip of her pretty nose. "But it's worth it to have you. Gwyn, I love you. I want you to be my wife. And if that is what's required, I will do it."

"Do you really mean that?"

"I do. I can't go on without you, dearling."

Tears welled in her eyes. "That is . . . the sweetest thing any man has ever said to me, *done* for me."

"So you'll marry me?"

"Yes," she whispered and kissed him soundly. "Yes."

"Good," he rasped. "Because I think I hear someone in the hall, so it's probably time we get dressed."

"Joshua!" she cried. "You should have said something!"

"And ruin our special moment? Not on your life." He left her to hop over to the settee so he could sit down and drag on his stockings. After he tied the garters, he pulled on his drawers and buttoned them up, trying not to look at her as she drew up her bodice.

She hadn't yet said she loved him, but she'd called him her love, and that was good enough for now. Especially because she'd agreed to marry him.

He looked over to find her slipping off the console table and fluffing out her skirts. "Damn, woman," he murmured. "You barely look disheveled."

"Yes, but underneath, I'm a ruin of dishevelment."

"Don't start talking like that," he grumbled. "I still have to don my trousers, not to mention my boots."

"Can I help?" she asked, coyly sashaying toward him.

"No." He drew on his trousers, then buttoned them. "Just the sight of you swinging your hips will soon have me rousing again."

"What a pity we can't do anything about that," she said flirtatiously and a bit too loudly.

This time he distinctly heard footsteps in the hall. He could tell she'd heard them, too, for her eyes widened. Hastily, he pulled on one boot as the footsteps paused and came back toward the door. It was probably just her maid, but he didn't like being unprepared.

Damnation. He took the pistol out of his other boot, which made her gasp. Then he slid it into the waistband of his trousers in back. Holding a finger to his lips, he gestured to her to get his cane for him where he'd left it by the console table. Nodding, she tiptoed toward it.

She'd just got it in her hand when the door swung open. Joshua had forgotten she had unlocked the door.

A man appeared in the doorway, his face in shadow because of the candles in the sconce on the wall behind him.

"Lionel?" Gwyn said.

Before Joshua could even rise, Malet grabbed her and held a blade to her neck. "Ah, ah, Major. Don't even attempt to come at me or she dies. I can slice her from ear to ear before you can limp one step forward."

Joshua's heart dropped into his stomach. This was his worst nightmare come to life. He dared not reach for his pistol because Malet would see that. And he had no other weapon ready to hand, nothing with which to thwart Malet. His gaze shot to Gwyn, who looked pale as death in the candlelight.

But she made sure that he noticed that his cane was in her right hand, though she'd moved it into the folds of her skirts. At least *she'd* have something to defend herself. Although right now that was little consolation. Because there might be more adversaries. The Frenchman might have come here, too. Joshua had to know what he was up against before he acted.

"You know damned well I won't let you leave this house with her," Joshua said, fighting to keep his terror from bleeding into his voice. "I don't even know how you got past the footman."

"I didn't have to. I came in through the kitchen door downstairs and slipped up here. Your footman was half-asleep when I got him by the throat and threatened to kill him if he didn't tell me where you were. He said you were in the kitchen, but I knew you weren't."

"You'd better not have hurt John!" Gwyn cried. "He's done nothing to you!"

"He's tied and gagged in a closet, my dear girl," Malet said. "I don't want to hurt anyone. As long as I get what I want, we'll all end up happily."

Somehow Joshua doubted that, but he had to keep Malet talking, had to distract him until he could get to his weapon. At least now he knew that Malet had come here alone.

Joshua pressed on the arm of the settee so he could rise. "What do you want?"

Malet's gaze narrowed on him. "Where's your cane?"

"Somewhere under the settee." He made as if he were going to bend over. "But if you'll give me a minute—"

"Stop! I'm not fool enough to let you gain access to your favorite weapon."

Joshua straightened, then shrugged. "I don't know about favorite. But it would do in a pinch."

Malet scowled at him. "Which is why I'm not about to let you hunt for the damned thing." He scoured the room. "Where did you put the Frenchman's purse?"

"It's still in my coat pocket." Joshua pointed to where his greatcoat lay over the chair. "You're welcome to look for it."

He had to get Malet away from Gwyn somehow.

"You seem to think I'm stupid," Malet growled. "You want me to let her go so I can look for the purse while you get hold of your cane and stab me with it."

Joshua shrugged. "It was worth a try."

"Fortunately, I am too clever for you." He nodded at Joshua's greatcoat. "Get the purse out of there and throw it to me. Come to think of it, while you're at it, throw me the papers I sold the Frenchman. I daresay he'll pay me for them again."

"Lionel!" Gwyn exclaimed. "Are you . . . are you spying for the French?"

"This doesn't concern you, Gwyn. It's between me and your lame champion there."

Joshua fought his urge to react in anger. He dared not risk Gwyn. "Speaking of lameness, how am I to walk without my cane?"

"I don't care. I just want the money."

"Very well." Joshua hopped toward his coat.

"Wait!" Malet cried. "You have your pistols in there, too, don't you? No wonder you were so amenable."

"Lionel, how could you even *consider* hurting me?" Gwyn wheedled. "Especially after all we meant to each other."

"Shut up, Gwyn! I need to think."

Gwyn cast Joshua a meaningful look and closed her fingers around the head of his cane. Damnation, she intended to try something. He'd better be ready.

Malet's knife hand wavered at her neck. "Here's what you're going to do, Major. You're going to grab your greatcoat by the collar and toss it over here so that it lands at my feet, do you hear?"

"There are two loaded pistols in the pockets of that greatcoat," Joshua lied calmly. "I daresay neither of us wants to risk them going off."

The bastard cast him a truly evil smile. "Then you'll just have to throw it carefully, won't you?"

"Fine," Joshua said in an annoyed tone that he hoped sounded convincing, given the fear he felt for Gwyn.

He hopped toward the chair where his greatcoat was draped, but he made sure to angle himself so that he could lean against the table beside the chair for support. Then he grabbed his greatcoat with his left hand and tossed it into the air.

While Malet's attention was on the greatcoat, Joshua thrust his right hand beneath his frock coat and drew his pistol. As the coat landed, Gwyn pushed the button to release the sword from Joshua's cane and jammed it down as hard as she could into Malet's calf.

The man howled and moved the knife from her neck for a fraction of a second, just long enough for her to duck under Malet's arm and for Joshua to fire.

And Malet crumpled.

# Chapter Twenty-Four

Gwyn looked down at Lionel and realized he wasn't moving. Besides which, there was an awful lot of blood on his waistcoat and the floor. Joshua pushed Lionel's knife away with the toe of his boot just in case.

"Do you think he's dead?" she asked Joshua.

"Probably. I aimed to kill." Joshua shoved his spent pistol into the fall of his trousers, then stepped forward to the console table. He held on to it so he could bend down and check Lionel's neck. "I can safely say he is dead."

"Thank heaven," she murmured, even as a chill seeped through her bones. She and Joshua had come so close to death themselves.

Joshua lifted a brow. "That's a bit bloodthirsty, don't you think?"

"I do not." She thrust out her chin. "I was so afraid he might get to one of those pistols in your greatcoat and shoot you!"

"You do know how to prick a man's pride," he said dryly as he pulled her against him.

That was when she realized what she'd said. "I didn't mean it that way. I merely feared you would be so worried for *me* that you would do something reckless."

"You mean, like stab a fellow in the leg while he's holding a knife to your throat?"

"Yes, I suppose that *was* reckless. I should have left the matter in your clearly capable hands." She gazed up into his face. "But I had to do *something*. I wasn't going to let Lionel get away with whatever he planned to do."

"You nearly gave me heart failure," he said hoarsely. "If he had cut your throat—"

The sound of people running around upstairs brought them both to their senses. Obviously, everyone in the house had heard the gunshot. She and Joshua would have to make explanations.

He ushered her past Lionel's body and into the hall just as her mother—in nightdress, wrapper, and mobcap—rounded the staircase baluster and saw them together.

"What happened?" Mama cried.

Sheridan came up behind her, wearing a dressing gown and slippers. "We heard a shot."

Then Heywood appeared. "A gunshot," Heywood said, as if that needed clarification. "Loud enough to wake me on the third floor, though Cass miraculously slept right through it."

"Yes, it was indeed a gunshot." Joshua squeezed Gwyn's waist as if to caution silence. "Malet got into the house somehow and tried to kidnap Gwyn at knifepoint. I was forced to shoot him."

"Then thank goodness you were here!" Mama said. "Shall I fetch a doctor for him?"

"There's no reason," Gwyn said. "Mr. Malet is dead." And with him died her fear of what he might say about her to the world, what scandal he might foment.

It sank in that she no longer had to worry. She'd never realized until just that moment how much her past with Malet had dogged her throughout her life. And now, what a weight his death had taken off her shoulders!

By that point, half a dozen servants were amassing behind Mama and Sheridan, and they began to murmur among themselves.

Immediately, Joshua turned into Major Wolfe and took charge of the situation, pointing to individual servants as he barked orders. "You there, let John out of the coat closet where Mr. Malet locked him, and get him out of his bindings. You there, find a sheet or something else with which to cover Mr. Malet's body. And you there, come with me. I need you to carry a message to Lucius Fitzgerald, undersecretary to the War Secretary."

Oh, right. Joshua's new secret employer.

Sheridan lifted a brow at Joshua's commanding tone. "What does the undersecretary to the War Office have to do with Malet?"

Blast. What could Joshua say to *that*?

"Malet was cashiered, yet he was still using his rank as if he hadn't been," Joshua said smoothly. "The undersecretary mentioned the problem to me when I was at the War Office asking about my half-pay. I told Fitzgerald that if I encountered the man, I'd be sure to let the War Office know. I encountered him. He tried to abduct Gwyn. I shot him. Now I am letting the War Office know."

Although Heywood, himself a retired officer, looked a bit skeptical, Sheridan seemed to accept Joshua's story, for he nodded to the servants to obey Joshua's orders.

"We should also send for Thorn," Heywood said. "He'll want to be included in this, because it involves Gwyn."

"Of course," Joshua said. "Feel free to handle that." He turned to Mama. "Aunt Lydia, why don't you call for tea to be served in the drawing room? I imagine Gwyn could use a cup."

"Indeed," Mama said, then took Gwyn by the arm to draw her off.

Normally, Gwyn would want to be in the midst of all the excitement, but this had been a very long day, and right now she would relish some quiet moments alone with Mama. She knew it was probably neither the time nor the place for her to talk to Mama about her own experiences giving birth, but ever since Beatrice and Joshua had planted doubts in her own head about her miscarriage, she'd been burning to question Mama. She just had to find a way to broach the subject.

As soon as they were settled in the drawing room with the door closed and their pot of tea steeping, Mama sat Gwyn down on the sofa next to her. "Are you all right, my dear? It cannot be easy to see a man shot dead before your very eyes."

It had been much easier than watching Joshua shot dead would have been, so she couldn't find it in her heart to mourn Lionel.

"I'm fine, Mama. Or I will be soon enough. Mr. Malet proved to be an awful fellow in more ways than you can possibly imagine. Trust me when I say that Joshua had no choice but to shoot him."

"I've no doubt of that. My nephew isn't reckless in the least. But you're sure you weren't harmed?"

"I wasn't harmed, Mama." She patted her mother's hand. "But I do need to talk to you about something important."

Her mother paled. "I swear, Gwyn, I didn't speak a word to Sheridan. He must have hoped for the same thing himself because *he* was the one who mentioned it to *me*."

"What are you talking about?"

Mama blinked. "Oh. What you wanted to discuss wasn't the possibility of you and Joshua marrying?"

"Wait—Sheridan is hoping I'll marry Joshua?"

"I told him not to even mention it to you because you get very annoyed by the subject, but he insisted—"

"This isn't about me and Joshua!" She paused a moment. "Well, we *are* getting married, but—"

"I *knew* it!" Mama seized her hands. "I am *so* happy!"

"Mama! I need you to pay attention for a moment. I have a question that I promised a friend I'd ask you, and it's been weighing heavily on me."

Her mother narrowed her gaze suspiciously. "Which friend?"

"It doesn't matter. I promised not to reveal her name."

"All right," Mama said in a wary voice. "What's the question?"

"Did you ever lose a baby?"

"What do you mean? While I was taking a walk with one in the park or something?"

Gwyn sighed. "No. I mean, have a miscarriage."

"Oh." Her mother pondered that a moment, then eyed Gwyn warily. "You and Joshua haven't—"

"Mama!" she said with all the outrage she could muster, knowing that she would have a hard time lying to her mother.

"Wait a minute—did Bea lose Grey's child?" her mother asked, heartbreak in her voice.

"No, Mama," Gwyn said hastily.

"Oh, I do hope it's not Cass and Heywood," Mama said worriedly.

"They've only been married a month," Gwyn pointed out. "There hasn't been enough time for that."

Her mother arched one brow. "Hasn't there? They got engaged at Christmas, and it's Easter. Besides, don't you think it odd that she slept through the gunshot that woke the rest of us?"

"I'm not speaking of anyone in the family, Mama." This was going to take all night. "It's just a married friend who had a miscarriage and is very concerned she won't ever be able to bear a child. *Please* answer the question, so I'll know what to tell her."

"Fine. I did lose one babe." She got a faraway look in her eyes. "I had just found out I was enceinte, and I was so excited because it was with your father. Of my three husbands, he was the only one I truly loved, you know."

"I do," Gwyn said, emotion clogging her throat.

Thorn and Gwyn had learned long ago that the Duke of Thornstock had been the love of their mother's life. Grey's father had essentially bought their mother, and the marriage between the eventual Duke of Armitage and Mama had been one between friends.

"Not that I didn't enjoy my marriage to Sheridan and Heywood's father," Mama continued, "but it wasn't the same. Anyway, that's why the loss of our baby hit me so hard."

How had Gwyn never known about her mother's miscarriage? The very idea of it gave her hope. "You mean, Thorn and I might have had an older brother or sister?"

Her mother nodded sadly. "Your father and I were devastated when I lost the babe. And when your father died before you and Thorn were even born, I thought I would never recover." She wiped away a tear, then broke into a smile. "But after your births, when I was still grieving the loss of your father, a good friend pointed out that I'd been given two children to make up for my having lost the one before, and I thought of it that way forever after."

"That was a very good friend, indeed." She patted Mama's hand, wondering how to frame her question without rousing her mother's suspicions. "So . . . it's possible to lose a child, but then have another one be born with no issues?"

"Possible? It happens more often than that. I've had a few friends who miscarried two or three times and yet have had children born fine, too. Nothing is ever certain when you're dealing with Mother Nature."

"Apparently not," Gwyn said, fighting to keep her elation in check.

All these years, she'd lived in fear. Granted, she might still be unable to have a child, but at least she now knew it was possible. And that was good enough for her. In such a case, she was willing to risk it.

"So," her mother said, "about this secret married friend of yours—"

The door burst open and Thorn ran in, then rushed to Gwyn's side. "Are you all right? Did that bastard hurt you?"

"No," she said, touched by his concern. "I'm fine. Joshua killed him."

Thorn ran his fingers through his hair. "I can't believe Malet broke in here. I never expected that."

"Nor did I." She gazed at her mother. "Mama, would you mind terribly if Thorn and I had a moment alone?"

"Of course not, my dear." She squeezed Gwyn's hand. "We'll talk later."

The meaningful glance her mother gave her told Gwyn that eventually Mama would want to know everything. And perhaps it was time that Gwyn told her. Perhaps it was time Gwyn told Thorn the truth, too.

As soon as Mama was through the door, Gwyn said, "Fortunately, Joshua was prepared for such a contingency. He handled everything brilliantly."

"And you thought you didn't need a bodyguard." Thorn crossed his arms over his chest. "I was right. Ha!"

"Yes, you were," Gwyn said. "About *that* anyway."

Thorn eyed her askance. "What are you saying?"

"Ten years ago, when you paid Malet to leave Berlin without me, what prompted that action? Did he do something to convince you that it was necessary?"

His gaze grew shuttered as he dropped onto the sofa next

to her. "That was a long time ago, *Liebchen*. And aren't you glad I intervened? He was obviously an arse."

"He was, yes. But I still want an answer to my question. What did Lionel do to alert you to his bad character? Or did you merely act as your usual arrogant self?"

Thorn sighed. "A friend of mine warned me that his cousin had been seduced by Malet. He ruined her utterly, then refused to marry her. Unlike you, she had no dowry, so she was of no use to Malet except as a bed partner." He fixed her with an intent look. "From what I understand, that sort of behavior is exactly what got him cashiered years later."

That wouldn't surprise her. "So why didn't you tell me of your reasoning? If you had laid out everything he'd done wrong, I might have listened and cut my ties to him. Instead, you assumed I was too stupid to recognize that your logic was sound."

Pure shock showed in Thorn's face. "I never for one moment considered you stupid. How could you even think that?"

"Because you acted without consulting me. And that implies that you didn't trust me to be as rational and logical as you."

"You were in love. Even I know that no one is rational and logical about that. I expected you to behave like anyone else in that situation." He released a frustrated breath. "And was what I did so very wrong, anyway? I was trying to protect you."

Now was her chance. She could tell him that Lionel had seduced her, that Thorn's actions had resulted in her spending a few terrifying months afraid of being found out by a pregnancy Thorn hadn't accounted for. That she'd spent years hating herself for letting Lionel have his way with her.

Then again, all of that had already happened by the time Thorn paid Lionel off, so the result would have been the same. Or worse. She would have been ruined, and thus would have felt forced to marry Lionel. She might have lost the child either way. And Lionel would have looted her fortune and made her miserable.

As for the blackmail, well, if not for that, she wouldn't have gained Joshua, the real love of her life.

So perhaps Mama was right. It was time to let bygones be bygones. Telling Thorn how she'd suffered would only pile guilt on his head. It certainly wouldn't change the past.

She smiled at her twin. "The only thing you did wrong was not trust me to weigh the evidence and decide for myself about Malet. But you're right. I fancied myself in love. I might have ignored it all. So I forgive you."

Thorn gazed at her. "You do? Really? You truly forgive me?"

"I do. I only wish it hadn't taken me so long."

To her surprise, he grabbed her in an intense hug that nearly knocked the breath out of her. "I missed you," he whispered in her ear. "You have no idea how much. You understand me better than anyone."

"I missed you, too," she said and realized it was true. She pushed him back so she could cup his head in her hands. "But if you ever try to pay off a suitor of mine again, I will throttle you. I mean it."

He laughed as he took her hands in his. "I doubt that situation will ever come up again. Or are you dragging your feet about accepting the major?"

She gaped at him. "How did you know about the major?"

"Did I neglect to mention that he came to see me earlier this evening? He was spitting mad about my not revealing your previous history with Malet because, and I quote, 'I could have handled my task better if I'd had that bit of crucial information.'"

"That's probably true. But that doesn't explain how you knew that the major has asked me to marry him."

He rose from the sofa. "Remember, you said you forgive me."

She scowled at him as she rose, too. "Thorn, what did you do?"

"I asked if I was going to have to buy him off, too."

"You didn't!"

Thorn's face clouded over. "Why? Do you think he would have accepted?"

"Of course not. I'm merely surprised he didn't stuff your offer down your throat."

Breaking into a grin, Thorn walked toward the door. "He did say I was welcome to try, but that I wouldn't like the outcome." He opened the door. "Now come on, Sis. Let's go see what has happened to your future husband."

"How do you know I said yes?" she asked as she walked toward him.

"Because any sister of mine can see the man is a catch."

She sniffed. "I'm glad you recognize it."

"Don't misunderstand me. I will insist upon a very stringent settlement."

"You can insist all you wish." She smiled. "He says he doesn't want my money."

That seemed to give Thorn pause. "None of it?"

"None of it," Joshua said from behind him, making Thorn jump. "Unless we have children, and then it can be held for them." Joshua looked past Thorn to where Gwyn was still smiling. "Come, dearling. There's someone who'd like to meet you."

As she joined him, he murmured, "This will probably be the only time you'll have dealings with Fitzgerald unless it's socially, so ask whatever you need to know."

"He came that quickly?" she said as they approached the back parlor.

"I mean, ask *him*, not me."

"I knew what you meant. I'm just . . . well, when you said you had a post, I didn't realize—"

"That it was so important? Neither did I. Then again, we did have a dead body in your family's parlor. And yours is a very prominent family, whose late patriarch was a noted ambassador before becoming a duke."

*Did* have a dead body?

They'd reached the parlor, where she was shocked to find that Lionel's body had disappeared. There were spots of blood on the wallpaper, but the blood that had been on the floor and the console table had already been scrubbed away.

"Mr. Fitzgerald," Joshua said, "may I present my fiancée, Lady Gwyn Drake? Gwyn, this is Mr. Lucius Fitzgerald, undersecretary to the War Office."

*Fiancée.* What a lovely word.

Mr. Fitzgerald bowed and took the hand she offered as they exchanged greetings.

"I understand that congratulations are in order," Mr. Fitzgerald said. "Have you chosen the date and place for your wedding?"

She laughed. "Major Wolfe only just proposed and I only just accepted, so no. And do forgive us for calling you to the house so late in the evening."

"I'm used to it," Mr. Fitzgerald said. "My position requires that I be available at odd hours."

Taking Joshua at his word about the questions, she asked, "And will that be true of my husband as well?"

"I'm afraid so. Is that a problem?"

"Of course not. I'm proud of whatever he does to serve his country." She closed the parlor door. "I don't suppose you can tell me what that will be."

"No," Fitzgerald said. "Nor can he."

"I see. Then I cannot say he works for the War Office?"

"No. He is merely a retired decorated officer who happens to also be the grandson of a duke and the husband of a duke's daughter. Although there will be instances when neither of those will be his role."

"So he's to be a spy," she said.

"I did not say that."

She heard Joshua softly chuckling beside her. When she glared at him, he said, "I believe you've met your match for keeping secrets and giving enigmatic answers."

"I already met my match for that. I'm about to marry him." She turned to Fitzgerald. "Then tell me this, sir. Is it dangerous work?"

"No more dangerous than going back to the war, which was your fiancé's previous suggestion."

"That's hardly a helpful answer," she grumbled. "And what happened to Mr. Malet's body? I have to tell my family *something* about your presence here."

When she caught a suspicious glint in Mr. Fitzgerald's eye, she realized he was enjoying this, curse him.

"Tell them that the War Office handles the inquests for any deaths involving our officers. Which happens to be true."

"Oh. I didn't realize that." She flashed him a coy smile. "So I should *not* tell them that Mr. Malet had sold important government papers to the French and that you're here to retrieve them?" When Mr. Fitzgerald's gaze shot to Joshua in alarm, she added, "Mr. Malet was very chatty while holding me at knifepoint."

"Ah," Mr. Fitzgerald said. "Now, Lady Gwyn, if you don't mind, I should like to leave. I still have a few more matters to attend to involving Mr. Malet's death."

"And his spying for the French."

Joshua bent to murmur, "You made your point, dearling. No need to rub it in."

Mr. Fitzgerald laughed. "I can see that you two will make a formidable couple. I'm glad you're on our side."

When he left, Joshua closed the door and took her in his arms. "I believe you have made a conquest of Fitzgerald. Not that I'm surprised. Everywhere you go, men are smitten."

"You, sir, know exactly the right thing to say to a woman."

"I've had an excellent tutor in that regard." He kissed her tenderly but briefly. "I suppose we cannot linger long in here with the door closed or your family will be up in arms. At the very least, we should go announce our engagement."

"Too late for that. I already told Mama, so I daresay the news has made it to the *Times* already."

He laughed. "And what else were you telling your mother while we were disposing of a body?"

"I asked her about miscarriages. It turns out she had one before she bore me and Thorn. She says that it's not unusual for a woman to have one occasionally and then have a perfectly healthy child."

He searched her face. "Dare I hope that means you're willing to risk having a child with me?"

"After fearing for your life—and mine—I am no longer afraid to risk anything." She headed for the door. "Indeed, I was thinking that perhaps I could help you with your work."

"No," he said firmly as he opened the door.

"You could teach me to shoot—a pistol, I mean—and I could pick off your enemies from a distance."

"God, no."

"All right. I will settle for shooting them with arrows."

"There will be no shooting of any kind. Not for you anyway."

She pretended to pout. "You suck the fun out of everything, Major."

"Fortunately, my dear, you put the fun back in." He gazed down at her with love in his eyes. "So we make the perfect couple."

"At last," she said, pressing a fond kiss to his cheek, "something we both can agree upon."

# Epilogue

*September 1809*

Joshua couldn't figure out what he and his wife were doing outside some stranger's town house. Gwyn had said she wanted to show him something, so he was glad to oblige, but before she'd brought him here he'd been half-afraid it might be a pistol-shooting match.

He suspected that her twin had been teaching her to shoot, despite Joshua's objections. Admittedly, those objections had become less strenuous the more he thought about how close Malet might have come to killing her five months before. And whenever he did voice an objection in front of her family and his, Beatrice pointed out that he was a hypocrite, because he'd taught *her* to shoot.

But this was some seemingly random town house in Mayfair.

Then it hit him. "Ah, you admire the architecture. This is to be another of *those* outings."

Gwyn planted her hands on her hips. "What do you mean, 'another of *those* outings'?"

"You know—where you take me somewhere in town so I can admire the 'bones' of the building, as you put it.

Although I confess that this one looks like all the others in this vicinity, just a touch more grand."

"Do you like it?" Gwyn asked slyly.

"We've been through this before, dearling. You know I can't tell a double-hung sash window from a single-hung one. I can look at a ship and instantly tell you what rate it is, how many guns it carries, and what poundage they are, but I daresay that's not useful to you."

"Not particularly. But I still want to know how you like the looks of this house. Speaking generally."

"It's attractive enough, I suppose. Why? What are we admiring on it this time?"

"Everything," she said enigmatically.

She walked up the front steps and knocked boldly on the entrance door.

"Gwyn!" he hissed. "What are you doing?"

"I know the owner," she said and gestured for him to follow her.

He climbed the steps with his cane in hand. "All right, but I can tell you that looking at the architecture on the inside is just as dull for me as looking at it on the outside."

Joshua was only halfway up when the door opened, and a gentleman ushered her inside, then waited for Joshua to follow.

"This way, Major," the man said.

They were expected, apparently. How else did the fellow know his rank? But when Joshua crossed the threshold, it was not to enter some stranger's house. The place was empty—no furniture, no paintings, no vases . . . nothing.

"What do you think?" Gwyn asked again.

He caught the gentleman who'd let them inside watching him expectantly.

Enough. Joshua was going to get to the bottom of this

right now. "Would you please excuse me and my wife?" he told the gentleman.

The man bowed and headed up the rather impressive staircase.

"All right, Gwyn. What is this about?"

She swallowed hard. "We-e-ell, I know you said that you didn't want my dowry—that I could save it for our children, and that if we didn't have any, I could spend it as I liked. But I was thinking that this would be a fine way to invest the money for their future. And . . . that is . . ."

"And what?" he demanded.

"It would also be a good place to live."

It took him a minute to comprehend what she was trying to tell him. "You *bought* it for us to live in?"

"Not yet," she said hastily. "Good Lord, I wouldn't buy a house without consulting you. I'm not as daft as all that. But you haven't been comfortable at Armitage House ever since you found out that it was one of the servants there who provided Malet with his information about our jaunts."

"I should have shot the servant, too," he groused, "especially because the damned fellow was also the one to let Malet in through the kitchen the night the bastard nearly killed you."

"It's a good thing you *didn't* shoot the servant. I daresay Fitzy wouldn't have approved of that. Or conveniently carried off the body for you."

Joshua eyed her sternly, though he was struggling hard not to laugh. "One day, you are going to call my employer 'Fitzy' in his hearing and lose me my post."

"Don't be absurd," she said with a wave of her lovely hand. "Fitzy has already increased your 'secret' pay twice. He considers you valuable." She narrowed her gaze. "You're changing the subject. The point is—"

"That you want to buy us this house so we will have a place of our own."

She blinked. "Well, *yes*. It's affordable now, but it won't be forever."

"And I suppose your dowry will pay for the furnishings, etcetera?"

A secretive smile crossed her lips. "It should. It will also cover a few other things, like a carriage and servants." She walked up to take his hand. "But if you hate it, just say so, and we will return to being, as you said, 'beholding' to your cousin."

"When you put it that way," he said, "how can I resist?"

Her eyes went wide. "Do you mean that? Truly?"

"I mean that I will seriously consider it. But first I want to see all the financial details—to make sure you aren't fudging the numbers to get what you want."

"Me? Fudge numbers? Never!"

"Right. What was I thinking?" He shook his head ruefully, knowing that this wasn't an argument he would win. "I also want to see the whole place from top to bottom before we even think of making an offer."

"Of course! That's why we're here, after all."

For the next two hours, she took him around the place, showing him the rooms and the impressive kitchen, with its new oven, and the garden in back. The only place they didn't go was the servants' quarters because Gwyn had said all servants' quarters looked alike.

Joshua asked questions of the gentleman he'd initially thought was the owner but who was actually the agent in charge of selling the place. Then he asked questions of Gwyn about why *she* liked the place.

When they were done with the tour, she asked breathlessly, "What do you think?"

"I think it would suit us very well."

She squealed and flung herself at him, then covered his face with kisses. "I was hoping you would say that." She waved her hand at the agent, and he disappeared down the hall.

Joshua was just contemplating kissing her more thoroughly when the entirety of their two families appeared just behind her. "Good God, what are you lot doing here?" he asked.

"Two hours, Joshua," Gwyn's mother said as she brushed off her sleeves. "We were in the servants' quarters for two *hours*. How long does it *take* you to decide where you wish to live?"

"I must say," Beatrice remarked, "I agree with Aunt Lydia. There were spiders down there, for pity's sake. I do not like spiders."

"There was *one* spider and I killed it for you," Greycourt said. "I had no idea that a woman as forthright as you could be felled by the sight of a spider."

"At least you had somewhere to sit," Thornstock complained as he dusted off his trousers. "Two hours is a long time to spend leaning against a wall."

"You were drinking champagne, Thorn," Sheridan said. "I don't know why that was so awful for any of you. I quite enjoyed the champagne."

Gwyn scowled at them. "The champagne was for our celebration!"

"You were that sure I would agree?" Joshua asked, amused when his wife colored.

"Of course not," she said. "But I wanted to be prepared in case you did."

Thornstock came up to clap Joshua on the shoulder. "Let me know when you want to look at the finances part. It's as I told Gwyn—you can rent it or buy it. I don't care which, as long as you decide soon. I've got two people already lined up to rent it if you don't."

"Wait a minute!" Joshua rounded on his wife. "Your *brother* owns this place?"

She smiled weakly. "I . . . I wanted you to see it without being biased, that's all. And I *did* say I knew the owner."

"Let me get this straight, Sis," Greycourt said. "Major Wolfe said he didn't want your dowry unless it was to go to your children. So you're using your dowry to buy the place as an investment for your children, and you're buying it from your brother, who is essentially in charge of providing the money for the dowry yet is getting the money back at the same time."

Gwyn screwed up her face in thought, then nodded. "That's about right. Assuming we buy and not rent."

As they all laughed, Joshua shook his head. "You lot are mad," he grumbled. "And you'd better not be counting on hiding in the servants' quarters ever again. If I know Gwyn, she'll want to put servants there."

They all began to talk at once, telling Gwyn their impressions of the house and congratulating Joshua—for what, he wasn't sure, because he'd had no voice in picking the place. But he had to admit it was ideal. It was easy to slip out the back and into the mews without being seen, even by the servants. It had enough rooms for raising a family, but not so many that they might not be able to afford it.

"By the way, Wolfe," Thorn said, "did you ever figure out whether Malet was the one who paid that stranger in Cambridge to unscrew the bolts on our carriage's perch?"

"He said it wasn't him," Joshua said.

"And I believe he told the truth," Gwyn said. "He truly looked bewildered by Joshua's accusation."

Thornstock and Sheridan exchanged glances with Greycourt. Joshua walked over to whisper in Beatrice's ear.

With a nod, she went up to Aunt Lydia. "I have to show you the garden, Aunt. I don't think you saw it."

"I didn't!" she said. "That would be lovely, Bea, thank you."

After they disappeared, Thornstock looked at Gwyn, but before he could say anything, she told him, "You're not packing me off with the other ladies. I was *there* when that stranger tampered with the coach. I'm as concerned about it as my brothers."

"Fine," her twin said. He turned to the others. "The thing is, we were considering the possibility that our fathers were all murdered, and that it had something to do with Mother. But if someone tried to murder Mother and me and Gwyn, not to mention Joshua, that muddies the waters a bit."

"Or it was a case of the villain not really caring who else got hurt," Joshua said. "So it could still have something to do with your mother. The question you should be asking is, who has made her—or the entire family—the object of his anger?"

"Wolfe is right," Greycourt said. "And not just this family, but Wolfe and Beatrice's family, too. Whoever the murderer is, he set Wolfe up to be blamed for Maurice's murder."

"Ah, but that could just have been in order to throw suspicion off himself," Joshua said.

"Or herself," Gwyn put in. When her brothers all shot her a skeptical look, she added, "What? Women can be villainous, too."

"She has a point," Joshua said. "And it still could just have been a matter of highwaymen hoping to rob us after the carriage broke down."

The others looked as skeptical as he felt. Then he noticed that Gwyn's mother and Beatrice were returning. "I'll tell you what. I'll nose around in London, see what more I can find out after you lot return to the country. Then I will let you know what I learn."

"Sounds good." Thornstock offered Joshua his hand, and they shook. "Thank you."

By then, their mother had returned. "I'm so happy to see you two becoming friendly. And I'm sure this house will bring you even closer."

Joshua certainly hoped so. Thornstock had proved to be not quite what he seemed, and Joshua found that encouraging. Besides, Gwyn loved her brother. So Joshua should at least try to *like* the fellow.

One by one, the others said they were ready to go and left. Beatrice stopped on her way out with Greycourt to give Joshua a kiss on the cheek and tuck something into his great-coat pocket.

As soon as everyone was gone, Gwyn sidled up to Joshua and took his arm. "I want to show you one other thing upstairs."

They climbed the stairs together, both flights, and when they reached the top, she started toward the nearest door.

"I already saw the nursery, dearling."

"I know. But I couldn't say much about it in the presence of the agent."

"Ah."

He walked with her into the room, which also adjoined another room that could be used as a schoolroom—or a bedroom for a governess.

She placed both hands on her stomach. "You may not have noticed but—"

"You're going to have our child."

She gaped at him. "You *did* notice."

"Of course I noticed. Did you think I was unaware of your breasts increasing or your throwing up your breakfast? I pay attention, my love. To everything, but, in particular, to everything involving *you*."

That brought a beaming smile to her lips. "Why didn't you say anything?"

"Honestly? I didn't know what to say. I was giving you time to tell me. I didn't know how you felt about it."

"Elated, actually. I went to a midwife recommended by Lady Hornsby, and she examined me and told me she saw no reason for me not to have a perfectly normal child. But, she said, even if I lost the babe, it wouldn't necessarily mean I couldn't have another."

"Did she say how far along you are?"

"She thinks it's five months. Apparently the first time is the charm with me."

"Five months. That's good, isn't it?"

"She thought it was."

His heart leaped into his throat. "Why didn't you tell me?"

"At first I was waiting to be sure. Then I went to see her. I'd already been talking to Thorn about buying or renting this place, so I wanted to wait until I was sure that would happen. I wanted to surprise you." She cupped his cheek. "It looks as if I waited too late for that."

"Are you daft? You surprise me every single day. You surprised me when you chose me to be your bodyguard, you surprised me the first time you responded to my kiss, and you downright shocked me by agreeing to marry me. If anything, I should be trying to surprise you."

He pulled out the rose Beatrice had plucked for him in the garden and offered it to her. "When we were taking the tour, I noticed that all the blooms on the exotic-looking rosebush outside had blown . . . except for this one. It's a September rose. Like you, it holds on through thick and thin to end up triumphant later in the season."

"Why, Joshua," she said softly, "I do believe you're getting very good at saying poetic things. That describes me perfectly." She tucked the rose into the ribbon on her bonnet so she could pull him close. "But it also describes *you* very well. So I think as long as we stay entwined, we will bloom and bloom forever."

He kissed her then, hard and long and deep. He'd been right all along: she had definitely had her pick of the men in London. And she'd picked *him*, thank God.

He was the bachelor no more.